Herman Melville (1819—1891)

Two Tales by

HERMAN MELVILLE

Billy Budd

AND

Benito Cereno

With an introduction by MAXWELL GEISMAR

and paintings by ROBERT SHORE

The 100 Greatest Books Ever Written

COLLECTOR'S EDITION
Bound in Genuine Leather

The Easton Press
NORWALK, CONNECTICUT

The present edition is published by advance reservation
exclusively for subscribers to the Easton Press collection of
The 100 Greatest Books Ever Written.

This book is printed on archival quality paper especially milled for this
edition. It is acid-neutral and conforms to all guidelines established for
permanence and durability by the Council of Library Resources and the
American National Standards Institute. ♾ ™

Printed and bound in the United States of America.

Publisher's Preface

HERMAN MELVILLE'S FATHER, Allan Melville, was a Boston merchant who relocated in New York where Herman was born August 1, 1819. Allan Melville's business failed and he died penniless in 1832. Herman was sent to live with relatives on a farm in upstate New York. He attended school in Albany until he was fifteen and became a bank clerk. Banking was not to his liking, and he shipped before the mast on a Liverpool-bound freighter. Following his experience, he took a job as a school teacher but was restless and unhappy and, in 1841 at the age of twenty-two, he took to the sea again, this time on a whaler.

The three years that followed supplied him with the material that would become his life work. He jumped ship in the Marquesas, spent several months on an island inhabited exclusively by natives (*Typee* was the product of this adventure), escaped to the Society Islands, which were inhabited by natives and Europeans (see *Omoo*), thence to Hawaii, where he enlisted on a ship of the United States Navy to get a ride home.

Typee and *Omoo* were instant successes. Published in 1846 and 1847 respectively, they were followed by *Mardi, Redburn*, and *White Jacket*. In 1853 he published his masterpiece — *Moby Dick*.

The thirty-eight years of Melville's life that followed *Moby Dick* were not unproductive, but they were nothing like the eight years preceding them. His next books included two verse titles, one a collection of Civil War "pieces and aspects" and the other a sort of two-volume epic about the Holy Land called *Clarel*, which he tried to suppress.

Herman Melville died in New York on September 28, 1891. It was not until thirty years after his death that his work became fully appreciated, when a young Columbia professor named Raymond Weaver published *Herman Melville: Mariner and Mystic*. Raymond Weaver's interest in Melville had led to his discovery of a granddaughter of Melville's, Mrs. Eleanor Melville Metcalf, who had been ten years old when the old whaleman died and who therefore had some clear and authentic memories of him. She had also preserved a trunkful of Melville memorabilia (certainly an "old battered trunk" — no other kind is permitted in the premises). Among this material was the manuscript (340 sheets of yellow paper) of *Billy Budd* (begun November 16, 1888, said an annotation, and finished April 19, 1891, less than half a year before Melville's death). Mrs. Metcalf allowed Raymond Weaver to copy the manuscript, and it was published for the first time in London in 1924. Until very recently that was the text printed in the anthologies.

Now Melville was an old man when he put his final story on paper; he had done most of his writing in a day when an author left his punctuation up to the printer (who knew more about it anyway); Melville's handwriting was ferociously undecipherable; he used his own systems of abbreviations; he was an indifferent speller, and, to add a capstone to this tower of difficulties, he wrote with a pencil.

Mrs. Metcalf gave her Melville papers to the Houghton Library of Harvard University. It was inevitable that someone should take another look at the *Billy Budd* manuscript and discover that the current published text was full of errors of transcription — pardonable errors, but serious nonetheless. The first time this happened was in 1948, when the story was re-edited from the original manuscript by F. Barron Freeman. Since then it has been re-re-edited by Elizabeth Treeman of the Harvard University Press, and it is on this super-corrected text that our edition is based.

The second unit in our salt-of-the-sea package caused much less difficulty than the first, both to Herman Melville and to us. It is *Benito Cereno*, a tale of an African slaver that is generally considered the best of the stories which Melville assembled as *The Piazza Tales* in 1856. We say "generally considered," and we may also say "specifically considered" in the case of the critic Maxwell Geismar, who regards *Benito Cereno* as the greatest of *The Piazza Tales* and says as much in his preface.

Maxwell Geismar, author of the introduction to our pair of Melville masterpieces, was graduated from Columbia University in 1931 and taught English at Sarah Lawrence College in Bronxville, New York, for ten years. A Guggenheim fellowship and a National Institute of Arts and Letters grant helped him to launch his *Writers in Crisis*, a multi-volume series on the American novel and American novelists from 1840 to 1940.

The illustrator for this volume is Robert Shore, whose training has included courses at Cranbrook Academy in Michigan, Borough Polytechnic in London, and the Royal Academy at Liège in Belgium. In 1952 he studied under a Fulbright Fellowship, and in 1957 he won first prize for sculpture in the Young American Craftsman Show. He has taught at Cooper Union and at the School of Visual Arts.

Robert Shore then lived on New York's East 25th Street. Not until he began work on the illustrations for *Billy Budd* and *Benito Cereno* did he become aware of the fact, noted in Raymond Weaver's Melville researches, that Herman Melville had once lived only a block away. Melville's later years, in fact, were passed at 104 East 26th Street; it was there that he wrote *Billy Budd*; it was there that he died.

The frontispiece portrait of Herman Melville which graces this edition is the work of Robert Handville. Born in New Jersey, this artist is a graduate of Pratt Institute. His work has been exhibited by such groups as The Smithsonian Institute, the Institute of Graphic Arts and the Butler Art Institute. Handville was the designer and painter of the Yellowstone National Park Commemorative U.S. postage stamp.

The intricate binding design which enhances the cover of this volume is the work of Tony Hom of Michael Mendelsohn Design in New York City. This fine design and the other special features such as the elegant endpapers and the ribbon page marker are touches rarely found in books today and make this edition of *Billy Budd* and *Benito Cereno* a worthy addition to the Easton Press collection of *The 100 Greatest Books Ever Written*.

EASTON PRESS

Introduction

I WAS ABOUT TO SAY that Herman Melville is surely our genius in the national letters, but not our best novelist. That honor I reserve for Theodore Dreiser, strange as it may seem, for reasons I can't go into here. For Melville was in fact a metaphysical poet staging great dramas of the human condition. On another level he is a pre-Freudian depth psychologist of fantastic proportions; on a third level he is one of the most peculiar and fascinating psychological case histories in literature; on still another—but there are so many levels of complexity in Melville's writing that this introduction to *Benito Cereno* and *Billy Budd* could never hold them all.

Suffice it to add that Herman Melville is a perfect American cross between Dostoevski and Tolstoi; what more can be said? Except that the man who wrote a whole series of tremendous short stories in the eighteen-fifties, from *Bartleby the Scrivener* to *Benito Cereno*—stories that are utterly unique in our literature, or any other; stories that make Hemingway's dark tales in the late nineteen-thirties look somewhat shallow—how could such a writer *not* have been our greatest fictionist? And indeed Melville should have been that, and perhaps would have been if, after writing these stories, he had not collapsed completely, retired into the shell of anonymity (like Bartleby himself), retreated into that conservatism and caste which the Yale professors admire so much, and, publishing his own volumes of poetry, given up. Still that is not the whole story either, as to origins, causes, and true nature, nor as to final results, which were again, in Melville's case, to be startling and magnificent.

Melville's case! How to really make sense of it, how to get at the final truth resting beneath so many levels of ambiguity, how to present all the different facets of whatever truth we can finally reach there? No wonder that the despairing Harvard professor of psychology, attempting to interpret *Pierre,* threw together every possible theory from every possible system of psychology in a potpourri of speculation which is probably all true. No wonder that the more conservative, cautious, and canny Princeton professor of American literature announced that Melville's central tragedy was "a failure of communication"—which is surely bringing Madison Avenue to Nantucket, and all the men in the gray flannel suits to those deliciously nude Typees. Well, we can do better than that, and let us modestly make a beginning (while also pointing out that it would take a book to make this clear, and that no book on Melville, from Lewis Mumford to Newton Arvin, has yet done the job, despite the fact that current American scholarship on Melville is prodigious).

Although this vast body of scholarship may—as in the case, say, of Yale's R.W. B. Lewis—apprise us of all the facts in Melville's strange history, it gives us everything *but* the truth; and perhaps the trouble is that the possible truth in Melville's case is stranger than his fiction. Yet I am also afraid to tackle this head-on, directly, and am looking for Melvillean linked-symbols to express the complexity of ambiguity underneath which lurks the ultimate horror. What *was* the horror which pervades *Benito Cereno* in particular and all these stories in general? that horror in nature or in humanity which suddenly, in mid-career and at the height of his powers, Melville felt he had discovered? That horror which he also felt or projected upon his own exuberant, hopeful, optimistic nineteenth-century society, ever developing in those blind Darwinian leaps to new peaks of progress, and which makes Melville such a prophetic writer today, *post* Hitler and *post* Stalin. That faceless horror embedded perhaps at the very core of life itself, which destroys Benito's own will to live even after he has been rescued and saved, and which he bluntly attributes to "the Negro" in the story, although, as I think, wrongly. That horror which did indeed finally render Melville himself as impotent and panic-stricken as Benito was, as defiantly voiceless, nameless, homeless as the clerical Bartleby of "the dead-letter office"—but which, despite all the odds, Melville himself lived to conquer all over again, so marvelously, so brilliantly, so triumphantly as to bring tears to your eyes, in the deathbed masterpiece of *Billy Budd*.

First of all, it really had nothing to do with the complete and utter rejection of *Moby Dick* when Melville was at the first crest of his powers, and knew he had written a masterpiece. It was a rejection both popular and critical, moral and social, a rejection that threw a pall of silence over Melville's name for almost seventy years, until a Columbia teacher named Raymond Weaver needed a subject for his Ph.D. dissertation. It is almost impossible to believe that a genius could have been utterly discredited, outlawed, and tabooed in nineteenth-century America. Yet there is absolutely no mention of Melville, save for his early adventure tales, in Henry James, say, or in Mark Twain, or in any of his literary successors that I know about. There is no mention of Melville, after *Moby Dick*, in the writings of his contemporary and close friend Hawthorne, who knew which way the wind was blowing and had no mind to get into another scandal. But Melville's collapse had nothing to do with his worldly and literary failure—unless you are an economic determinist and believe that the worldly conditions which surround a genius may have the same effect upon him as upon the human race in general.

Melville's mysterious tale of *Bartleby the Scrivener* is crucial here. In a brilliant essay the poet-critic-professor Ruth Miller of State University of New York at Stony Brook even demonstrates that it is a purely literary story, complete with profile sketches of the popular hack writers of the period, while the one authentic genius is reduced to mute rebellion, to a kind of insane form of passive resistance, still ending up, however, as the unmourned corpse in a public institution.

But perhaps this was Bartleby's own will to die, in reaction to some mysterious crime perpetrated upon him and never touched on in the story proper. The gruff, decent, jolly, Dickensian and humanitarian narrator-lawyer of the story is not unakin to the early Melville himself, successful author of five or six rattling good adventure tales with enough social protest to give them bite. At base, *Bartleby the Scrivener* is a divided-personality story, and may indicate why the earlier Melville took such a kindly interest, if an unavailing one, in the later and mutely defiant outcast, prisoner, corpse. And in Bartleby, in turn, it is possible to see another phase of the psychological panic that shakes Don Benito, cripples him, makes him faint, and prevents him from telling the terrifying truth until a last desperate burst of energy lands him in the good American captain's whaleboat of escape and freedom.

All these figures were the revolving phases and facets of Herman Melville's spiritual state when he wrote those tremendous self-portraits of the eighteen-fifties, dramatized to the hilt. The successful, conventional, well-meaning Wall Street lawyer of *Bartleby* was a blood-brother of the kindly Captain Delano of *Benito Cereno*, this New England innocent and man of good will who dwells uneasily but hopefully in the very center of human cunning, depravity, cruelty, horror; who wishes to refurbish the very ship of human evil. Innocent, indeed! Aren't the very names of all these figures—Bartleby, Benito, and even Billy Budd—too similar for it to be a coincidence? Yes, and Benito Cereno—the victim of the slave revolt, the terrorized prisoner of the blacks who never does reveal the final atrocities which have confirmed his collapse—the Spanish Benito Cereno is not unrelated by name also to Amasa Delano of Duxbury, Massachusetts, who is in fact again his "better half," or at least his earlier, hopeful, capable, and innocent self. Ah, what a spiritual ruin was impending there in Melville's own psyche which he kept describing over and over again, brilliantly and with marvelous acuity, in all these fantastically mad tales! A ruin which he projected as the description of man himself, or of nature and human nature, of the innermost meaning of life.

Is Benito, the chained master, also related, then, to Babo, the perfect Negro servant, as Delano the New England Southerner believes so innocently again, and so arrogantly, and so stupidly? For Babo is the mastermind of the conspiracy and even, in a sense—in all these shifting lights of the narrative where everything keeps changing shape and form and meaning before our eyes—the story's tragic hero. (Babo, like Bartleby, is mute again when he is dragged off to the gallows, his body burned, his head exhibited as a warning by the "superior"—and kindly?—white men.) The dependence of Benito upon Babo, described with infinite twists of the dramatic imagination, is that of the victim upon his black master; it is a dependence of terror and fear and death in the panicked and ravaged mind, fainting and swooning and starting and swaying, all unhinged.

Note that while the mad Spaniard blames the Negro for the depths of his own degradation and collapse, their relationship of false master and false slave, *à la Waiting for Godot*, is not without emotional compulsion either, or even a curious kind of mutual involvement and dependence. For, still on the psychological plane of *Benito Cereno*, what else is that whole fantastic Negro crew—the industrious hatchet-polishers, the perched oakum-pickers, the sexually inciting Ashantee Negresses—except the Dark Furies which have taken command of Benito Cereno's and Herman Melville's soul alike?

Take it on another level, that of social-cultural commentary, from whence Melville started and which—immense rebel, profound revolutionary that he was at heart—he never (as we shall see in *Billy Budd*) abandoned to the day of his death: What a great parable of slavery, written at the dawn of the Civil War, he had evolved in *Benito Cereno!* We have already noticed Amasa Delano's genial ignorance of the true nature of these "black children" and "perfect servants"; there is more than an inkling of the deeper love-hatred bond between Benito and Babo, tragic brothers indeed under the skin. A natural Hegelian, an early Marxian dialectician just as he was a pre-Freudian Freudian, there were times when Herman Melville seemed to see the whole universe in terms of white and black, through whose deepest opposition and deeper affinity the truth might yet be perceived—if there was any truth in the universe, which was just the point at question.

It is almost inconceivable that Melville had not heard of the Nat Turner slave rebellion, despite all the desperate Southern attempts to keep this and a long series of other such uprisings from the public eye. The South, like Don Benito, an uneasy master chained to his hypocritical slaves, lived in perpetual fear and panic; and hence the brutality, the coarsening of the spirit, the dehumanization of the white soul as well as of the Negro body. And when looked at from this angle, what, after all, did these magnificent Melvillean blacks do that was so terrible, or that was not logical, or that did not show only their intelligence, their immense theatricality (so appealing to Melville), their overweening desire for freedom? True, these perfect loving servants, these natural children indeed of a self-deluded and corrupt white plantation aristocracy; these domestic intimates so trusted they bore no chains—ah, that was the mistake!—turned savage killers, torturers, cannibals, or worse. To their natural jungle cruelty, perhaps, or sudden childlike changes from anger to applause, they added only the calculated savagery of their white masters, the brainwashing through utter fear, the psychological lessons of slavery which they had learned so well. (Go read such a book as Thomas Wentworth Higginson's *Army Life in a Black Regiment* to see what miracles of bravery, ingenuity, gallantry these same black slaves were capable of when given a chance at true freedom.)

When you come down to it, what *was* the true horror of the universe which this whole group of dark stories—and most notably perhaps *Benito Cereno*—not only hint at but somehow convey in emotional, though not rational, terms? What is so horrid, what was so horrible to Melville himself? Just the knowledge that in fact there was no truth in the universe, that man lived by a series of illusions, and that *this* knowledge was a knife at man's throat? We can take that, we accept it, we work from that premise, though it may have been harder in Melville's own day and age; though it was indeed a "modern" discovery which he had got on to. (It has been declared that Melville boarded the Transcendental bark and brought back bad news.) Was it the fact, as Melville suggests, that absolute evil could reign in the world, as it did symbolically aboard the blood-stained *San Dominick*? That nature was not only blind and indifferent to man's fate but actively conspiring against him?

That is bad news, if true; and since then we have been through the Nazi terror, revealing the utmost depths of human degradation and human potential for rational evil, of such proportions as to make the antics of the black Jacobins aboard the decayed grandeur of the ex-Spanish man-o'-war look like child's play indeed. We have been through the worst phase of the Russian revolution when a mad dictator controlled a whole culture, and perhaps even changed the future history of the world. But then, was it really not so much the fact (if true) that man is inherently evil, but that society, and particularly modern society, had already, by the mid-nineteenth century, corrupted whatever traces of original grace he had carried with him from that Edenite garden of his visions?

I think that in some part all these conclusions were reached by Herman Melville in the mid-fifties, and that all of them are in some part reflected in this intertwined fashion—complexity made more complex—in the great short stories which come to culmination in *Benito Cereno.* But that there was something else here too is apparent in Melville's history before these stories and after them, right up to *Billy Budd,* right up to his own death.

† † † † †

HE was the innocent. *He* had been betrayed by life, ensnared by that bland, happy, progressive, rational, and scientific nineteenth-century society which first acclaimed Melville's adventure tales, good as they were, and then blindly and hypocritically, and perhaps even malignantly, repudiated his masterpiece, *Moby Dick;* from then on abjuring all respect, all admiration, all loyalty, all public mention even, or private and personal acknowledgment of the great artist called Herman Melville.

That was the vista of human desolation, of the arid reaches of the spirit which paraded under the illusion of the Encantadas, the Enchanted Isles, and under the black treachery of appearances in *Benito Cereno.* What these stories reveal as a group—a group dark and damned and close to madness in the controlled insanity of great art—is simply Herman Melville's loss of faith in Herman Melville. Which, being the unique metaphysical poet that he was, he had to project into universal truths, universal states of man, universal modes of nature and being. And Melville being the man of talent that he was, the stories have a tremendous appeal to us because they are true reflections of certain phases of man's spirit that, up to Melville's time, or perhaps up to ours, no other artist had caught so accurately and dramatized so brilliantly. And that was the end of it—almost.

It was the end of it, at least, for some twenty-five years during which Melville wrote two poor novels, and also some dubious verse that I am not qualified to judge. He tried to become a public lecturer, was refused a consulship, moved to New York City from his Massachusetts farm, worked as a customs inspector—and then, nearing death, completely obscure and unheard of, neglected to the extreme, wrote *Billy Budd.*

Of such tormented and compulsive creativity we can never have enough.

With this, through the contrarieties and oppositions of the dialectical method, he made the complete circle of his thought and came out with whatever facts of existence we can arrive at in a deceptive, veiled (and sometimes better-to-be-veiled) universe. In this connection it is instructive to compare Melville's first book, *Typee,* in 1846, with his last one, *Billy Budd,* finished but unpublished when Melville died in 1891.

Typee is almost the reverse of *The Piazza Tales,* about which we have been talking, in that its hero is cast away in what he thinks is a barbaric and savage Polynesian tribe of cannibals, witch doctors, and idol-worshippers. But these fearsome tan primitives also knock their gods over when angry at them. They do nothing except to enjoy life to the hilt; they are beautiful in body and spirit and culture. The shaking Melville had landed, in short, in a primitive paradise, a coppery Eden, from which he never recovered, and which gave him some second thoughts about progress and civilization in nineteenth-century America.

Heretical thoughts, then, which brought about a *Moby Dick* and for which, in a way, nineteenth-century America was right to outlaw its author. But the point is that Billy Budd himself, as the hero of Melville's last book, is a Typee in white-face, as Melville says several times in the story. He is a natural man, angelic, beautiful, innocent, defenseless, who is trapped by the evil Claggart. There are homosexual undertones to this relation, which would also account for Claggart's jealousy and rage at Billy, and his desire for revenge on the beautiful sailor boy, but which Melville appears to ignore when talking about Claggart's "natural evil."

Claggart we can deal with, however. Since Melville was also, without any question, the greatest of American satirists, Claggart may even be a decoy. In fact Melville, in a very Henry Jamesian way, filled this last epic tale with a series of decoys and red herrings and with screens upon screens of a final blasting ambiguity. Another of these decoys is, to me, the whole concept of Billy Budd as a second Christ Crucified for the mutinous sailors—a concept which most of current academic scholarship hails as Melville's "final acquiescence" to God, but which means only that sometimes Melville considered *himself* to be the crucified Christ, and had a certain identification with their common suffering.

No, the real villain of *Billy Budd* is obviously Captain Vere, that noble English gentleman of culture and moderation and reason and justice and conformity to the *status quo*. He knows, Starry Vere, that Billy is innocent. He knows that Claggart is a schemer and a liar. He even loves Billy like his own son, this blond, pagan, Adamite charmer who is really good; he thinks of him as an angel. "Yet the angel must hang!" Why, and why in such haste, when the case could wait, could have further legal scrutiny, and when Vere's own officers think their captain has become demented? Because Captain Vere, just like Captain Benito Cereno, is in a panic. He fears that the naval mutinies ignited by the blood and fire of the French Revolution will spread, as they have already spread in the English navy, unless justice is fast and harsh and violent, even if absolutely unjust. The gallows, like Bartleby's Tombs prison, have now become the Halls of Justice.

But between the naval world of *Billy Budd* and the naval world of *Benito Cereno* there is a whole difference of mood and moral and meaning that—had it not been concealed by Melville's final and ultimate depths of irony—would be clear even to those critics who equate the stories and their message. For one thing, the panicked captain is not the hero of *Billy Budd*. And in another sense, the villain Vere—the straightforward, truthful, honorable, even starry Captain Vere, who is all verity and who at the fatal, crucial point does indeed veer from his own nature and principles†—Vere is also the victim of the social order he represents, the social order at war with the French Revolution and struggling so desperately, as it believed, for its own survival. In such cases, angels do hang with equal ease in reactionary and radical quarters alike. But, then, even Claggart—hailed by contemporary criticism as justifying both Melville's and our own view of natural, immutable, hereditary evil; or, it might be said, embodying anew the hoary doctrine of original sin—isn't Claggart too the victim of his unacknowledged personal passions and of his personal repressions?

But why skirmish around so much? I am not saying that Melville denied the existence of evil in nature or in man or in society. But Melville was *not* saying in *Billy Budd*—as he was beginning to intimate in *Moby Dick*, as he said out loud and quite madly in *Benito Cereno*—that evil was at the *core* of the universe, that evil was the guiding principle of man, life, and society. That is what our current rash of historians and critics alike

†In case you think I am making too much of Melville's name-dropping, let me remind you I have not mentioned Billy *Budd* as the budding man, or the potential good man, now destroyed—in his primitive, barbaric state at least—by "civilization" in the form of Captain Vere and Claggart. And we've seen how Billy Budd is related by name-sound to the Babo of *Benito Cereno*, his primitive black brother equally destroyed by slavery as another mode of society.

are trying to find in Melville, or are trying to make out of Melville. That is what I am opposing here because such an idea is in fact the sign of a diseased culture as well as of a diseased nature. And Herman Melville must be brought back to the side of humanity and love and life—dark-lined though it all is, as nobody would deny, as art knows best of all. But still, alive! And with all the luxury and pleasure and comfort and grace of life, which sometimes makes all the rest bearable.

And artistically, what a character is this Claggart, cowardly braggart with the clink of chains in his name; with his ingratiating deference, his "austere patriotism" (note well), his mania for a secret police, his rabies of the heart! But once again, Melville's discussion of Claggart's evil is planned along the several planes of philosophy, metaphysics, religion, *and* history, society, economics: all interwoven, all fused in this great art exactly as they are in life. Nothing is omitted here, and nothing is simplified.

Claggart is above all a "man of reason" just as Captain Vere is. I suspect that Melville hated most those rationalists, noble or criminal, who had repressed their own moving emotions and hence were unaware of them. Those are the true madmen (as I wrote about Melville some years ago), who give every appearance of decency, respectability, sobriety, "calm judgment," and, in Vere's case, of the class, property, and position to which Claggart aspired. Yes, Claggart is the direct reverse of a saint, but: "To pass from a normal nature to him one must cross 'the deadly space between.' " His depravity partook of nothing "of the sordid or sensual," no vulgar alloy of the brute, but was indeed dominated by intellectuality. "Civilization, especially of the austerer sort," was auspicious to such types!

In this sense Claggart is a later phase of Ahab, hunting down not a whale but a doe. Billy is all innocent love of life. Claggart is all repressed, rational, "civilized" evil—the incipient potential, as it turned out, of Melville's own beneficent, hopeful, bustling Western society to whom (just as the bankers, industrialists, and respectable middle class capitulated to a Hitler) the panicked Vere himself surrenders all his probity and decency. In this last great fable Melville had returned to and was quite aware of *all* the levels of human behavior and culture.

But the real reason I claim that Billy Budd was the Typeean natural man—or the way man should be if civilization did not corrupt him—rather than the Christ Crucified that he is to our modern Melvillean metaphysicians, is simply the fact that during the days of his final agony, directly before his death, Billy refuses to see the ship's chaplain. He remains "a barbarian," as Melville said, and then Melville also asked: Just what is the purpose of a chaplain, anyhow, aboard a man-o'-war? What is the Prince of Peace doing so close to the god of war? *Why is he there?* "Bluntly put, . . . because he indirectly subserves the purpose attested by the cannon; because, too, he lends the sanction of the religion of the meek to that which practically is the abrogation of everything but brute force."

That is to say, because our religious institutions also have been corrupted by modern civilization "in its martial phase." There is that final aside about the battle lanterns which hang over Billy's chained and imprisoned body: "Fed with the oil supplied by the war contractors (whose gains, honest or otherwise, are in every land an anticipated portion of the harvest of death), with flickering splashes of dirty yellow light they pollute the pale moonshine . . ." An aside which in such miraculous language confirms the true moral of the tale. For how could *Billy Budd* possibly be construed as a document of religious repentance, conversion, acceptance? Was Melville another Claggart, a false informer about man's condition and destiny? And how can you still say that *Billy Budd* is a parable of evil incarnate, natural corruption, original sin, etc.?

No. After the terrible depths of dark despair in the mid-fifties, after that horrifying vision of a universal core of evil, that madness and loss of faith and loss even of physical control, Melville had returned to his original radical premises about life and about American life. Cast out, like the rebellious angel, he never recanted. Like the Typees he loved, who were liquidated by the whaling captains and the missionaries, he too remained a barbarian. He is no true aid and comfort to the conservatives and reactionaries of our own age who keep insisting on his "levels of ambiguity." For in the end all this ambiguity, fascinating to unravel, reduces itself to an eminently simple proposition. THESIS: Man's natural innocence and goodness. ANTITHESIS: Man's (or nature's) natural evil and corruption. SYNTHESIS: A nature and a world, like the microcosm of a whaling ship or a man-o'-war, composed of both good and evil, innocence and corruption, where man could, depending on his society and culture, do and be anything he wished. Q.E.D.

A simple and a sound resolution, and one that makes sense. But in the process of achieving this simplicity, what great and complex art Melville demonstrated!

One last thing: If, depending on his society and culture, man could become anything he wished to, the fact is that towards the middle and end of the last century Western man was not quite making out as well as those "primitives" he had displaced and destroyed for the sake of private enterprise, profits, Christianity, and colonization. This was what Melville suggested in both his first fable and his last fable; this was what the raging Mark Twain told us in no uncertain terms at the very end of his life. This is what all our major nineteenth-century writers (with the exception perhaps of that incurable somnambulist, Henry James) knew and felt in their bones at the peak and decline of Western culture.

In Melville's own work and career, what you had was an incredible peak, followed by an awesome decline celebrated in his art, a madness, an inertia, a death, a silence—and then: another peak! Talk about Satan; talk about the human will. . . .

MAXWELL GEISMAR

Harrison, New York
March 5, 1965

A Note on the Text of "Billy Budd"

CALLING IT "Billy Budd, Foretopman," Raymond Weaver gave the story its first publication in 1924. Melville had not transcribed *Billy Budd* for the press, and Weaver's reading of the ms. had many inaccuracies, several of them serious. The present edition, for the most part, follows the Harvard University Press text established by F. Barron Freeman in 1948 and corrected by Elizabeth Treeman in 1956. Variant and archaic spellings were permitted to stand; but punctuation and an occasional preposition or article have been added when essential for sense, frequently in accordance with emendations by the editors of *The American Tradition in Literature*, published in 1957 (W.W. Norton & Company, Inc.), and by Milton R. Stern, whose edition was published in 1958 (E. P. Dutton & Co., Inc.).

Our reading of a sentence in Chapter 18 utilizes a conjecture of Raymond Weaver's as well as those of Milton Stern and the editors of the Harvard text, and a phrase in Chapter 26 departs from the Harvard version in favor of Weaver's.

Billy Budd, Sailor

☛ An inside narrative.

What BEFELL him
in the year of the GREAT MUTINY.

DEDICATED to JACK CHACE, Englishman,
wherever that great heart may now be,
here on earth or harboured in paradise.
Captain of the maintop in the year 1843
in the U. S. Frigate *United States*.

Preface

THE YEAR 1797, the year of this narrative, belongs to a period which, as every thinker now feels, involved a crisis for Christendom not exceeded in its undetermined momentousness at the time by any other era whereof there is record. The opening proposition made by the Spirit of that Age involved rectification of the Old World's hereditary wrongs. In France, to some extent, this was bloodily effected. But what then? Straightway the Revolution itself became a wrongdoer, one more oppressive than the Kings. Under Napoleon it enthroned upstart kings, and initiated that prolonged agony of continual war whose final throe was Waterloo. During those years not the wisest could have foreseen that the outcome of all would be what to some thinkers apparently it has since turned out to be—a political advance along nearly the whole line for Europeans.

Now, as elsewhere hinted, it was something caught from the Revolutionary Spirit that at Spithead emboldened the man-of-war's men to rise against real abuses, long-standing ones, and afterwards at the Nore to make inordinate and aggressive demands—successful resistance to which was confirmed only when the ringleaders were hung for an admonitory spectacle to the anchored fleet. Yet in a way analogous to the operation of the Revolution at large—the Great Mutiny, though by Englishmen naturally deemed monstrous at the time, doubtless gave the first latent prompting to most important reforms in the British Navy.

IN THE TIME before steamships, or then more frequently than now, a stroller along the docks of any considerable sea-port would occasionally have his attention arrested by a group of bronzed mariners, man-of-war's men or merchant-sailors in holiday attire ashore on liberty. In certain instances they would flank, or, like a body-guard quite surround some superior figure of their own class, moving along with them like Aldebaran among the lesser lights of his constellation. That signal object was the "Handsome Sailor" of the less prosaic time alike of the military and merchant navies. With no perceptible trace of the vainglorious about him, rather with the off-hand unaffectedness of natural regality, he seemed to accept the spontaneous homage of his shipmates. A somewhat remarkable instance recurs to me. In Liverpool, now half a century ago, I saw under the shadow of the great dingy street-wall of Prince's Dock (an obstruction long since removed) a common sailor, so intensely black that he must needs have been a native African of the unadulterate blood of Ham. A symmetric figure much above the average height. The two ends of a gay silk handkerchief thrown loose about the neck danced upon the displayed ebony of his chest; in his ears were big hoops of gold, and a Scotch Highland bonnet with a tartan band set off his shapely head.

It was a hot noon in July; and his face, lustrous with perspiration, beamed with barbaric good humor. In jovial sallies right and left, his white teeth flashing into view, he rollicked along, the centre of a company of his shipmates. These were made up of such an assortment of tribes and complexions as would have well fitted them to be marched up by Anacharsis Cloots before the bar of the first French Assembly as Representatives of the Human Race. At each spontaneous tribute rendered by the wayfarers to this black pagod of a fellow—the tribute of a pause and stare, and less frequent an exclamation,—the motley retinue showed that they took that sort of pride in the evoker of it which the Assyrian priests doubtless showed for their grand sculptured Bull when the faithful prostrated themselves.

To return.

If in some cases a bit of a nautical Murat in setting forth his person ashore, the Handsome Sailor of the period in question evinced nothing of the dandified Billy-be-Damn, an amusing character all but extinct now, but occasionally to be encountered, and in a form yet more amusing than the original, at the tiller of the boats on the tempestuous Erie Canal or, more likely, vaporing in the groggeries along the tow-path. Invariably a proficient in his perilous calling, he was also more or less of a mighty boxer or wrestler. It was strength and beauty. Tales of his prowess were recited. Ashore he was the champion; afloat the spokesman; on every suitable occasion always foremost. Close-reefing top-sails in a gale, there he was, astride the weather yard-arm-end, foot in the Flemish horse as "stirrup," both hands tugging at the "earring" as at a bridle, in very much the attitude of young Alexander curbing the fiery Bucephalus. A superb figure, tossed up as by the horns of Taurus against the thunderous sky, cheerily hallooing to the strenuous file along the spar.

The moral nature was seldom out of keeping with the physical make. Indeed, except as toned by the former, the comeliness and power, always attractive in masculine conjunction, hardly could have drawn the sort of honest homage the Handsome Sailor in some examples received from his less gifted associates.

Such a cynosure, at least in aspect, and something such too in nature, though with important variations made apparent as the story proceeds, was welkin-eyed Billy Budd, or Baby Budd, as more familiarly under circumstances hereafter to be given he at last came to be called, aged twenty-one, a foretopman of the British fleet toward the close of the last decade of the eighteenth century. It was not very long prior to the time of the narration that follows that he had entered the King's Service, having been impressed on the Narrow Seas from a homeward-bound English merchantman into a seventy-four outward-bound, H.M.S. *Indomitable;* which ship, as was not unusual in those hurried days, having been obliged to put to sea short of her proper complement of men. Plump upon Billy at first sight in the gangway the boarding officer Lieutenant Ratcliff pounced, even before the merchantman's crew was formally mustered on the quarter-deck for his deliberate inspection. And him only he elected. For whether it was because the other men when ranged before him showed to ill advantage after Billy, or whether he had some scruples in view of the merchantman being rather short-handed, however it might be, the officer contented himself with his first spontaneous choice. To the surprise of the ship's company, though much to the Lieutenant's satisfaction, Billy made no demur. But, indeed, any demur would have been as idle as the protest of a goldfinch popped into a cage.

Noting this uncomplaining acquiescence, all but cheerful one might say, the shipmates turned a surprised glance of silent reproach at the sailor. The Shipmaster was one of those worthy mortals found in every vocation, even the humbler ones—the sort of person whom everybody agrees in calling "a respectable man." And—nor so strange to report as it may appear to be—though a ploughman of the troubled waters, life-long contending with the intractable elements, there was nothing this honest soul at heart loved better than simple peace and quiet. For the rest, he was fifty or thereabouts, a little inclined to corpulence, a prepossessing face, unwhiskered, and of an agreeable color—a rather full face, humanely intelligent in expression. On a fair day with a fair wind and all going well, a certain musical chime in his voice seemed to be the veritable unobstructed outcome of the innermost man. He had much prudence, much conscientiousness, and there were occasions when these virtues were the cause of overmuch disquietude in him. On a passage, so long as his craft was in any proximity to land, no sleep for Captain Graveling. He took to heart those serious responsibilities not so heavily borne by some shipmasters.

Now while Billy Budd was down in the forecastle getting his kit together, the *Indomitable's* Lieutenant, burly and bluff, nowise disconcerted by Captain Graveling's omitting to proffer the customary hospitalities on an occasion so unwelcome to him, an omission simply caused by preoccupation of thought, unceremoniously invited himself into the cabin, and also to a flask from the spirit-locker, a receptacle which his experienced eye instantly discovered. In fact he was one of those sea-dogs in whom all the hardship and peril of naval life in the great prolonged wars of his time never impaired the natural instinct for sensuous enjoyment. His duty he always faithfully did; but duty is sometimes a dry obligation, and he was for irrigating its aridity, whensoever possible, with a fertilizing decoction of strong waters. For the cabin's proprietor there was nothing left but to play the part of the enforced host with whatever grace and alacrity were practicable. As necessary adjuncts to the flask, he silently placed tumbler and water-jug before the irrepressible guest. But excusing himself from partaking just then, he dismally watched the unembarrassed officer deliberately diluting his grog a little, then tossing it off in three swallows, pushing the empty tumbler away, yet not so far as to be beyond easy reach, at the same time settling himself in his seat and smacking his lips with high satisfaction, looking straight at the host.

These proceedings over, the Master broke the silence; and there lurked a rueful reproach in the tone of his voice: "Lieutenant, you are going to take my best man from me, the jewel of 'em."

"Yes, I know," rejoined the other, immediately drawing back the tumbler preliminary to a replenishing; "Yes, I know. Sorry."

"Beg pardon, but you don't understand, Lieutenant. See here now. Before I shipped that young fellow, my forecastle was a rat-pit of quarrels. It was black times, I tell you, aboard the *Rights* here. I was worried to that degree my pipe had no comfort for me. But Billy came; and it was like a Catholic priest striking peace in an Irish shindy. Not that he preached to them or said or did anything in particular; but a virtue went out of him, sugaring the sour ones. They took to him like hornets to treacle; all but the buffer of the gang, the big shaggy chap with the fire-red whiskers. He indeed out of envy, perhaps, of the newcomer, and thinking such a 'sweet and pleasant fellow,' as he mockingly designated him to the others, could hardly have the spirit of a game-cock, must needs bestir himself in trying to get up an ugly row with him. Billy forebore with him and reasoned with him in a pleasant way—he is something like myself, Lieutenant, to whom aught like a quarrel is hateful—but nothing served. So, in the second dog-watch one day the Red Whiskers in presence of the others, under pretence of showing Billy just whence a sirloin steak was cut—for the fellow had once been a butcher—insultingly gave him a dig under the ribs. Quick as lightning Billy let fly his arm. I dare say he never meant to do quite as much as he did, but anyhow he gave the burly fool a terrible drubbing. It took about half a minute, I should think. And, lord bless you, the lubber was astonished at the celerity. And will you believe it, Lieutenant, the Red Whiskers now really loves Billy—loves him, or is the biggest hypocrite that ever I heard of. But they all love him. Some of 'em do his washing, darn his old trousers for him; the carpenter is at odd times making a pretty little chest of drawers for him. Anybody will do anything for Billy Budd; and it's the happy family here. But now, Lieutenant, if that young fellow goes—I know how it will be aboard the *Rights*. Not again very soon shall I, coming up from dinner, lean over the capstan smoking a quiet pipe—no, not very soon again, I think. Ay, Lieutenant, you are going to take away the jewel of 'em; you are going to take away my peacemaker!" And with that the good soul had really some ado in checking a rising sob.

"Well," said the officer who had listened with amused interest to all this, and now waxing merry with his tipple; "Well, blessed are the peacemakers, especially the fighting peacemakers! And such are the seventy-four beauties some of which you see poking their noses out of the port-holes of yonder war-ship lying-to for me," pointing thro' the cabin window at the *Indomitable*. "But courage! don't look so downhearted, man. Why, I pledge you in advance the royal approbation. Rest assured that His Majesty will be delighted to know that in a time when his hard tack is not sought for by sailors with such avidity as should be; a time also when some shipmasters privily resent the borrowing from them a tar or two for the service; His Majesty, I say, will be delighted to learn that *one* shipmaster at least cheerfully surrenders to the King, the flower of his flock, a sailor who with equal loyalty makes no dissent.—But where's my beauty? Ah," looking through the cabin's open door, "Here he comes; and, by Jove—lugging along his chest—Apollo with his portmanteau!—My man," stepping out to him, "you can't take that big box aboard a war-ship. The boxes there are mostly shot-boxes. Put your duds in a bag, lad. Boot and saddle for the cavalry-man, bag and hammock for the man-of-war's man."

The transfer from chest to bag was made. And, after seeing his man into the cutter and then following him down, the Lieutenant pushed off from the *Rights-of-Man*. That was the merchant-ship's name; tho' by her master and crew abbreviated in sailor fashion into *The Rights*. The hard-headed Dundee owner was a staunch admirer of Thomas Paine whose book in rejoinder to Burke's arraignment of the French Revolution had then been published for some time and had gone everywhere. In christening his vessel after the title of Paine's volume, the man of Dundee was something like his contemporary shipowner, Stephen Girard of Philadelphia, whose sympathies, alike with his native land and its liberal philosophers, he evinced by naming his ships after Voltaire, Diderot, and so forth.

But now, when the boat swept under the merchantman's stern, and officer and oarsmen were noting—some bitterly and others with a grin,—the name emblazoned there; just then it was that the new recruit jumped up from the bow where the coxswain had directed him to sit, and waving his hat to his silent shipmates sorrowfully looking over at him from the taffrail, bade the lads a genial good-bye. Then, making a salutation as to the ship herself, "And good-bye to you too, old *Rights-of-Man*."

"Down, Sir!" roared the Lieutenant, instantly assuming all the rigour of his rank, though with difficulty repressing a smile.

To be sure, Billy's action was a terrible breach of naval decorum. But in that decorum he had never been instructed; in consideration of which the Lieutenant would hardly have been so energetic in reproof but for the concluding farewell to the ship. This he rather took as meant to convey a covert sally on the new recruit's part, a sly slur at impressment in general, and that of himself in especial. And yet, more likely, if satire it was in effect, it was hardly so by intention, for Billy, tho' happily endowed with the gayety of high health, youth, and a free heart, was yet by no means of a satirical turn. The will to it and the sinister dexterity were alike wanting. To deal in double meanings and insinuations of any sort was quite foreign to his nature.

As to his enforced enlistment, that he seemed to take pretty much as he was wont to take any vicissitude of weather. Like the animals, though no philosopher, he was, without knowing it, practically a fatalist. And, it may be, that he rather liked this adventurous turn in his affairs, which promised an opening into novel scenes and martial excitements.

Aboard the *Indomitable* our merchant-sailor was forthwith rated as an able-seaman and assigned to the starboard watch of the fore-top. He was soon at home in the service, not at all disliked for his unpretentious good looks and a sort of genial happy-go-lucky air. No merrier man in his mess: in marked contrast to certain other individuals included like himself among the impressed portion of the ship's company; for these when not actively employed were sometimes, and more particularly in the last dog-watch when the drawing near of twilight induced revery, apt to fall into a saddish mood which in some partook of sullenness. But they were not so young as our foretopman, and no few of them must have known a hearth of some sort; others may have had wives and children left, too probably, in uncertain circumstances, and hardly any but must have had acknowledged kith and kin, while for Billy, as will shortly be seen, his entire family was practically invested in himself.

2

Though our new-made foretopman was well received in the top and on the gun decks, hardly here was he that cynosure he had previously been among those minor ship's companies of the merchant marine, with which companies only had he hitherto consorted.

He was young; and despite his all but fully developed frame, in aspect looked even younger than he really was, owing to a lingering adolescent expression in the as yet smooth face, all but feminine in purity of natural complexion, but where, thanks to his seagoing, the lily was quite suppressed and the rose had some ado visibly to flush through the tan.

To one essentially such a novice in the complexities of factitious life, the abrupt transition from his former and simpler sphere to the ampler and more knowing world of a great war-ship; this might well have abashed him had there been any conceit or vanity in his composition. Among her miscellaneous multitude, the *Indomitable* mustered several individuals who, however inferior in grade, were of no common natural stamp, sailors more signally susceptive of that air which continuous martial discipline and repeated presence in battle can in some degree impart even to the average man. As the Handsome Sailor, Billy Budd's position aboard the seventy-four was something analogous to that of a rustic beauty transplanted from the provinces and brought into competition with the highborn dames of the court. But this change of circumstances he scarce noted. As little did he observe that something about him provoked an ambiguous smile in one or two harder faces among the blue-jackets. Nor less unaware was he of the peculiar favorable effect his person and demeanour had upon the more intelligent gentlemen of the quarter-deck. Nor could this well have been otherwise. Cast in a mould peculiar to the finest physical examples of those Englishmen in whom the Saxon strain would seem not at all to partake of any Norman or other admixture, he showed in face that humane look of reposeful good nature which the Greek sculptor in some instances gave to his heroic strong man, Hercules. But this again was subtly modified by another and pervasive quality. The ear, small and shapely, the arch of the foot, the curve in mouth and nostril, even the indurated hand dyed to the orange-tawny of the toucan's bill, a hand telling alike of the halyards and tar-bucket; but, above all, something in the mobile expression, and every chance attitude and movement, something suggestive of a mother eminently favored by Love and the Graces; all this strangely indicated a lineage in direct contradiction to his lot. The mysteriousness here became less mysterious through a matter-of-fact elicited when Billy, at the capstan, was being formally mustered into the service. Asked by the officer, a small brisk little gentleman, as it chanced among other questions, his place of birth, he replied, "Please, Sir, I don't know."

"Don't know where you were born?—Who was your father?"

"God knows, Sir."

Struck by the straightforward simplicity of these replies, the officer next asked, "Do you know anything about your beginning?"

"No, Sir. But I have heard that I was found in a pretty silk-lined basket hanging one morning from the knocker of a good man's door in Bristol."

"*Found* say you? Well," throwing back his head and looking up and down the new recruit; "Well, it turns out to have been a pretty good find. Hope they'll find some more like you, my man; the fleet sadly needs them."

Yes, Billy Budd was a foundling, a presumable by-blow, and, evidently, no ignoble one. Noble descent was as evident in him as in a blood horse.

For the rest, with little or no sharpness of faculty or any trace of the wisdom of the serpent, nor yet quite a dove, he possessed that kind and degree of intelligence going along with the unconventional rectitude of a sound human creature, one to whom not yet has been proffered the questionable apple of knowledge. He was illiterate; he could not read, but he could sing, and like the illiterate nightingale was sometimes the composer of his own song.

Of self-consciousness he seemed to have little or none, or about as much as we may reasonably impute to a dog of Saint Bernard's breed.

Habitually living with the elements and knowing little more of the land than as a beach, or, rather, that portion of the terraqueous globe providentially set apart for dance-houses, doxies and tapsters, in short what sailors call a "fiddlers'-green," his simple nature remained unsophisticated by those moral obliquities which are not in every case incompatible with that manufacturable thing known as respectability. But are sailors, frequenters of "fiddlers'-greens," without vices? No; but less often than with landsmen do their vices, so called, partake of crookedness of heart, seeming less to proceed from viciousness than exuberance of vitality after long constraint; frank manifestations in accordance with natural law. By his original constitution aided by the cooperating influences of his lot, Billy in many respects was little more than a sort of upright barbarian, much such perhaps as Adam presumably might have been ere the urbane Serpent wriggled himself into his company.

And here be it submitted that apparently going to corroborate the doctrine of man's fall, a doctrine now popularly ignored, it is observable that where certain virtues pristine and unadulterate peculiarly characterize anybody in the external uniform of civilization, they will upon scrutiny seem not to be derived from custom or convention, but rather to be out of keeping with these, as if indeed exceptionally transmitted from a period prior to Cain's city and citified man. The character marked by such qualities has to an unvitiated taste an untampered-with flavor like that of berries, while the man thoroughly civilized, even in a fair specimen of the breed, has to the same moral palate a questionable smack as of a compounded wine. To any stray inheritor of these primitive qualities found, like Caspar Hauser, wandering dazed in any Christian capital of our time, the good-natured poet's famous invocation, near two thousand years ago, of the good rustic out of his latitude in the Rome of the Cesars, still appropriately holds:—

"Honest and poor, faithful in word and thought,
What has thee, Fabian, to the city brought?"

Though our Handsome Sailor had as much of masculine beauty as one can expect anywhere to see; nevertheless, like the beautiful woman in one of Hawthorne's minor tales, there was just one thing amiss in him. No visible blemish, indeed, as with the lady; no, but an occasional liability to a vocal defect. Though in the hour of elemental uproar or peril he was everything that a sailor should be, yet under sudden provocation of strong heart-feeling, his voice otherwise singularly musical, as if expressive of the harmony within, was apt to develop an organic hesitancy, in fact, more or less of a stutter or even worse. In this particular Billy was a striking instance that the arch interferer, the envious marplot of Eden, still has more or less to do with every human consignment to this planet of earth. In every case, one way or another he is sure to slip in his little card, as much as to remind us—I too have a hand here.

The avowal of such an imperfection in the Handsome Sailor should be evidence not alone that he is not presented as a conventional hero, but also that the story in which he is the main figure is no romance.

3

At the time of Billy Budd's arbitrary enlistment into the *Indomitable* that ship was on her way to join the Mediterranean fleet. No long time elapsed before the junction was effected. As one of that fleet the seventy-four participated in its movements, tho' at times, on account of her superior sailing qualities, in the absence of frigates, despatched on separate duty as a scout and at times on less temporary service. But with all this the story has little concernment, restricted as it is to the inner life of one particular ship and the career of an individual sailor.

It was the summer of 1797. In the April of that year had occurred the commotion at Spithead followed in May by a second and yet more serious outbreak in the fleet at the Nore. The latter is known, and without exaggeration in the epithet, as the Great Mutiny. It was indeed a demonstration more menacing to England than the contemporary manifestoes and conquering and proselyting armies of the French Directory.

To the British Empire the Nore Mutiny was what a strike in the fire-brigade would be to London threatened by general arson. In a crisis when the kingdom might well have anticipated the famous signal that some years later published along the naval line of battle what it was that upon occasion England expected of Englishmen; *that* was the time when at the mast-heads of the three-deckers and seventy-fours moored in her own roadstead—a fleet, the right arm of a Power then all but the sole free conservative one of the Old World—the blue-jackets, to be numbered by thousands, ran up with huzzas the British colors with the union and cross wiped out;

by that cancellation transmuting the flag of founded law and freedom defined, into the enemy's red meteor of unbridled and unbounded revolt. Reasonable discontent growing out of practical grievances in the fleet had been ignited into irrational combustion, as by live cinders blown across the Channel from France in flames.

The event converted into irony for a time those spirited strains of Dibdin—as a song-writer no mean auxiliary to the English Government at the European conjuncture—strains celebrating, among other things, the patriotic devotion of the British tar:

"And as for my life, 'tis the King's!"

Such an episode in the Island's grand naval story her naval historians naturally abridge; one of them (G. P. R. James) candidly acknowledging that fain would he pass it over did not "impartiality forbid fastidiousness." And yet his mention is less a narration than a reference, having to do hardly at all with details. Nor are these readily to be found in the libraries. Like some other events in every age befalling states everywhere, including America, the Great Mutiny was of such character that national pride along with views of policy would fain shade it off into the historical background. Such events can not be ignored, but there is a considerate way of historically treating them. If a well-constituted individual refrains from blazoning aught amiss or calamitous in his family, a nation in the like circumstance may without reproach be equally discreet.

Though after parleyings between Government and the ringleaders, and concessions by the former as to some glaring abuses, the first uprising—that at Spithead—with difficulty was put down, or matters for the time pacified; yet at the Nore the unforeseen renewal of insurrection on a yet larger scale, and emphasized in the conferences that ensued by demands deemed by the authorities not only inadmissible but aggressively insolent, indicated—if the Red Flag did not sufficiently do so—what was the spirit animating the men. Final suppression, however, there was; but only made possible perhaps by the unswerving loyalty of the marine corps and voluntary resumption of loyalty among influential sections of the crews.

To some extent the Nore Mutiny may be regarded as analogous to the distempering irruption of contagious fever in a frame constitutionally sound, and which anon throws it off.

At all events, of these thousands of mutineers were some of the tars who not so very long afterwards—whether wholly prompted thereto by patriotism, or pugnacious instinct, or by both,—helped to win a coronet for Nelson at the Nile, and the naval crown of crowns for him at Trafalgar. To the mutineers those battles, and especially Trafalgar, were a plenary absolution and a grand one: For all that goes to make up scenic naval display, heroic magnificence in arms, those battles, especially Trafalgar, stand unmatched in human annals.

4

Concerning "The greatest sailor since our world began."
TENNYSON

In this matter of writing, resolve as one may to keep to the main road, some by-paths have an enticement not readily to be withstood. I am going to err into such a by-path. If the reader will keep me company I shall be glad. At the least we can promise ourselves that pleasure which is wickedly said to be in sinning, for a literary sin the divergence will be.

Very likely it is no new remark that the inventions of our time have at last brought about a change in sea-warfare in degree corresponding to the revolution in all warfare effected by the original introduction from China into Europe of gunpowder. The first European fire-arm, a clumsy contrivance, was, as is well known, scouted by no few of the knights as a base implement, good enough peradventure for weavers too craven to stand up crossing steel with steel in frank fight. But as ashore, knightly valor, tho' shorn of its blazonry, did not cease with the knights, neither on the seas, though nowadays in encounters there a certain kind of displayed gallantry be fallen out of date as hardly applicable under changed circumstances, did the nobler qualities of such naval magnates as Don

John of Austria, Doria, Van Tromp, Jean Bart, the long line of British Admirals and the American Decaturs of 1812 become obsolete with their wooden walls.

Nevertheless, to anybody who can hold the Present at its worth without being inappreciative of the Past, it may be forgiven, if to such an one the solitary old hulk at Portsmouth, Nelson's *Victory*, seems to float there, not alone as the decaying monument of a fame incorruptible, but also as a poetic reproach, softened by its picturesqueness, to the *Monitors* and yet mightier hulls of the European ironclads. And this not altogether because such craft are unsightly, unavoidably lacking the symmetry and grand lines of the old battle-ships, but equally for other reasons.

There are some, perhaps, who while not altogether inaccessible to that poetic reproach just alluded to, may yet on behalf of the new order, be disposed to parry it; and this to the extent of iconoclasm, if need be. For example, prompted by the sight of the star inserted in the *Victory's* quarter-deck designating the spot where the Great Sailor fell, these martial utilitarians may suggest considerations implying that Nelson's ornate publication of his person in battle was not only unnecessary, but not military, nay, savored of foolhardiness and vanity. They may add, too, that at Trafalgar it was in effect nothing less than a challenge to death; and death came; and that but for his bravado the victorious Admiral might possibly have survived the battle; and so, instead of having his sagacious dying injunctions overruled by his immediate successor in command, he himself, when the contest was decided, might have brought his shattered fleet to anchor, a proceeding which might have averted the deplorable loss of life by shipwreck in the elemental tempest that followed the martial one.

Well, should we set aside the more disputable point whether for various reasons it was possible to anchor the fleet, then plausibly enough the Benthamites of war may urge the above.

But the *might-have-been* is but boggy ground to build on. And, certainly, in foresight as to the larger issue of an encounter, and anxious preparations for it—buoying the deadly way and mapping it out, as at Copenhagen—few commanders have been so painstakingly circumspect as this same reckless declarer of his person in fight.

Personal prudence even when dictated by quite other than selfish considerations surely is no special virtue in a military man; while an excessive love of glory, impassioning a less burning impulse, the honest sense of duty, is the first. If the name *Wellington* is not so much of a trumpet to the blood as the simpler name *Nelson*, the reason for this may perhaps be inferred from the above. Alfred in his funeral ode on the victor of Waterloo ventures not to call him the greatest soldier of all time, tho' in the same ode he invokes Nelson as "the greatest sailor since our world began."

At Trafalgar, Nelson, on the brink of opening the fight, sat down and wrote his last brief will and testament. If under the presentiment of the most magnificent of all victories to be crowned by his own glorious death, a sort of priestly motive led him to dress his person in the jewelled vouchers of his own shining deeds; if thus to have adorned himself for the altar and the sacrifice were indeed vainglory, then affectation and fustian is each more heroic line in the great epics and dramas, since in such lines the poet but embodies in verse those exaltations of sentiment that a nature like Nelson, the opportunity being given, vitalizes into acts.

5

Yes, the outbreak at the Nore was put down. But not every grievance was redressed. If the contractors, for example, were no longer permitted to ply some practices peculiar to their tribe everywhere, such as providing shoddy cloth, rations not sound, or false in the measure, not the less impressment, for one thing, went on. By custom sanctioned for centuries, and judicially maintained by a Lord Chancellor as late as Mansfield, that mode of manning the fleet, a mode now fallen into a sort of abeyance but never formally renounced, it was not practicable to give up in those years. Its abrogation would have crippled the indispensable fleet, one wholly under canvas, no steam-power, its innumerable sails and thousands of cannon, everything in short, worked by muscle alone; a fleet the more insatiate in demand for men, because then multiplying its ships of all grades against contingencies present and to come of the convulsed Continent.

Discontent foreran the Two Mutinies, and more or less it lurkingly survived them. Hence it was not unreasonable to apprehend some return of trouble, sporadic or general. One instance of such apprehensions: In the same year with this story, Nelson, then Vice-Admiral Sir Horatio, being with the fleet off the Spanish coast, was directed by the Admiral in command to shift his pennant from the *Captain* to the *Theseus;* and for this reason: that the latter ship having newly arrived on the station from home where it had taken part in the Great Mutiny, danger was apprehended from the temper of the men; and it was thought that an officer like Nelson was the one, not indeed to terrorize the crew into base subjection, but to win them, by force of his mere presence, back to an allegiance if not as enthusiastic as his own, yet as true. So it was that for a time on more than one quarter-deck anxiety did exist. At sea precautionary vigilance was strained against relapse. At short notice an engagement might come on. When it did, the lieutenants assigned to batteries felt it incumbent on them, in some instances, to stand with drawn swords behind the men working the guns.

6

But on board the seventy-four in which Billy now swung his hammock, very little in the manner of the men and nothing obvious in the demeanour of the officers would have suggested to an ordinary observer that the Great Mutiny was a recent event. In their general bearing and conduct the commissioned officers of a warship naturally take their tone from the Commander, that is if he have that ascendancy of character that ought to be his.

Captain the Honorable Edward Fairfax Vere, to give his full title, was a bachelor of forty or thereabouts, a sailor of distinction even in a time prolific of renowned seamen. Though allied to the higher nobility, his advancement had not been altogether owing to influences connected with that circumstance. He had seen much service, been in various engagements, always acquitting himself as an officer mindful of the welfare of his men, but never tolerating an infraction of discipline; thoroughly versed in the science of his profession, and intrepid to the verge of temerity, though never injudiciously so. For his gallantry in the West Indian waters as Flag-Lieutenant under Rodney in that Admiral's crowning victory over De Grasse, he was made a Post-Captain.

Ashore in the garb of a civilian, scarce anyone would have taken him for a sailor, more especially that he never garnished unprofessional talk with nautical terms, and grave in his bearing, evinced little appreciation of mere humor. It was not out of keeping with these traits that on a passage when nothing demanded his paramount action, he was the most undemonstrative of men. Any landsman observing this gentleman, not conspicuous by his stature and wearing no pronounced insignia, emerging from his cabin to the open deck, and noting the silent deference of the officers retiring to leeward, might have taken him for the King's guest, a civilian aboard the King's-ship, some highly honorable discreet envoy on his way to an important post. But in fact this unobtrusiveness of demeanour may have proceeded from a certain unaffected modesty of manhood sometimes accompanying a resolute nature, a modesty evinced at all times not calling for pronounced action, and which shown in any rank of life suggests a virtue aristocratic in kind.

As with some others engaged in various departments of the world's more heroic activities, Captain Vere, though practical enough upon occasion, would at times betray a certain dreaminess of mood. Standing alone on the weather-side of the quarter-deck, one hand holding by the rigging, he would absently gaze off at the blank sea. At the presentation to him then of some minor matter interrupting the current of his thoughts he would show more or less irascibility; but instantly he would control it.

In the navy he was popularly known by the appellation—Starry Vere. How such a designation happened to fall upon one who, whatever his sterling qualities, was without any brilliant ones was in this wise: A favorite kinsman, Lord Denton, a free-hearted fellow, had been the first to meet and congratulate him upon his return to

England from his West Indian cruise; and but the day previous turning over a copy of Andrew Marvell's poems, had lighted, not for the first time however, upon the lines entitled *Appleton House*, the name of one of the seats of their common ancestor, a hero in the German wars of the seventeenth century, in which poem occur the lines,

> "This 'tis to have been from the first
> In a domestic heaven nursed,
> Under the discipline severe
> Of Fairfax and the starry Vere."

And so, upon embracing his cousin fresh from Rodney's great victory wherein he had played so gallant a part, brimming over with just family pride in the sailor of their house, he exuberantly exclaimed, "Give ye joy, Ed; give ye joy, my starry Vere!" This got currency, and the novel prefix serving in familiar parlance readily to distinguish the *Indomitable's* Captain from another Vere his senior, a distant relative, an officer of like rank in the navy, it remained permanently attached to the surname.

7

In view of the part that the Commander of the *Indomitable* plays in scenes shortly to follow, it may be well to fill out that sketch of his outlined in the previous chapter.

Aside from his qualities as a sea-officer, Captain Vere was an exceptional character. Unlike no few of England's renowned sailors, long and arduous service with signal devotion to it, had not resulted in absorbing and *salting* the entire man. He had a marked leaning toward everything intellectual. He loved books, never going to sea without a newly replenished library, compact but of the best. The isolated leisure, in some cases so wearisome, falling at intervals to commanders even during a war-cruise, never was tedious to Captain Vere. With nothing of that literary taste which less heeds the thing conveyed than the vehicle, his bias was toward those books to which every serious mind of superior order occupying any active post of authority in the world naturally inclines;

books treating of actual men and events no matter of what era—history, biography and unconventional writers, who, free from cant and convention, like Montaigne, honestly and in the spirit of common sense philosophize upon realities.

In this line of reading he found confirmation of his own more reasoned thoughts—confirmation which he had vainly sought in social converse, so that as touching most fundamental topics, there had got to be established in him some positive convictions, which he forefelt would abide in him essentially unmodified so long as his intelligent part remained unimpaired. In view of the troubled period in which his lot was cast this was well for him. His settled convictions were as a dyke against those invading waters of novel opinion, social, political and otherwise, which carried away as in a torrent no few minds in those days, minds by nature not inferior to his own. While other members of that aristocracy to which by birth he belonged were incensed at the innovators mainly because their theories were inimical to the privileged classes, not alone Captain Vere disinterestedly opposed them because they seemed to him incapable of embodiment in lasting institutions, but at war with the peace of the world and the true welfare of mankind.

With minds less stored than his and less earnest, some officers of his rank, with whom at times he would necessarily consort, found him lacking in the companionable quality, a dry and bookish gentleman, as they deemed. Upon any chance withdrawal from their company one would be apt to say to another, something like this: "Vere is a noble fellow, Starry Vere. Spite the gazettes, Sir Horatio" (meaning him with the Lord title) "is at bottom scarce a better seaman or fighter. But between you and me now, don't you think there is a queer streak of the pedantic running thro' him? Yes, like the King's yarn in a coil of navy-rope?"

Some apparent ground there was for this sort of confidential criticism; since not only did the Captain's discourse never fall into the jocosely familiar, but in illustrating of any point touching the stirring personages and events of the time he would be as apt to cite some historic character or incident of antiquity as that he would cite from the moderns. He seemed unmindful of the circumstance that to his bluff company such remote allusions, however pertinent they might really be, were altogether alien to men whose reading was mainly confined to the journals. But considerateness in such matters is not easy to natures constituted like Captain Vere's. Their honesty prescribes to them directness, sometimes far-reaching like that of a migratory fowl that in its flight never heeds when it crosses a frontier.

8

The lieutenants and other commissioned gentlemen forming Captain Vere's staff it is not necessary here to particularize, nor needs it to make any mention of any of the warrant-officers. But among the petty-officers was one who having much to do with the story, may as well be forthwith introduced. His portrait I essay, but shall never hit it. This was John Claggart, the Master-at-arms. But that sea-title may to landsmen seem somewhat equivocal. Originally, doubtless, that petty-officer's function was the instruction of the men in the use of arms, sword or cutlas. But very long ago, owing to the advance in gunnery making hand-to-hand encounters less frequent and giving to nitre and sulphur the preeminence over steel, that function ceased; the Master-at-arms of a great war-ship becoming a sort of Chief of Police, charged among other matters with the duty of preserving order on the populous lower gun decks.

Claggart was a man about five and thirty, somewhat spare and tall, yet of no ill figure upon the whole. His hand was too small and shapely to have been accustomed to hard toil. The face was a notable one; the features all except the chin cleanly cut as those on a Greek medallion; yet the chin, beardless as Tecumseh's, had something of strange protuberant heaviness in its make that recalled the prints of the Rev. Dr. Titus Oates, the historic deponent with the clerical drawl in the time of Charles II and the fraud of the alleged Popish Plot. It served Claggart in his office that his eye could cast a tutoring glance. His brow was of the sort phrenologically associated with more than average intellect; silken jet curls partly clustering over it, making a foil to the pallor below, a pallor tinged with a faint shade of amber akin to the hue of time-tinted marbles of old. This complexion, singularly contrasting with the red or deeply bronzed visages of the sailors, and in part the result of his official seclusion from the sunlight, tho' it was not exactly displeasing, nevertheless seemed to hint of something defective or abnormal in the constitution and blood. But his general aspect and manner were so suggestive of an education and career incongruous with his naval function that when not actively engaged in it he looked a man of high quality, social and moral, who for reasons of his own was keeping incog. Nothing was known of his former life. It might be that he was an Englishman; and yet there lurked a bit of accent in his speech suggesting that possibly he was not such by birth, but through naturalization in early childhood. Among certain grizzled sea-gossips of the gun decks and forecastle went a rumor perdue that the Master-at-arms was a *chevalier* who had volunteered into the King's Navy by way of compounding for some mysterious swindle whereof he had been arraigned at the King's Bench. The fact that nobody could substantiate this report was, of course, nothing against its secret currency. Such a rumor once started on the gun decks in reference to almost anyone below the rank of a commissioned officer would, during the period assigned to this narrative, have seemed not altogether wanting in credibility to the tarry old wiseacres of a man-of-war crew. And indeed a man of Claggart's accomplishments, without prior nautical experience, entering the navy at mature life, as he did, and necessarily allotted at the start to the lowest grade in it; a man, too, who never made allusion to his previous life ashore; these were circumstances which in the dearth of exact knowledge as to his true antecedents opened to the invidious a vague field for unfavorable surmise.

But the sailors' dog-watch gossip concerning him derived a vague plausibility from the fact that now for some period the British Navy could so little afford to be squeamish in the matter of keeping up the muster-rolls, that not only were press-gangs notoriously abroad both afloat and ashore, but there was little or no secret about another matter, namely that the London police were at liberty to capture any able-bodied suspect, any questionable fellow at large and summarily ship him to dockyard or fleet. Furthermore, even among voluntary enlistments there were instances where the motive thereto partook neither of patriotic impulse nor yet of a random desire to experience a bit of sea-life and martial adventure. Insolvent debtors of minor grade, together with the promiscuous lame ducks of morality found in the Navy a convenient and secure refuge. Secure, because once enlisted aboard a King's-ship, they were as much in sanctuary, as the transgressor of the Middle Ages harboring himself under the shadow of the altar. Such sanctioned irregularities, which for obvious reasons the Government would hardly think to parade at the time, and which consequently, and as affecting the least influential class of mankind, have all but dropped into oblivion, lend color to something for the truth whereof I do not vouch, and hence have some scruple in stating; something I remember having seen in print, though the book I can not recall; but the same thing was personally communicated to me now more than forty years ago by an old pensioner in a cocked hat with whom I had a most interesting talk on the terrace at Greenwich, a Baltimore Negro, a Trafalgar man. It was to this effect: In the case of a war-ship short of hands whose speedy sailing was imperative, the deficient quota in lack of any other way of making it good, would be eked out by draughts culled direct from the jails. For reasons previously suggested it would not perhaps be easy at the present day directly to prove or disprove the allegation. But allowed as a verity, how significant would it be of England's straits at the time, confronted by those wars which like a flight of harpies rose shrieking from the din and dust of the fallen Bastille. That era appears measurably clear to us who look back at it, and but read of it. But to the grandfathers of us graybeards, the more thoughtful of them, the genius of it presented an aspect like that of Camoëns' Spirit of the Cape, an eclipsing menace mysterious and prodigious. Not America was exempt from apprehension. At the height of Napoleon's unexampled conquests, there were Americans who had fought at Bunker Hill who looked forward to the possibility that the Atlantic might prove no barrier against the ultimate schemes of this French upstart from the revolutionary chaos who seemed in act of fulfilling judgement prefigured in the Apocalypse.

But the less credence was to be given to the gun-deck talk touching Claggart, seeing that no man holding his office in a man-of-war can ever hope to be popular with the crew. Besides, in derogatory comments upon anyone against whom they have a grudge, or for any reason or no reason mislike, sailors are much like landsmen; they are apt to exaggerate or romance it.

About as much was really known to the *Indomitable's* tars of the Master-at-arms' career before entering the service as an astronomer knows about a comet's travels prior to its first observable appearance in the sky. The verdict of the sea quid-nuncs has been cited only by way of showing what sort of moral impression the man made upon rude uncultivated natures whose conceptions of human wickedness were necessarily of the narrowest, limited to ideas of vulgar rascality,—a thief among the swinging hammocks during a night-watch, or the man-brokers and land-sharks of the sea-ports.

It was no gossip, however, but fact, that though, as before hinted, Claggart upon his entrance into the navy was, as a novice, assigned to the least honourable section of a man-of-war's crew, embracing the drudgery, he did not long remain there.

The superior capacity he immediately evinced, his constitutional sobriety, ingratiating deference to superiors, together with a peculiar ferreting genius manifested on a singular occasion; all this capped by a certain austere patriotism abruptly advanced him to the position of Master-at-arms.

Of this maritime Chief of Police the ship's-corporals, so called, were the immediate subordinates, and compliant ones; and this, as is to be noted in some business departments ashore, almost to a degree inconsistent with entire moral volition. His place put various converging wires of underground influence under the Chief's control, capable when astutely worked thro' his understrappers, of operating to the mysterious discomfort, if nothing worse, of any of the sea-commonalty.

9

Life in the fore-top well agreed with Billy Budd. There, when not actually engaged on the yards yet higher aloft, the topmen, who as such had been picked out for youth and activity, constituted an aerial club lounging at ease against the smaller stun'sails rolled up into cushions, spinning yarns like the lazy gods, and frequently amused with what was going on in the busy world of the decks below. No wonder then that a young fellow of Billy's disposition was well content in such society. Giving no cause of offence to anybody, he was always alert at a call. So in the merchant service it had been with him. But now such a punctiliousness in duty was shown that his topmates would sometimes good-naturedly laugh at him for it. This heightened alacrity had its cause, namely, the impression made upon him by the first formal gangway-punishment he had ever witnessed, which befell the day following his impressment. It had been incurred by a little fellow, young, a novice, an after-guardsman absent from his assigned post when the ship was being put about; a dereliction resulting in a rather serious hitch to that manoeuvre, one demanding instantaneous promptitude in letting go and making fast. When Billy saw the culprit's naked back under the scourge gridironed with red welts, and worse; when he marked the dire expression on the liberated man's face as with his woolen shirt flung over him by the executioner he rushed forward from the spot to bury himself in the crowd, Billy was horrified. He resolved that never through remissness would he make himself liable to such a visitation or do or omit aught that might merit even verbal reproof. What then was his surprise and concern when ultimately he found himself getting into petty trouble occasionally about such matters as the stowage of his bag or something amiss in his hammock, matters under the police oversight of the ship's-corporals of the lower decks, and which brought down on him a vague threat from one of them.

So heedful in all things as he was, how could this be? He could not understand it, and it more than vexed him. When he spoke to his young topmates about it they were either lightly incredulous or found something comical in his unconcealed anxiety. "Is it your bag, Billy?" said one. "Well, sew yourself up in it, bully boy, and then you'll be sure to know if anybody meddles with it."

Now there was a veteran aboard who because his years began to disqualify him for more active work had been recently assigned duty as mainmastman in his watch, looking to the gear belayed at the rail roundabout that great spar near the deck. At off-times the Foretopman had picked up some acquaintance with him, and now in his trouble it occurred to him that he might be the sort of person to go to for wise counsel. He was an old Dansker long anglicized in the service, of few words, many wrinkles and some honorable scars. His wizened face, time-tinted and weather-stained to the complexion of an antique parchment, was here and there peppered blue by the chance explosion of a gun-cartridge in action. He was an *Agamemnon*-man; some two years prior to the time of this story having served under Nelson, when but Sir Horatio, in that ship immortal in naval memory, and which, dismantled and in part broken up to her bare ribs, is seen a grand skeleton in Haydon's etching. As one of a boarding-party from the *Agamemnon* he had received a cut slantwise along one temple and cheek, leaving a long scar like a streak of dawn's light falling athwart the dark visage. It was on account of that scar and the affair in which it was known that he had received it, as well as from his blue-peppered complexion, that the Dansker went among the *Indomitable's* crew by the name of "Board-her-in-the-smoke."

Now the first time that his small weazel-eyes happened to light on Billy Budd, a certain grim internal merriment set all his ancient wrinkles into antic play. Was it that his eccentric unsentimental old sapience, primitive in its kind, saw or thought it saw something which, in contrast with the war-ship's environment, looked oddly incongruous in the Handsome Sailor? But after slyly studying him at intervals, the old Merlin's equivocal merriment was modified; for now when the twain would meet, it would start in his face a quizzing sort of look, but it would be but momentary and sometimes replaced by an expression of speculative query as to what might eventually befall a nature like that, dropped into a world not without some man-traps and against whose subtleties simple courage, lacking experience and address and without any touch of defensive ugliness, is of little avail; and where such innocence as man is capable of does yet in a moral emergency not always sharpen the faculties or enlighten the will.

However it was, the Dansker in his ascetic way rather took to Billy. Nor was this only because of a certain philosophic interest in such a character. There was another cause. While the old man's eccentricities, sometimes bordering on the ursine, repelled the juniors, Billy, undeterred thereby, revering him as a salt hero, would make advances, never passing the old *Agamemnon*-man without a salutation marked by that respect which is seldom lost on the aged however crabbed at times or whatever their station in life.

There was a vein of dry humor, or what not, in the mast-man; and, whether in freak of patriarchal irony touching Billy's youth and athletic frame, or for some other and more recondite reason, from the first in addressing him he always substituted Baby for Billy. The Dansker in fact being the originator of the name by which the Foretopman eventually became known aboard ship.

Well then, in his mysterious little difficulty, going in quest of the wrinkled one, Billy found him off duty in a dog-watch ruminating by himself, seated on a shot-box of the upper gun deck, now and then surveying with a somewhat cynical regard certain of the more swaggering promenaders there. Billy recounted his trouble, again wondering how it all happened. The salt seer attentively listened, accompanying the Foretopman's recital with queer twitchings of his wrinkles and problematical little sparkles of his small ferret eyes. Making an end of his story, the Foretopman asked, "And now, Dansker, do tell me what you think of it."

The old man, shoving up the front of his tarpaulin and deliberately rubbing the long slant scar at the point where it entered the thin hair, laconically said, "Baby Budd, *Jimmy Legs*" (meaning the Master-at-arms) "is down on you."

"*Jimmy Legs!*" ejaculated Billy, his welkin eyes expanding; "what for? Why he calls me *the sweet and pleasant young fellow*, they tell me."

"Does he so?" grinned the grizzled one; then said, "Ay, Baby Lad, a sweet voice has Jimmy Legs."

"No, not always. But to me he has. I seldom pass him but there comes a pleasant word."

"And that's because he's down upon you, Baby Budd."

Such reiteration along with the manner of it, incomprehensible to a novice, disturbed Billy almost as much as the mystery for which he had sought explanation. Something less unpleasingly oracular he tried to extract; but the old sea-Chiron, thinking perhaps that for the nonce he had sufficiently instructed his young Achilles, pursed his lips, gathered all his wrinkles together and would commit himself to nothing further.

Years, and those experiences which befall certain shrewder men subordinated life-long to the will of superiors, all this had developed in the Dansker the pithy guarded cynicism that was his leading characteristic.

∽ 10 ∽

The next day an incident served to confirm Billy Budd in his incredulity as to the Dansker's strange summing-up of the case submitted. The ship at noon, going large before the wind, was rolling on her course, and he, below at dinner and engaged in some sportful talk with the members of his mess, chanced in a sudden lurch to spill the entire contents of his soup-pan upon the new scrubbed deck. Claggart, the Master-at-arms, official rattan in hand, happened to be passing along the battery in a bay of which the mess was lodged, and the greasy liquid streamed just across his path. Stepping over it, he was proceeding on his way without comment, since the matter was nothing to take notice of under the circumstances, when he happened to observe who it was that had done the spilling. His countenance changed. Pausing, he was about to ejaculate something hasty at the sailor, but checked himself, and pointing down to the streaming soup, playfully tapped him from behind with his rattan, saying in a low musical voice peculiar to him at times, "Handsomely done, my lad! And handsome is as handsome did it too!" And with that passed on. Not noted by Billy, as not coming within his view, was the involuntary smile, or rather grimace, that accompanied Claggart's equivocal words. Aridly it drew down the thin corners of his shapely mouth. But everybody taking his remark as meant for humourous, and at which therefore as coming from a superior they were bound to laugh "with counterfeited glee," acted accordingly; and Billy tickled, it may be, by the allusion to his being the handsome sailor, merrily joined in; then addressing his messmates exclaimed, "There now, who says that Jimmy Legs is down on me!" "And who said he was, Beauty?" demanded one Donald with some surprise. Whereat the Foretopman looked a little foolish, recalling that it was only one person, Board-her-in-the-smoke, who had suggested what to him was the smoky idea that this Master-at-arms was in any peculiar way hostile to him. Meantime that functionary, resuming his path, must have momentarily worn some expression less guarded than that of the bitter smile, and usurping the face from the heart, some distorting expression perhaps; for a drummer-boy heedlessly frolicking along from the opposite direction and chancing to come into light collision with his person was strangely disconcerted by his aspect. Nor was the impression lessened when the official, impulsively giving him a sharp cut with the rattan, vehemently exclaimed, "Look where you go!"

11

What was the matter with the Master-at-arms? And, be the matter what it might, how could it have direct relation to Billy Budd with whom, prior to the affair of the spilled soup, he had never come into any special contact, official or otherwise? What indeed could the trouble have to do with one so little inclined to give offence as the merchant-ship's *peacemaker*, even him who in Claggart's own phrase was "the sweet and pleasant young fellow"? Yes, why should *Jimmy Legs*, to borrow the Dansker's expression, be *down* on the Handsome Sailor? But, at heart and not for nothing,

as the late chance encounter may indicate to the discerning, down on him, secretly down on him, he assuredly was.

Now to invent something touching the more private career of Claggart, something involving Billy Budd, of which something the latter should be wholly ignorant, some romantic incident implying that Claggart's knowledge of the young blue-jacket began at some period anterior to catching sight of him on board the seventy-four —all this, not so difficult to do, might avail in a way more or less interesting to account for whatever of enigma may appear to lurk in the case. But in fact there was nothing of the sort. And yet the cause, necessarily to be assumed as the sole one assignable, is in its very realism as much charged with that prime element of Radcliffian romance, *the mysterious*, as any that the ingenuity of the author of the *Mysteries of Udolpho* could devise. For what can more partake of the mysterious than an antipathy spontaneous and profound, such as is evoked in certain exceptional mortals by the mere aspect of some other mortal, however harmless he may be, if not called forth by this very harmlessness itself?

Now there can exist no irritating juxtaposition of dissimilar personalities comparable to that which is possible aboard a great war-ship fully manned and at sea. There, every day among all ranks almost every man comes into more or less of contact with almost every other man. Wholly there to avoid even the sight of an aggravating object one must needs give it Jonah's toss or jump overboard himself. Imagine how all this might eventually operate on some peculiar human creature the direct reverse of a saint?

But for the adequate comprehending of Claggart by a normal nature, these hints are insufficient. To pass from a normal nature to him one must cross "the deadly space between." And this is best done by indirection.

Long ago an honest scholar my senior, said to me in reference to one who like himself is now no more, a man so unimpeachably respectable that against him nothing was ever openly said tho' among the few something was whispered, "Yes, X——— is a nut not to be cracked by the tap of a lady's fan. You are aware that I am the adherent of no organized religion much less of any philosophy built into a system. Well, for all that, I think that to try and get into X———, enter his labyrinth and get out again, without a clue derived from some source other than what is known as *knowledge of the world*—that were hardly possible, at least for me."

"Why," said I, "X———, however singular a study to some, is yet human, and knowledge of the world assuredly implies the knowledge of human nature, and in most of its varieties."

"Yes, but a superficial knowledge of it, serving ordinary purposes. But for anything deeper, I am not certain whether to know the world and to know human nature be not two distinct branches of knowledge, which while they may coexist in the same heart, yet either may exist with little or nothing of the other. Nay, in an average man of the world, his constant rubbing with it blunts that fine spiritual insight indispensable to the understanding of the essential in certain exceptional characters, whether evil ones or good. In a matter of some importance I have seen a girl wind an old lawyer about her little finger. Nor was it the dotage of senile love. Nothing of the sort. But he knew law better than he knew the girl's heart. Coke and Blackstone hardly shed so much light into obscure spiritual places as the Hebrew prophets. And who were they? Mostly recluses."

At the time my inexperience was such that I did not quite see the drift of all this. It may be that I see it now. And, indeed, if that lexicon which is based on Holy Writ were any longer popular, one might with less difficulty define and denominate certain phenomenal men. As it is, one must turn to some authority not liable to the charge of being tinctured with the Biblical element.

In a list of definitions included in the authentic translation of Plato, a list attributed to him, occurs this: "Natural Depravity: a depravity according to nature." A definition which tho' savoring of Calvinism, by no means involves Calvin's dogmas as to total mankind. Evidently its intent makes it applicable but to individuals. Not many are the examples of this depravity which the gallows and jail supply. At any rate for notable instances, since these have no vulgar alloy of the brute in them, but invariably are dominated by intellectuality, one must go elsewhere. Civilization, especially if of the austerer sort, is auspicious to it. It folds itself in the mantle of respectability. It has its certain negative virtues serving as silent auxiliaries. It never allows wine to get within its guard. It is not going too far to say that it is without vices or small sins. There is a phenomenal pride in it that excludes them from anything mercenary or avaricious. In short the depravity here meant partakes nothing of the sordid or sensual. It is serious, but free from acerbity. Though no flatterer of mankind it never speaks ill of it.

But the thing which in eminent instances signalizes so exceptional a nature is this: though the man's even temper and discreet bearing would seem to intimate a mind peculiarly subject to the law of reason, not the less in his heart he would seem to riot in complete exemption from that law, having apparently little to do with reason further than to employ it as an ambidexter implement for effecting the irrational. That is to say: Toward the accomplishment of an aim which in wantonness of malignity would seem to partake of the insane, he will direct a cool judgement sagacious and sound.

These men are true madmen, and of the most dangerous sort, for their lunacy is not continuous but occasional, evoked by some special object; it is probably secretive, which is as much to say it is self-contained, so that when moreover, most active, it is to the average mind not distinguishable from sanity, and for the reason above suggested that whatever its aims may be—and the aim is never declared—the method and the outward proceeding are always perfectly rational.

Now something such an one was Claggart, in whom was the mania of an evil nature, not engendered by vicious training or corrupting books or licentious living, but born with him and innate, in short "a depravity according to nature."

12

Lawyers, Experts, Clergy

AN EPISODE

By the way, can it be the phenomenon, disowned or at least concealed, that in some criminal cases puzzles the courts? For this cause have our juries at times not only to endure the prolonged contentions of lawyers with their fees, but also the yet more perplexing strife of the medical experts with theirs?—But why leave it to them? Why not subpoena as well the clerical proficients? Their vocation bringing them into peculiar contact with so many human beings, and sometimes in their least guarded hour, in interviews very much more confidential than those of physician and patient; this would seem to qualify them to know something about those intricacies involved in the question of moral responsibility; whether in a given case, say, the crime proceeded from mania in the brain or rabies of the heart. As to any differences among themselves these clerical proficients might develop on the stand, these could hardly be greater than the direct contradictions exchanged between the remunerated medical experts.

Dark sayings are these, some will say. But why? Is it because they somewhat savor of Holy Writ in its phrase "mysteries of iniquity"? If they do, such savor was far from being intended, for little will it commend these pages to many a reader of to-day.

The point of the present story turning on the hidden nature of the Master-at-arms has necessitated this chapter. With an added hint or two in connection with the incident at the mess, the resumed narrative must be left to vindicate, as it may, its own credibility.

13

Pale ire, envy and despair

That Claggart's figure was not amiss, and his face, save the chin, well moulded, has already been said. Of these favorable points he seemed not insensible, for he was not only neat but careful in his dress. But the form of Billy Budd was heroic; and if his face was without the intellectual look of the pallid Claggart's, not the less was it lit, like his, from within, though from a different source. The bonfire in his heart made luminous the rose-tan in his cheek.

In view of the marked contrast between the persons of the twain, it is more than probable that when the Master-at-arms in the scene last given applied to the sailor the proverb *Handsome is as handsome does*, he there let escape an ironic inkling, not caught by the young sailors who heard it, as to what it was that had first moved him against Billy, namely, his significant personal beauty.

Now envy and antipathy, passions irreconcilable in reason, nevertheless in fact may spring conjoined like Chang and Eng in one birth. Is Envy then such a monster? Well, though many an arraigned mortal has in hopes of mitigated penalty pleaded guilty to horrible actions, did ever anybody seriously confess to envy? Something there is in it universally felt to be more shameful than even felonious crime. And not only does everybody disown it, but the better sort are inclined to incredulity when it is in earnest imputed to an intelligent man. But since its lodgement is in the heart not the brain, no degree of intellect supplies a guarantee against it. But Claggart's was no vulgar form of the passion. Nor, as directed toward Billy Budd, did it partake of that streak of apprehensive jealousy that marred Saul's visage perturbedly brooding on the comely young David. Claggart's envy struck deeper. If askance he eyed the good looks, cheery health and frank enjoyment of young life in Billy Budd, it was because these went along with a nature that, as Claggart magnetically felt, had in its simplicity never willed malice or experienced the reactionary bite of that serpent. To him, the spirit lodged within Billy, and looking out from his welkin eyes as from windows, that ineffability it was which made the dimple in his dyed cheek, suppled his joints, and dancing in his yellow curls made him preeminently the Handsome Sailor. One person excepted, the Master-at-arms was perhaps the only man in the ship intellectually capable of adequately appreciating the moral phenomenon presented in Billy Budd. And the insight but intensified his passion, which assuming various secret forms within him, at times assumed that of cynic disdain—disdain of innocence. To be nothing more than innocent! Yet in an aesthetic way he saw the charm of it, the courageous free-and-easy temper of it, and fain would have shared it, but he despaired of it.

With no power to annul the elemental evil in him, tho' readily enough he could hide it; apprehending the good, but powerless to be it; a nature like Claggart's surcharged with energy as such natures almost invariably are, what recourse is left to it but to recoil upon itself and like the scorpion for which the Creator alone is responsible, act out to the end the part allotted it.

14

Passion, and passion in its profoundest, is not a thing demanding a palatial stage whereon to play its part. Down among the groundlings, among the beggars and rakers of the garbage, profound passion is enacted. And the circumstances that provoke it, however trivial or mean, are no measure of its power. In the present instance the stage is a scrubbed gun deck, and one of the external provocations a man-of-war's-man's spilled soup.

Now when the Master-at-arms noticed whence came that greasy fluid streaming before his feet, he must have taken it—to some extent wilfully, perhaps—not for the mere accident it assuredly was, but for the sly escape of a spontaneous feeling on Billy's part more or less answering to the antipathy on his own. In effect a foolish demonstration he must have thought, and very harmless, like the futile kick of a heifer, which yet were the heifer a shod stallion, would not be so harmless. Even so was it that into the gall of Claggart's envy he infused the vitriol of his contempt. But the incident confirmed to him certain tell-tale reports purveyed to his ear by *Squeak*, one of his more cunning Corporals, a grizzled little man, so nicknamed by the sailors on account of his squeaky voice, and sharp visage ferreting about the dark corners of the lower decks after interlopers, satirically suggesting to them the idea of a rat in a cellar.

From his Chief's employing him as an implicit tool in laying little traps for the worriment of the Foretopman—for it was from the Master-at-arms that the petty persecutions heretofore adverted to had proceeded—the Corporal having naturally enough concluded that his master could have no love for the sailor, made it his business, faithful understrapper that he was, to foment the ill blood by perverting to his Chief certain innocent frolics of the good-natured Foretopman, besides inventing for his mouth sundry contumelious epithets he claimed to have overheard him let fall. The Master-at-arms never suspected the veracity of these reports, more especially as to the epithets, for he well knew how secretly unpopular may become a master-at-arms, at least a master-at-arms of those days zealous in his function, and how the blue-jackets shoot at him in private their raillery and wit; the nickname by which he goes among them (*Jimmy Legs*) implying under the form of merriment their cherished disrespect and dislike.

But in view of the greediness of hate for patrolmen, it hardly needed a purveyor to feed Claggart's passion. An uncommon prudence is habitual with the subtler depravity, for it has everything to hide. And in case of an injury but suspected, its secretiveness voluntarily cuts it off from enlightenment or disillusion; and, not unreluctantly, action is taken upon surmise as upon certainty. And the retaliation is apt to be in monstrous disproportion to the supposed offence; for when in anybody was revenge in its exactions aught else but an inordinate usurer? But how with Claggart's conscience? For though consciences are unlike as foreheads, every intelligence, not excluding the Scriptural devils who "believe and tremble," has one. But Claggart's conscience being but the lawyer to his will, made ogres of trifles, probably arguing that the motive imputed to Billy in spilling the soup just when he did, together with the epithets alleged, these, if nothing more, made a strong case against him; nay, justified animosity into a sort of retributive righteousness. The Pharisee is the Guy Fawkes prowling in the hid chambers underlying the Claggarts. And they can really form no conception of an unreciprocated malice. Probably, the Master-at-arms' clandestine persecution of Billy was started to try the temper of the man; but it had not developed any quality in him that enmity could make official use of or even pervert into plausible self-justification; so that the occurrence at the mess, petty if it were, was a welcome one to that peculiar conscience assigned to be the private mentor of Claggart. And, for the rest, not improbably it put him upon new experiments.

15

Not many days after the last incident narrated, something befell Billy Budd that more gravelled him than aught that had previously occurred.

It was a warm night for the latitude; and the Foretopman, whose watch at the time was properly below, was dozing on the uppermost deck whither he had ascended from his hot hammock, one of hundreds suspended so closely wedged together over a lower gun deck that there was little or no swing to them. He lay as in the shadow of a hill-side, stretched under the lee of the booms, a piled ridge of spare spars amidships between fore-mast and main-mast and among which the ship's largest boat, the launch, was stowed. Alongside of three other slumberers from below, he lay near that end of the booms which approaches the fore-mast; his station aloft on duty as a foretopman being just over the deck-station of the forecastlemen, entitling him according to usage to make himself more or less at home in that neighbourhood.

Presently he was stirred into semi-consciousness by somebody, who must have previously sounded the sleep of the others, touching his shoulder, and then as the Foretopman raised his head, breathing into his ear in a quick whisper, "Slip into the lee fore-chains, Billy; there is something in the wind. Don't speak. Quick, I will meet you there"; and disappeared.

Now Billy like sundry other essentially good-natured ones had some of the weaknesses inseparable from essential good-nature; and among these was a reluctance, almost an incapacity of plumply saying *no* to an abrupt proposition not obviously absurd, on the face of it, nor obviously unfriendly, nor iniquitous. And being of warm blood he had not the phlegm tacitly to negative any proposition by unresponsive inaction. Like his sense of fear, his apprehension as to aught outside of the honest and natural was seldom very quick. Besides, upon the present occasion, the drowse from his sleep still hung upon him.

However it was, he mechanically rose, and sleepily wondering what could be in the wind, betook himself to the designated place, a narrow platform, one of six, outside of the high bulwarks and screened by the great dead-eyes and multiple columned lanyards of the shrouds and back-stays; and, in a great war-ship of that time, of dimensions commensurate with the hull's magnitude; a tarry balcony, in short, overhanging the sea, and so secluded that one mariner of the *Indomitable*, a non-conformist old tar of a serious turn, made it even in daytime his private oratory.

In this retired nook the stranger soon joined Billy Budd. There was no moon as yet; a haze obscured the star-light. He could not distinctly see the stranger's face. Yet from something in the outline and carriage, Billy took him to be, and correctly, one of the after-guard.

"Hist! Billy," said the man in the same quick cautionary whisper as before; "You were impressed, weren't you? Well, so was I"; and he paused, as to mark the effect. But Billy, not knowing exactly what to make of this, said nothing. Then the other: "We are not the only impressed ones, Billy. There's a gang of us.—Couldn't you—help—at a pinch?"

"What do you mean?" demanded Billy, here thoroughly shaking off his drowse.

"Hist, hist!" the hurried whisper now growing husky, "see here"; and the man held up two small objects faintly twinkling in the nightlight; "see, they are yours, Billy, if you'll only—"

But Billy broke in, and in his resentful eagerness to deliver himself his vocal infirmity somewhat intruded: "D-D-Damme, I don't know what you are d-d-driving at, or what you mean, but you had better g-g-go where you belong!" For the moment the fellow, as confounded, did not stir; and Billy springing to his feet, said, "If you d-don't start I'll t-t-toss you back over the r-rail!" There was no mistaking this and the mysterious emissary decamped disappearing in the direction of the main-mast in the shadow of the booms.

"Hallo, what's the matter?" here came growling from a forecastleman awakened from his deck-doze by Billy's raised voice. And as the Foretopman reappeared and was recognized by him; "Ah, *Beauty*, is it you? Well, something must have been the matter for you st-st-stuttered."

"O," rejoined Billy, now mastering the impediment; "I found an afterguardsman in our part of the ship here and I bid him be off where he belongs."

"And is that all you did about it, Foretopman?" gruffly demanded another, an irascible old fellow of brick-colored visage and hair, and who was known to his associate forecastlemen as *Red Pepper*; "Such sneaks I should like to marry to the gunner's daughter!" by that expression meaning that he would like to subject them to disciplinary castigation over a gun.

However, Billy's rendering of the matter satisfactorily accounted to these inquirers for the brief commotion, since of all the sections of a ship's company, the forecastlemen, veterans for the most part and bigoted in their sea-prejudices, are the most jealous in resenting territorial encroachments, especially on the part of any of the afterguard, of whom they have but a sorry opinion, chiefly landsmen, never going aloft except to reef or furl the mainsail and in no wise competent to handle a marlinspike or turn in a *dead-eye*, say.

16

This incident sorely puzzled Billy Budd. It was an entirely new experience; the first time in his life that he had ever been personally approached in underhand intriguing fashion. Prior to this encounter he had known nothing of the afterguardsman, the two men being stationed wide apart, one forward and aloft during his watch, the other on deck and aft.

What could it mean? And could they really be guineas, those two glittering objects the interloper had held up to his eyes? Where could the fellow get guineas? Why even spare buttons are not so plentiful at sea. The more he turned the matter over, the more he was non-plussed, and made uneasy and discomforted. In his disgustful recoil from an overture which tho' he but ill comprehended he instinctively knew must involve evil of some sort, Billy Budd was like a young horse fresh from the pasture suddenly inhaling a vile whiff from some chemical factory, and by repeated snortings tries to get it out of his nostrils and lungs. This frame of mind barred all desire of holding further parley with the fellow, even were it but for the purpose of gaining some enlightenment as to his design in approaching him. And yet he was not without natural curiosity to see how such a visitor in the dark would look in broad day.

He espied him the following afternoon, in his first dog-watch, below, one of the smokers on that forward part of the upper gun deck allotted to the pipe. He recognized him by his general cut and build, more than by his round freckled face and glassy eyes of pale blue, veiled with lashes all but white. And yet Billy was a bit uncertain whether indeed it were he—yonder chap about his own age chatting and laughing in free-hearted way, leaning against a gun; a genial young fellow enough to look at, and something of a rattlebrain, to all appearance. Rather chubby too for a sailor, even an afterguardsman. In short the last man in the world, one would think, to be overburthened with thoughts, especially those perilous thoughts that must needs belong to a conspirator in any serious project, or even to the underling of such a conspirator.

Altho' Billy was not aware of it, the fellow, with a sidelong watchful glance had perceived Billy first, and then noting that Billy was looking at him, thereupon nodded a familiar sort of friendly recognition as to an old acquaintance, without interrupting the talk he was engaged in with the group of smokers. A day or two afterwards, chancing in the evening promenade on a gun deck to pass Billy, he offered a flying word of good-fellowship, as it were, which by its unexpectedness, and equivocalness under the circumstances so embarrassed Billy that he knew not how to respond to it, and let it go unnoticed.

Billy was now left more at a loss than before. The ineffectual speculation into which he was led was so disturbingly alien to him, that he did his best to smother it. It never entered his mind that here was a matter which from its extreme questionableness, it was his duty as a loyal blue-jacket to report in the proper quarter. And, probably, had such a step been suggested to him, he would have been deterred from taking it by the thought, one of novice-magnanimity, that it would savor overmuch of the dirty work of a telltale. He kept the thing to himself. Yet upon one occasion, he could not forbear a little disburthening himself to the old Dansker, tempted thereto perhaps by the influence of a balmy night when the ship lay becalmed; the twain, silent for the most part, sitting together on deck, their heads propped against the bulwarks. But it was only a partial and anonymous account that Billy gave, the unfounded scruples above referred to preventing full disclosure to anybody. Upon hearing Billy's version, the sage Dansker seemed to divine more than he was told; and after a little meditation during which his wrinkles were pursed as into a point, quite effacing for the time that quizzing expression his face sometimes wore,—"Didn't I say so, Baby Budd?"

"Say what?" demanded Billy.

"Why, *Jimmy Legs* is *down* on you."

"And what," rejoined Billy in amazement, "has *Jimmy Legs* to do with that cracked afterguardsman?"

"Ho, it was an afterguardsman then. A cat's-paw, a cat's-paw!" And with that exclamation, which, whether it had reference to a light puff of air just then coming over the calm sea, or subtler relation to the afterguardsman there is no telling, the old Merlin gave a twisting wrench with his black teeth at his plug of tobacco, vouchsafing no reply to Billy's impetuous question, tho' now repeated, for it was his wont to relapse into grim silence when interrogated in skeptical sort as to any of his sententious oracles, not always very clear ones, rather partaking of that obscurity which invests most Delphic deliverances from any quarter.

Long experience had very likely brought this old man to that bitter prudence which never interferes in aught and never gives advice.

17

Yes, despite the Dansker's pithy insistence as to the Master-at-arms being at the bottom of these strange experiences of Billy on board the *Indomitable,* the young sailor was ready to ascribe them to almost anybody but the man who, to use Billy's own expression, "always had a pleasant word for him." This is to be wondered at. Yet not so much to be wondered at. In certain matters, some sailors even in mature life remain unsophisticated enough. But a young seafarer of the disposition of our athletic Foretopman, is much of a child-man. And yet a child's utter innocence is but its blank ignorance, and the innocence more or less wanes as intelligence waxes. But in Billy Budd intelligence, such as it was, had advanced, while yet his simplemindedness remained for the most part unaffected. Experience is a teacher indeed; yet did Billy's years make his experience small. Besides, he had none of that intuitive knowledge of the bad which in natures not good or incompletely so foreruns experience, and therefore may pertain, as in some instances it too clearly does pertain, even to youth.

And what could Billy know of man except of man as a mere sailor? And the old-fashioned sailor, the veritable man-before-the-mast, the sailor from boyhood up, he, tho' indeed of the same species as a landsman, is in some respects singularly distinct from him. The sailor is frankness, the landsman is finesse. Life is not a game with the sailor, demanding the long head; no intricate game of chess where few moves are made in straightforwardness, and ends are attained by indirection; an oblique, tedious, barren game hardly worth that poor candle burnt out in playing it.

Yes, as a class, sailors are in character a juvenile race. Even their deviations are marked by juvenility. And this more especially holding true with the sailors of Billy's time. Then, too, certain things which apply to all sailors, do more pointedly operate, here and there, upon the junior one. Every sailor, too, is accustomed to obey orders without debating them; his life afloat is externally ruled for him; he is not brought into that promiscuous commerce with mankind where unobstructed free agency on equal terms—equal superficially, at least—soon teaches one that unless upon occasion he exercise a distrust keen in proportion to the fairness of the appearance, some foul turn may be served him. A ruled undemonstrative distrustfulness is so habitual, not with business-men so much, as with men who know their kind in less shallow relations than business, namely, certain men-of-the-world, that they come at last to employ it all but unconsciously; and some of them would very likely feel real surprise at being charged with it as one of their general characteristics.

18

But after the little matter at the mess Billy Budd no more found himself in strange trouble at times about his hammock or his clothesbag or what not. While, as to that smile that occasionally sunned him, and the pleasant passing word, these were if not more frequent, yet if anything, more pronounced than before.

But for all that, there were certain other demonstrations now. When Claggart's unobserved glance happened to light on belted Billy rolling along the upper gun deck in the leisure of the second dog-watch, exchanging passing broadsides of fun with other young promenaders in the crowd; that glance would follow the cheerful sea-Hyperion with a settled meditative and melancholy expression, his eyes strangely suffused with incipient feverish tears. Then would Claggart look like the man of sorrows. Yes, and sometimes the melancholy expression would have in it a touch of soft yearning, as if Claggart could even have loved Billy but for fate and ban. But this was an evanescence, and quickly repented of, as it were, by an immitigable look, pinching and shrivelling the visage into the momentary semblance of a wrinkled walnut. But sometimes catching sight in advance of the Foretopman coming in his direction, he would, upon their nearing, step aside a little to let him pass, dwelling upon Billy for the moment with the glittering dental satire of a Guise. But upon any abrupt unforeseen encounter a red light would flash forth from his eye like a spark from an anvil in a dusk smithy. That quick fierce light was a strange one, darted from orbs which in repose were of a color nearest approaching a deeper violet, the softest of shades.

Tho' some of these caprices of the pit could not but be observed by their object, yet were they beyond the construing of such a nature. And the *thews* of Billy were hardly compatible with that sort of sensitive spiritual organisation which in some cases instinctively conveys to ignorant innocence an admonition of the proximity of the malign. He thought the Master-at-arms acted in a manner rather queer at times. That was all. But the occasional frank air and pleasant word went for what they purported to be, the young sailor never having heard as yet of the "too fair-spoken man."

Had the Foretopman been conscious of having done or said anything to provoke the ill will of the official, it would have been different with him, and his sight might have been purged if not sharpened. As it was, innocence was his blinder.

So was it with him in yet another matter. Two minor officers—the Armorer and Captain of the Hold, with whom he had never exchanged a word, his position in the ship not bringing him into contact with them; these men now for the first began to cast upon Billy when they chanced to encounter him, that peculiar glance which evidences that the man from whom it comes has been some way tampered with and to the prejudice of him upon whom the glance lights. Never did it occur to Billy as a thing to be noted or a thing suspicious, tho' he well knew the fact, that the Armorer and Captain of the Hold, with the ship's-yeoman, apothecary, and others of that grade, were by naval usage, messmates of the Master-at-arms, men with ears convenient to his confidential tongue.

But the general popularity that our Handsome Sailor's manly forwardness bred upon occasion, and his irresistible good-nature, indicating no mental superiority tending to excite an invidious feeling, this good will on the part of most of his shipmates made him the less to concern himself about such mute aspects toward him as those whereto allusion has just been made, aspects he could not fathom as to infer their whole import.

As to the afterguardsman, tho' Billy for reasons already given necessarily saw little of him, yet when the two did happen to meet, invariably came the fellow's off-hand cheerful recognition, sometimes accompanied by a passing pleasant word or two. Whatever that equivocal young person's original design may really have been, or the design of which he might have been the deputy, certain it was from his manner upon these occasions, that he had wholly dropped it.

It was as if his precocity of crookedness (and every vulgar villain is precocious) had for once deceived him, and the man he had sought to entrap as a simpleton had, through his very simplicity, ignominiously baffled him.

But shrewd ones may opine that it was hardly possible for Billy to refrain from going up to the afterguardsman and bluntly demanding to know his purpose in the initial interview, so abruptly closed in the fore-chains. Shrewd ones may also think it but natural in Billy to set about sounding some of the other impressed men of the ship in order to discover what basis, if any, there was for the emissary's obscure suggestions as to plotting disaffection aboard. Yes, the shrewd may so think. But something more, or rather, something else than mere shrewdness is perhaps needful for the due understanding of such a character as Billy Budd's.

As to Claggart, the monomania in the man—if that indeed it were—as involuntarily disclosed by starts in the manifestations detailed, yet in general covered over by his self-contained and rational demeanour; this, like a subterranean fire was eating its way deeper and deeper in him. Something decisive must come of it.

After the mysterious interview in the fore-chains—the one so abruptly ended there by Billy—nothing especially german to the story occurred until the events now about to be narrated.

Elsewhere it has been said that in the lack of frigates (of course better sailers than line-of-battle ships) in the English squadron up the Straits at that period, the *Indomitable* was occasionally employed not only as an available substitute for a scout, but at times on detached service of more important kind. This was not alone because of her sailing qualities, not common in a ship of her rate, but quite as much, probably, that the character of her commander, it was thought, specially adapted him for any duty where under unforeseen difficulties a prompt initiative might have to be taken in some matter demanding knowledge and ability in addition to those qualities implied in good seamanship. It was on an expedition of the latter sort, a somewhat distant one, and when the *Indomitable* was almost at her furthest remove from the fleet, that in the latter part of an afternoon-watch she unexpectedly came in sight of a ship of the enemy. It proved to be a frigate. The latter perceiving thro' the glass that the weight of men and metal would be heavily against her, invoking her light heels, crowded sail to get away. After a chase urged almost against hope and lasting until about the middle of the first dog-watch, she signally succeeded in effecting her escape.

Not long after the pursuit had been given up, and ere the excitement incident thereto had altogether waned away, the Master-at-arms, ascending from his cavernous sphere, made his appearance cap in hand by the main-mast, respectfully waiting the notice of Captain Vere then solitary walking the weather-side of the quarter-deck, doubtless somewhat chafed at the failure of the pursuit. The spot where Claggart stood was the place allotted to men of lesser grades seeking some more particular interview either with the officer-of-the-deck or the Captain himself. But from the latter it was not often that a sailor or petty-officer of those days would seek a hearing; only some exceptional cause, would, according to established custom, have warranted that.

Presently, just as the Commander absorbed in his reflections was on the point of turning aft in his promenade, he became sensible of Claggart's presence, and saw the doffed cap held in deferential expectancy. Here be it said that Captain Vere's personal knowledge of this petty-officer had only begun at the time of the ship's last sailing from home, Claggart then for the first, in transfer from a ship detained for repairs, supplying on board the *Indomitable* the place of a previous master-at-arms disabled and ashore.

No sooner did the Commander observe who it was that deferentially stood awaiting his notice, than a peculiar expression came over him. It was not unlike that which uncontrollably will flit across the countenance of one at unawares encountering a person who, though known to him indeed, has hardly been long enough known for thorough knowledge, but something in whose aspect nevertheless now for the first provokes a vaguely repellent distaste. But coming to a stand, and resuming much of his wonted official manner, save that a sort of impatience lurked in the intonation of the opening word, he said, "Well? what is it, Master-at-arms?"

With the air of a subordinate grieved at the necessity of being a messenger of ill tidings, and while conscientiously determined to be frank, yet equally resolved upon shunning overstatement, Claggart, at this invitation or rather summons to disburthen, spoke up. What he said, conveyed in the language of no uneducated man, was to the effect following, if not altogether in these words, namely, that during the chase and preparations for the possible encounter he had seen enough to convince him that at least one sailor aboard was a dangerous character in a ship mustering some who not only had taken a guilty part in the late serious troubles, but others also who, like the man in question, had entered His Majesty's service under another form than enlistment.

At this point Captain Vere with some impatience interrupted him: "Be direct, man; say impressed men."

Claggart made a gesture of subservience, and proceeded.

Quite lately he (Claggart) had begun to suspect that on the

gun decks some sort of movement prompted by the sailor in question was covertly going on, but he had not thought himself warranted in reporting the suspicion so long as it remained indistinct. But from what he had that afternoon observed in the man referred to, the suspicion of something clandestine going on had advanced to a point less removed from certainty. He deeply felt, he added, the serious responsibility assumed in making a report involving such possible consequences to the individual mainly concerned, besides tending to augment those natural anxieties which every naval commander must feel in view of extraordinary outbreaks so recent as those which, he sorrowfully said it, it needed not to name.

Now at the first broaching of the matter Captain Vere, taken by surprise, could not wholly dissemble his disquietude. But as Claggart went on, the former's aspect changed into restiveness under something in the witness' manner in giving his testimony. However, he refrained from interrupting him. And Claggart, continuing, concluded with this: "God forbid, Your Honor, that the *Indomitable's* should be the experience of the—"

"Never mind that!" here peremptorily broke in the superior, his face altering with anger, instinctively divining the ship that the other was about to name, one in which the Nore Mutiny had assumed a singularly tragical character that for a time jeopardized the life of its commander. Under the circumstances he was indignant at the purposed allusion. When the commissioned officers themselves were on all occasions very heedful how they referred to the recent events, for a petty-officer unnecessarily to allude to them in the presence of his Captain, this struck him as a most immodest presumption. Besides, to his quick sense of self-respect, it even looked under the circumstances something like an attempt to alarm him. Nor at first was he without some surprise that one who so far as he had hitherto come under his notice had shown considerable tact in his function should in this particular evince such lack of it.

But these thoughts and kindred dubious ones flitting across his mind were suddenly replaced by an intuitional surmise which, though as yet obscure in form, served practically to affect his reception of the ill tidings. Certain it is, that long versed in everything pertaining to the complicated gun-deck life, which like every other form of life, has its secret mines and dubious side, the side popularly disclaimed, Captain Vere did not permit himself to be unduly disturbed by the general tenor of his subordinate's report. Furthermore, if in view of recent events prompt action should be taken at the first palpable sign of recurring insubordination, for all that, not judicious would it be, he thought, to keep the idea of lingering disaffection alive by undue forwardness in crediting an informer, even if his own subordinate, and charged among other things with police surveillance of the crew. This feeling would not perhaps have so prevailed with him were it not that upon a prior occasion the patriotic zeal officially evinced by Claggart had somewhat irritated him as appearing rather supersensible and strained. Furthermore, something even in the official's self-possessed and somewhat ostentatious manner in making his specifications strangely reminded him of a bandsman, a perjurous witness in a capital case before a court-martial ashore of which when a lieutenant, he, Captain Vere, had been a member.

Now the peremptory check given to Claggart in the matter of the arrested allusion was quickly followed up by this: "You say that there is at least one dangerous man aboard. Name him."

"William Budd. A foretopman, Your Honor—"

"William Budd," repeated Captain Vere with unfeigned astonishment; "and mean you the man that Lieutenant Ratcliff took from the merchantman not very long ago—the young fellow who seems to be so popular with the men—Billy, the 'Handsome Sailor,' as they call him?"

"The same, Your Honor; but for all his youth and good looks, a deep one. Not for nothing does he insinuate himself into the good will of his shipmates, since at the least all hands will at a pinch say a good word for him at all hazards. Did Lieutenant Ratcliff happen to tell Your Honor of that adroit fling of Budd's, jumping up in the cutter's bow under the merchantman's stern when he was being taken off? It is even masqued by that sort of good-humoured air that at heart he resents his impressment. You have but noted his fair cheek. A man-trap may be under his ruddy-tipped daisies."

Now the Handsome Sailor, as a signal figure among the crew, had naturally enough attracted the Captain's attention from the first. Tho' in general not very demonstrative to his officers, he had congratulated Lieutenant Ratcliff upon his good fortune in lighting on such a fine specimen of the genus homo, who in the nude might have posed for a statue of young Adam before the Fall.

As to Billy's adieu to the ship *Rights-of-Man,* which the boarding lieutenant had indeed reported to him, but in a deferential way more as a good story than aught else, Captain Vere, tho' mistakenly understanding it as a satiric sally, had but thought so much the better of the impressed man for it; as a military sailor, admiring the spirit that could take an arbitrary enlistment so merrily and sensibly. The Foretopman's conduct, too, so far as it had fallen under the Captain's notice, had confirmed the first happy augury, while the new recruit's qualities as a *sailor-man* seemed to be such that he had thought of recommending him to the executive officer for promotion to a place that would more frequently bring him under his own observation, namely, the captaincy of the mizzentop, replacing there in the starboard watch a man not so young whom partly for that reason he deemed less fitted for the post. Be it parenthesized here that since the mizzentopmen having not to handle such breadths of heavy canvas as the lower sails on the main-mast and fore-mast, a young man if of the right stuff not only seems best adapted to duty there, but in fact is generally selected for the captaincy of that top, and the company under him are light hands and often but striplings. In sum, Captain Vere had from the beginning deemed Billy Budd to be what in the naval parlance of the time was called a "*King's bargain,*" that is to say, for His Britannic Majesty's Navy a capital investment at small outlay or none at all.

After a brief pause during which the reminiscences above mentioned passed vividly through his mind and he weighed the import of Claggart's last suggestion conveyed in the phrase "man-trap under his daisies," and the more he weighed it the less reliance he felt in the informer's good faith, suddenly he turned upon him and in a low voice: "Do you come to me, Master-at-arms, with so foggy a tale? As to Budd, cite me an act or spoken word of his confirmatory of what you in general charge against him. Stay," drawing nearer to him, "heed what you speak. Just now, and in a case like this, there is a yard-arm-end for the false-witness."

"Ah, Your Honor!" sighed Claggart, mildly shaking his shapely head as in sad deprecation of such unmerited severity of tone. Then, bridling—erecting himself as in virtuous self-assertion, he circumstantially alleged certain words and acts, which collectively, if credited, led to presumptions mortally inculpating Budd. And for some of these averments, he added, substantiating proof was not far.

With gray eyes impatient and distrustful essaying to fathom to the bottom Claggart's calm violet ones, Captain Vere again heard him out; then for the moment stood ruminating. The mood he evinced, Claggart—himself for the time liberated from the other's scrutiny—steadily regarded with a look difficult to render, —a look curious of the operation of his tactics, a look such as might have been that of the spokesman of the envious children of Jacob deceptively imposing upon the troubled patriarch the blood-dyed coat of young Joseph.

Though something exceptional in the moral quality of Captain Vere made him, in earnest encounter with a fellow-man, a veritable touch-stone of that man's essential nature, yet now as to Claggart and what was really going on in him, his feeling partook less of intuitional conviction than of strong suspicion clogged by strange dubieties. The perplexity he evinced proceeded less from aught touching the man informed against—as Claggart doubtless opined —than from considerations how best to act in regard to the informer. At first indeed he was naturally for summoning that substantiation of his allegations which Claggart said was at hand. But such a proceeding would result in the matter at once getting abroad, which in the present stage of it, he thought, might undesirably affect the ship's company. If Claggart was a false witness,—that closed the affair. And therefore before trying the accusation, he would first practically test the accuser; and he thought this could be done in a quiet undemonstrative way.

The measure he determined upon involved a shifting of the scene, a transfer to a place less exposed to observation than the broad quarter-deck. For although the few gun-room officers there at the time had, in due observance of naval etiquette, withdrawn to leeward the moment Captain Vere had begun his promenade on the deck's weather-side; and tho' during the colloquy with Claggart they of course ventured not to diminish the distance; and though throughout the interview Captain Vere's voice was far from high, and Claggart's silvery and low; and the wind in the cordage and the wash of the sea helped the more to put them beyond earshot; nevertheless, the interview's continuance already had attracted observation from some topmen aloft and other sailors in the waist or further forward.

Having determined upon his measures, Captain Vere forthwith took action. Abruptly turning to Claggart he asked, "Master-at-arms, is it now Budd's watch aloft?"

"No, Your Honor." Whereupon, "Mr. Wilkes!" summoning the nearest midshipman, "tell Albert to come to me." Albert was the Captain's hammock-boy, a sort of sea-valet in whose discretion and fidelity his master had much confidence. The lad appeared. "You know Budd the Foretopman?"

"I do, Sir."

"Go find him. It is his watch off. Manage to tell him out of earshot that he is wanted aft. Contrive it that he speaks to nobody. Keep him in talk yourself. And not till you get well aft here, not till then let him know that the place where he is wanted is my cabin. You understand. Go.—Master-at-arms, show yourself on the decks below, and when you think it time for Albert to be coming with his man, stand by quietly to follow the sailor in."

20

Now when the Foretopman found himself closeted there, as it were, in the cabin with the Captain and Claggart, he was surprised enough. But it was a surprise unaccompanied by apprehension or distrust. To an immature nature essentially honest and humane, forewarning intimations of subtler danger from one's kind come tardily if at all. The only thing that took shape in the young sailor's mind was this: Yes, the Captain, I have always thought, looks kindly upon me. Wonder if he's going to make me his coxswain. I should like that. And maybe now he is going to ask the Master-at-arms about me.

"Shut the door there, sentry," said the Commander; "stand without, and let nobody come in.—Now, Master-at-arms, tell this man to his face what you told of him to me"; and stood prepared to scrutinize the mutually confronting visages.

With the measured step and calm collected air of an asylum-physician approaching in the public hall some patient beginning to show indications of a coming paroxysm, Claggart deliberately advanced within short range of Billy, and mesmerically looking him in the eye, briefly recapitulated the accusation.

Not at first did Billy take it in. When he did, the rose-tan of his cheek looked struck as by white leprosy. He stood like one impaled and gagged. Meanwhile the accuser's eyes removing not as yet from the blue dilated ones, underwent a phenomenal change, their wonted rich violet color blurring into a muddy purple. Those lights of human intelligence losing human expression, gelidly protruding like the alien eyes of certain uncatalogued creatures of the deep. The first mesmeric glance was one of serpent fascination; the last was as the hungry lurch of the torpedo-fish.

"Speak, man!" said Captain Vere to the transfixed one, struck by his aspect even more than by Claggart's, "Speak! defend yourself." Which appeal caused but a strange dumb gesturing and gurgling in Billy; amazement at such an accusation so suddenly sprung on inexperienced nonage; this, and, it may be, horror of the accuser, serving to bring out his lurking defect and in this instance for the time intensifying it into a convulsed tongue-tie; while the intent head and entire form straining forward in an agony of ineffectual eagerness to obey the injunction to speak and defend himself, gave an expression to the face like that of a condemned Vestal priestess in the moment of being buried alive, and in the first struggle against suffocation.

Though at the time Captain Vere was quite ignorant of Billy's liability to vocal impediment, he now immediately divined it, since vividly Billy's aspect recalled to him that of a bright young schoolmate of his whom he had once seen struck by much the same startling impotence in the act of eagerly rising in the class to be foremost in response to a testing question put to it by the master. Going close up to the young sailor, and laying a soothing hand on his shoulder, he said, "There is no hurry, my boy. Take your time, take your time." Contrary to the effect intended, these words so fatherly in tone, doubtless touching Billy's heart to the quick, prompted yet more violent efforts at utterance—efforts soon ending for the time in confirming the paralysis, and bringing to his face an expression which was as a crucifixion to behold. The next instant, quick as the flame from a discharged cannon at night, his right arm shot out, and Claggart dropped to the deck. Whether intentionally or but owing to the young athlete's superior height, the blow had taken effect fully upon the forehead, so shapely and intellectual-looking a feature in the Master-at-arms; so that the body fell over lengthwise, like a heavy plank tilted from erectness. A gasp or two, and he lay motionless.

"Fated boy," breathed Captain Vere in tone so low as to be almost a whisper, "what have you done! But here, help me."

The twain raised the felled one from the loins up into a sitting position. The spare form flexibly acquiesced, but inertly. It was like handling a dead snake. They lowered it back. Regaining erectness Captain Vere with one hand covering his face stood to all appearance as impassive as the object at his feet. Was he absorbed in taking in all the bearings of the event and what was best not only now at once to be done, but also in the sequel? Slowly he uncovered his face; and the effect was as if the moon emerging from eclipse should reappear with quite another aspect than that which had gone into hiding. The father in him, manifested towards Billy thus far in the scene, was replaced by the military disciplinarian. In his official tone he bade the Foretopman retire to a state-room aft (pointing it out), and there remain till thence summoned. This order Billy in silence mechanically obeyed. Then going to the cabin-door where it opened on the quarter-deck, Captain Vere said to the sentry without, "Tell somebody to send Albert here." When the lad appeared his master so contrived it that he should not catch sight of the prone one. "Albert," he said to him, "tell the Surgeon I wish to see him. You need not come back till called." When the Surgeon entered—a self-poised character of that grave sense and experience that hardly anything could take him aback,—Captain Vere advanced to meet him, thus unconsciously intercepting his view of Claggart, and interrupting the other's wonted ceremonious salutation, said, "Nay, tell me how it is with yonder man," directing his attention to the prostrate one.

The Surgeon looked, and for all his self-command, somewhat started at the abrupt revelation. On Claggart's always pallid complexion, thick black blood was now oozing from nostril and ear. To the gazer's professional eye it was unmistakably no living man that he saw.

"Is it so then?" said Captain Vere intently watching him. "I thought it. But verify it." Whereupon the customary tests confirmed the Surgeon's first glance, who now looking up in unfeigned concern, cast a look of intense inquisitiveness upon his superior. But Captain Vere, with one hand to his brow, was standing motionless.

Suddenly, catching the Surgeon's arm convulsively, he exclaimed, pointing down to the body—"It is the divine judgement on Ananias! Look!"

Disturbed by the excited manner he had never before observed in the *Indomitable's* Captain, and as yet wholly ignorant of the affair, the prudent Surgeon nevertheless held his peace, only again looking an earnest interrogation as to what it was that had resulted in such a tragedy.

But Captain Vere was now again motionless standing absorbed in thought. But again starting, he vehemently exclaimed—"Struck dead by an angel of God! Yet the angel must hang!"

At these passionate interjections, mere incoherences to the listener as yet unapprised of the antecedents, the Surgeon was profoundly discomposed. But now as recollecting himself, Captain

Vere in less passionate tone briefly related the circumstances leading up to the event.

"But come; we must despatch," he added. "Help me to remove him" (meaning the body) "to yonder compartment," designating one opposite that where the Foretopman remained immured. Anew disturbed by a request that as implying a desire for secrecy, seemed unaccountably strange to him, there was nothing for the subordinate to do but comply.

"Go now," said Captain Vere with something of his wonted manner—"Go now. I shall presently call a drum-head court. Tell the lieutenants what has happened, and tell Mr. Mordant," meaning the Captain of Marines, "and charge them to keep the matter to themselves."

21

Full of disquietude and misgiving the Surgeon left the cabin. Was Captain Vere suddenly affected in his mind, or was it but a transient excitement, brought about by so strange and extraordinary a happening? As to the drum-head court, it struck the Surgeon as impolitic, if nothing more. The thing to do, he thought, was to place Billy Budd in confinement and in a way dictated by usage, and postpone further action in so extraordinary a case to such time as they should rejoin the squadron, and then refer it to the Admiral. He recalled the unwonted agitation of Captain Vere and his excited exclamations so at variance with his normal manner. Was he unhinged? But assuming that he is, it is not so susceptible of proof. What then can he do? No more trying situation is conceivable than that of an officer subordinate under a Captain whom he suspects to be, not mad indeed, but yet not quite unaffected in his intellect. To argue his order to him would be insolence. To resist him would be mutiny.

In obedience to Captain Vere he communicated what had happened to the lieutenants and Captain of Marines; saying nothing as to the Captain's state. They fully shared his own surprise and concern. Like him too they seemed to think that such a matter should be referred to the Admiral.

∽ 22 ∽

Who in the rainbow can draw the line where the violet tint ends and the orange tint begins? Distinctly we see the difference of the colors, but where exactly does the one first blendingly enter into the other? So with sanity and insanity. In pronounced cases there is no question about them. But in some supposed cases, in various degrees supposedly less pronounced, to draw the exact line of demarkation few will undertake tho' for a fee some professional experts will. There is nothing namable but that some men will undertake to do it for pay.

Whether Captain Vere, as the Surgeon professionally and privately surmised, was really the sudden victim of any degree of aberration, one must determine for himself by such light as this narrative may afford.

That the unhappy event which has been narrated could not have happened at a worse juncture was but too true. For it was close on the heel of the suppressed insurrections, an aftertime very critical to naval authority, demanding from every English sea-commander two qualities not readily interfusable—prudence and rigour. Moreover there was something crucial in the case.

In the jugglery of circumstances preceding and attending the event on board the *Indomitable*, and in the light of that martial code whereby it was formally to be judged, innocence and guilt personified in Claggart and Budd in effect changed places. In a legal view the apparent victim of the tragedy was he who had sought to victimize a man blameless; and the indisputable deed of the latter, navally regarded, constituted the most heinous of military crimes. Yet more. The essential right and wrong involved in the matter, the clearer that might be, so much the worse for the responsibility of a loyal sea-commander inasmuch as he was not authorized to determine the matter on that primitive basis.

Small wonder then that the *Indomitable's* Captain, though in general a man of rapid decision, felt that circumspectness not less than promptitude was necessary. Until he could decide upon his course, and in each detail; and not only so, but until the concluding measure was upon the point of being enacted, he deemed it advisable, in view of all the circumstances, to guard as much as possible against publicity. Here he may or may not have erred. Certain it is, however, that subsequently in the confidential talk of more than one or two gun-rooms and cabins he was not a little criticized by some officers, a fact imputed by his friends and vehemently by his cousin, Jack Denton, to professional jealousy of *Starry Vere*. Some imaginative ground for invidious comment there was. The maintenance of secrecy in the matter, the confining all knowledge of it for a time to the place where the homicide occurred, the quarter-deck cabin; in these particulars lurked some resemblance to the policy adopted in those tragedies of the palace which have occurred more than once in the capital founded by Peter the Barbarian.

The case indeed was such that fain would the *Indomitable's* Captain have deferred taking any action whatever respecting it further than to keep the Foretopman a close prisoner till the ship rejoined the squadron, and then submitting the matter to the judgement of his Admiral.

But a true military officer is in one particular like a true monk. Not with more of self-abnegation will the latter keep his vows of monastic obedience than the former his vows of allegiance to martial duty.

Feeling that unless quick action was taken on it, the deed of the Foretopman, so soon as it should be known on the gun decks, would tend to awaken any slumbering embers of the Nore among the crew, a sense of the urgency of the case overruled in Captain Vere every other consideration. But tho' a conscientious disciplinarian, he was no lover of authority for mere authority's sake. Very far was he from embracing opportunities for monopolizing to himself the perils of moral responsibility, none at least that could properly be referred to an official superior, or shared with him by his official equals or even subordinates. So thinking, he was glad it would not be at variance with usage to turn the matter over to a summary court of his own officers, reserving to himself as the one on whom the ultimate accountability would rest, the right of maintaining a supervision of it, or formally or informally interposing at need. Accordingly a drum-head court was summarily convened, he electing the individuals composing it, the First Lieutenant, the Captain of Marines, and the Sailing Master.

In associating an officer of marines with the sea-lieutenants in a case having to do with a sailor, the Commander perhaps deviated from general custom. He was prompted thereto by the circumstance that he took that soldier to be a judicious person, thoughtful, and not altogether incapable of grappling with a difficult case unprecedented in his prior experience. Yet even as to him he was not without some latent misgiving, for withal he was an extremely good-natured man, an enjoyer of his dinner, a sound sleeper, and inclined to obesity, a man who tho' he would always maintain his manhood in battle might not prove altogether reliable in a moral dilemma involving aught of the tragic. As to the First Lieutenant and the Sailing Master, Captain Vere could not but be aware that though honest natures, of approved gallantry upon occasion, their intelligence was mostly confined to the matter of active seamanship and the fighting demands of their profession. The court was held in the same cabin where the unfortunate affair had taken place. This cabin, the Commander's, embraced the entire area under the poop-deck. Aft, and on either side, was a small state-room; the one room temporarily a jail and the other a dead-house, and a yet smaller compartment leaving a space between, expanding forward into a goodly oblong of length coinciding with the ship's beam. A skylight of moderate dimension was overhead and at each end of the oblong space were two sashed port-hole windows easily convertible back into embrasures for short carronades.

All being quickly in readiness, Billy Budd was arraigned, Captain Vere necessarily appearing as the sole witness in the case, and as such, temporarily sinking his rank, though singularly maintaining it in a matter apparently trivial, namely, that he testified from the ship's weather-side, with that object having caused the court to sit on the lee-side. Concisely he narrated all that had led up to the catastrophe, omitting nothing in Claggart's accusation and deposing as to the manner in which the prisoner had received it. At this testimony the three officers glanced with no little surprise at Billy Budd, the last man they would have suspected either of the mutinous design alleged by Claggart or the undeniable deed he himself had done.

The First Lieutenant, taking judicial primacy and turning toward the prisoner, said, "Captain Vere has spoken. Is it or is it not as Captain Vere says?" In response came syllables not so much impeded in the utterance as might have been anticipated. They were these: "Captain Vere tells the truth. It is just as Captain Vere says, but it is not as the Master-at-arms said. I have eaten the King's bread and I am true to the King."

"I believe you, my man," said the witness, his voice indicating a suppressed emotion not otherwise betrayed.

"God will bless you for that, Your Honor!" not without stammering said Billy, and all but broke down. But immediately was recalled to self-control by another question, to which with the same emotional difficulty of utterance he said, "No, there was no malice between us. I never bore malice against the Master-at-arms. I am sorry that he is dead. I did not mean to kill him. Could I have used my tongue I would not have struck him. But he foully lied to my face and in presence of my Captain, and I had to say something, and I could only say it with a blow, God help me!"

In the impulsive above-board manner of the frank one, the court saw confirmed all that was implied in words that just previously had perplexed them, coming as they did from the testifier to the tragedy and promptly following Billy's impassioned disclaimer of mutinous intent—Captain Vere's words, "I believe you, my man."

Next it was asked of him whether he knew of or suspected aught savoring of incipient trouble (meaning mutiny, tho' the explicit term was avoided) going on in any section of the ship's company.

The reply lingered. This was naturally imputed by the court to the same vocal embarrassment which had retarded or obstructed previous answers. But in main it was otherwise here; the question immediately recalling to Billy's mind the interview with the afterguardsman in the fore-chains. But an innate repugnance to playing a part at all approaching that of an informer against one's own shipmates—the same erring sense of uninstructed honor which had stood in the way of his reporting the matter at the time though as a loyal man-of-war-man it was incumbent on him, and failure so to do if charged against him and proven, would have subjected him to the heaviest of penalties; this, with the blind feeling now his, that nothing really was being hatched, prevailed with him. When the answer came it was a negative.

"One question more," said the officer of marines now first speaking and with a troubled earnestness. "You tell us that what the Master-at-arms said against you was a lie. Now why should he have so lied, so maliciously lied, since you declare there was no malice between you?"

At that question unintentionally touching on a spiritual sphere wholly obscure to Billy's thoughts, he was nonplussed, evincing a confusion indeed that some observers, such as can readily be imagined, would have construed into involuntary evidence of hidden guilt. Nevertheless he strove some way to answer, but all at once relinquished the vain endeavor, at the same time turning an appealing glance towards Captain Vere as deeming him his best helper and friend. Captain Vere who had been seated for a time rose to his feet, addressing the interrogator. "The question you put to him comes naturally enough. But how can he rightly answer it? or anybody else? unless indeed it be he who lies within there," designating the compartment where lay the corpse. "But the prone one there will not rise to our summons. In effect, tho', as it seems to me, the point you make is hardly material. Quite aside from any conceivable motive actuating the Master-at-arms, and irrespective of the provocation to the blow, a martial court must needs in the present case confine its attention to the blow's consequence, which consequence justly is to be deemed not otherwise than as the striker's deed."

This utterance, the full significance of which it was not at all likely that Billy took in, nevertheless caused him to turn a wistful interrogative look toward the speaker, a look in its dumb expres-

siveness not unlike that which a dog of generous breed might turn upon his master seeking in his face some elucidation of a previous gesture ambiguous to the canine intelligence. Nor was the same utterance without marked effect upon the three officers, more especially the soldier. Couched in it seemed to them a meaning unanticipated, involving a prejudgement on the speaker's part. It served to augment a mental disturbance previously evident enough.

The soldier once more spoke; in a tone of suggestive dubiety addressing at once his associates and Captain Vere: "Nobody is present—none of the ship's company, I mean—who might shed lateral light, if any is to be had, upon what remains mysterious in this matter."

"That is thoughtfully put," said Captain Vere; "I see your drift. Ay, there is a mystery; but, to use a Scriptural phrase, it is 'a mystery of iniquity,' a matter for psychologic theologians to discuss. But what has a military court to do with it? Not to add that for us any possible investigation of it is cut off by the lasting tongue-tie of—him—in yonder," again designating the mortuary stateroom. "The prisoner's deed,—with that alone we have to do."

To this, and particularly the closing reiteration, the marine soldier knowing not how aptly to reply, sadly abstained from saying aught. The First Lieutenant who at the outset had not unnaturally assumed primacy in the court, now overrulingly instructed by a glance from Captain Vere, a glance more effective than words, resumed that primacy. Turning to the prisoner, "Budd," he said, and scarce in equable tones, "Budd, if you have aught further to say for yourself, say it now."

Upon this the young sailor turned another quick glance toward Captain Vere; then, as taking a hint from that aspect, a hint confirming his own instinct that silence was now best, replied to the Lieutenant, "I have said all, Sir."

The marine—the same who had been the sentinel without the cabin-door at the time that the Foretopman followed by the Master-at-arms, entered it—he, standing by the sailor throughout these judicial proceedings, was now directed to take him back to the after compartment originally assigned to the prisoner and his custodian.

As the twain disappeared from view, the three officers as partially liberated from some inward constraint associated with Billy's mere presence, simultaneously stirred in their seats. They exchanged looks of troubled indecision, yet feeling that decide they must and without long delay. As for Captain Vere, he for the time stood unconsciously with his back toward them, apparently in one of his absent fits, gazing out from a sashed port-hole to windward upon the monotonous blank of the twilight sea. But the court's silence continuing, broken only at moments by brief consultations in low earnest tones, this seemed to arm him and energize him. Turning, he to-and-fro paced the cabin athwart; in the returning ascent to windward, climbing the slant deck in the ship's lee roll; without knowing it symbolizing thus in his action a mind resolute to surmount difficulties even if against primitive instincts strong as the wind and the sea. Presently he came to a stand before the three. After scanning their faces he stood less as mustering his thoughts for expression, than as one inly deliberating how best to put them to well-meaning men not intellectually mature, men with whom it was necessary to demonstrate certain principles that were axioms to himself. Similar impatience as to talking is perhaps one reason that deters some minds from addressing any popular assemblies.

When speak he did, something both in the substance of what he said and his manner of saying it, showed the influence of unshared studies modifying and tempering the practical training of an active career. This, along with his phraseology, now and then was suggestive of the grounds whereon rested that imputation of a certain pedantry socially alleged against him by certain naval men of wholly practical cast, captains who nevertheless would frankly concede that His Majesty's Navy mustered no more efficient officer of their grade than *Starry Vere.*

What he said was to this effect: "Hitherto I have been but the witness, little more; and I should hardly think now to take another tone, that of your coadjutor, for the time, did I not perceive in you, —at the crisis too—a troubled hesitancy, proceeding, I doubt not, from the clash of military duty with moral scruple—scruple vitalized by compassion. For the compassion, how can I otherwise than share it? But, mindful of paramount obligations I strive against scruples that may tend to enervate decision. Not, gentlemen, that I hide from myself that the case is an exceptional one. Speculatively regarded, it well might be referred to a jury of casuists. But for us here acting not as casuists or moralists, it is a case practical, and under martial law practically to be dealt with.

"But your scruples: do they move as in a dusk? Challenge them. Make them advance and declare themselves. Come now: do they import something like this? If, mindless of palliating circumstances, we are bound to regard the death of the Master-at-arms as the prisoner's deed, then does that deed constitute a capital crime whereof the penalty is a mortal one? But in natural justice is nothing but the prisoner's overt act to be considered? How can we adjudge to summary and shameful death a fellow-creature innocent before God, and whom we feel to be so?—Does that state it aright? You sign sad assent. Well, I too feel that, the full force of that. It is Nature. But do these buttons that we wear attest that our allegiance is to Nature? No, to the King. Though the ocean, which is inviolate Nature primeval, tho' this be the element where we move and have our being as sailors, yet as the King's officers lies our duty in a sphere correspondingly natural? So little is that true, that in receiving our commissions we in the most important regards ceased to be natural free-agents. When war is declared are we the commissioned fighters previously consulted? We fight at command. If our judgements approve the war, that is but coincidence. So in other particulars. So now. For suppose condemnation to follow these present proceedings. Would it be so much we ourselves that would condemn as it would be martial law operating through us? For that law and the rigour of it, we are not responsible. Our avowed responsibility is in this: That however pitilessly that law may operate, we nevertheless adhere to it and administer it.

"But the exceptional in the matter moves the hearts within you. Even so too is mine moved. But let not warm hearts betray heads that should be cool. Ashore in a criminal case will an upright judge allow himself off the bench to be waylaid by some tender kinswoman of the accused seeking to touch him with her tearful plea? Well the heart here denotes the feminine in man is as that piteous woman, and hard tho' it be, she must here be ruled out."

He paused, earnestly studying them for a moment; then resumed.

"But something in your aspect seems to urge that it is not solely the heart that moves in you, but also the conscience, the private conscience. But tell me whether or not, occupying the position we do, private conscience should not yield to that imperial one formulated in the code under which alone we officially proceed?"

Here the three men moved in their seats, less convinced than agitated by the course of an argument troubling but the more the spontaneous conflict within.

Perceiving which, the speaker paused for a moment; then abruptly changing his tone, went on.

"To steady us a bit, let us recur to the facts.—In war-time at sea a man-of-war's-man strikes his superior in grade, and the blow kills. Apart from its effect, the blow itself is, according to the Articles of War, a capital crime. Furthermore—"

"Ay, Sir," emotionally broke in the officer of marines, "in one sense it was. But surely Budd purposed neither mutiny nor homicide."

"Surely not, my good man. And before a court less arbitrary and more merciful than a martial one, that plea would largely extenuate. At the Last Assizes it shall acquit. But how here? We proceed under the law of the Mutiny Act. In feature no child can resemble his father more than that Act resembles in spirit the thing from which it derives—War. In His Majesty's service—in this ship indeed—there are Englishmen forced to fight for the King against their will. Against their conscience, for aught we know. Tho' as their fellow-creatures some of us may appreciate their position, yet as navy officers, what reck we of it? Still less recks the enemy. Our impressed men he would fain cut down in the same swath with our volunteers. As regards the enemy's naval conscripts, some of whom may even share our own abhorrence of the regicidal French Directory, it is the same on our side. War looks but to the frontage, the appearance. And the Mutiny Act, War's child, takes after the father. Budd's intent or non-intent is nothing to the purpose.

"But while, put to it by these anxieties in you which I can not but respect, I only repeat myself—while thus strangely we prolong proceedings that should be summary—the enemy may be sighted and an engagement result. We must do; and one of two things must we do—condemn or let go."

"Can we not convict and yet mitigate the penalty?" asked the junior Lieutenant here speaking, and falteringly, for the first.

"Lieutenant, were that clearly lawful for us under the circumstances, consider the consequences of such clemency. The people" (meaning the ship's company) "have native-sense; most of them are familiar with our naval usage and tradition; and how would they take it? Even could you explain to them—which our official position forbids—they, long moulded by arbitrary discipline have not that kind of intelligent responsiveness that might qualify them to comprehend and discriminate. No, to the people the Foretopman's deed, however it be worded in the announcement, will be plain homicide committed in a flagrant act of mutiny. What penalty for that should follow, they know. But it does not follow. *Why?* they will ruminate. You know what sailors are. Will they not revert to the recent outbreak at the Nore? Ay. They know the well-founded alarm—the panic it struck throughout England. Your clement sentence they would account pusillanimous. They would think that we flinch, that we are afraid of them—afraid of practising a lawful rigour singularly demanded at this juncture lest it should provoke new troubles. What shame to us such a conjecture on their part, and how deadly to discipline. You see then, whither, prompted by duty and the law, I steadfastly drive. But I beseech you, my friends, do not take me amiss. I feel as you do for this unfortunate boy. But did he know our hearts, I take him to be of that generous nature that he would feel even for us on whom in this military necessity so heavy a compulsion is laid."

With that, crossing the deck he resumed his place by the sashed port-hole, tacitly leaving the three to come to a decision. On the cabin's opposite side the troubled court sat silent. Loyal lieges, plain and practical, though at bottom they dissented from some points Captain Vere had put to them, they were without the faculty, hardly had the inclination, to gainsay one whom they felt to be an earnest man, one too not less their superior in mind than in naval rank. But it is not improbable that even such of his words as were not without influence over them, less came home to them than his closing appeal to their instinct as sea-officers in the forethought he threw out as to the practical consequences to discipline, considering the unconfirmed tone of the fleet at the time, should a man-of-war's-man's violent killing at sea of a superior in grade be allowed to pass for aught else than a capital crime demanding prompt infliction of the penalty.

Not unlikely they were brought to something more or less akin to that harassed frame of mind which in the year 1842 actuated the Commander of the U.S. brig-of-war *Somers* to resolve, under the so-called Articles of War, Articles modelled upon the English Mutiny Act, to resolve upon the execution at sea of a midshipman and two petty-officers as mutineers designing the seizure of the brig. Which resolution was carried out though in a time of peace and within not many days' sail of home. An act vindicated by a naval court of inquiry subsequently convened ashore. History, and here cited without comment. True, the circumstances on board the *Somers* were different from those on board the *Indomitable*. But the urgency felt, well-warranted or otherwise, was much the same.

Says a writer whom few know, "Forty years after a battle it is easy for a non-combatant to reason about how it ought to have been fought. It is another thing personally and under fire to direct the fighting while involved in the obscuring smoke of it. Much so with respect to other emergencies involving considerations both practical and moral, and when it is imperative promptly to act. The greater the fog the more it imperils the steamer, and speed is put on tho' at the hazard of running somebody down. Little ween the snug card-players in the cabin of the responsibilities of the sleepless man on the bridge."

In brief, Billy Budd was formally convicted and sentenced to be hung at the yard-arm in the early morning watch, it being now night. Otherwise, as is customary in such cases, the sentence would forthwith have been carried out. In war-time on the field or in the fleet, a mortal punishment decreed by a drum-head court—on the field sometimes decreed by but a nod from the General—follows without delay on the heel of conviction without appeal.

23

It was Captain Vere himself who of his own motion communicated the finding of the court to the prisoner; for that purpose going to the compartment where he was in custody and bidding the marine there to withdraw for the time.

Beyond the communication of the sentence what took place at this interview was never known. But in view of the character of the twain briefly closeted in that state-room, each radically sharing in the rarer qualities of our nature—so rare indeed as to be all but incredible to average minds however much cultivated—some conjectures may be ventured.

It would have been in consonance with the spirit of Captain Vere should he on this occasion have concealed nothing from the condemned one—should he indeed have frankly disclosed to him the part he himself had played in bringing about the decision, at the same time revealing his actuating motives. On Billy's side it is not improbable that such a confession would have been received in much the same spirit that prompted it. Not without a sort of joy indeed he might have appreciated the brave opinion of him implied in his Captain's making such a confidant of him. Nor, as to the sentence itself could he have been insensible that it was imparted to him as to one not afraid to die. Even more may have been. Captain Vere in the end may have developed the passion sometimes latent under an exterior stoical or indifferent. He was old enough to have been Billy's father. The austere devotee of military duty, letting himself melt back into what remains primeval in our formalized humanity, may in the end have caught Billy to his heart even as Abraham may have caught young Isaac on the brink of resolutely offering him up in obedience to the exacting behest. But there is no telling the sacrament, seldom if in any case revealed to the gadding world, wherever under circumstances at all akin to those here attempted to be set forth, two of great Nature's nobler order embrace. There is privacy at the time, inviolable to the survivor, and holy oblivion, the sequel to each diviner magnanimity, providentially covers all at last.

The first to encounter Captain Vere in act of leaving the compartment was the senior Lieutenant. The face he beheld, for the moment one expressive of the agony of the strong, was to that officer, tho' a man of fifty, a startling revelation. That the condemned one suffered less than he who mainly had effected the condemnation was apparently indicated by the former's exclamation in the scene soon perforce to be touched upon.

24

Of a series of incidents within a brief term rapidly following each other, the adequate narration may take up a term less brief, especially if explanation or comment here and there seem requisite to the better understanding of such incidents. Between the entrance into the cabin of him who never left it alive, and him who when he did leave it left it as one condemned to die; between this and the closeted interview just given, less than an hour and a half had elapsed. It was an interval long enough however to awaken speculations among no few of the ship's company as to what it was that could be detaining in the cabin the Master-at-arms and the sailor; for a rumor that both of them had been seen to enter it and neither of them had been seen to emerge, this rumor had got abroad upon the gun decks and in the tops; the people of a great war-ship being in one respect like villagers taking microscopic note of every outward movement or non-movement going on. When therefore in weather not at all tempestuous all hands were called in the second dog-watch, a summons under such circumstances not usual in those hours, the crew were not wholly unprepared for some announcement extraordinary, one having connection too with the continued absence of the two men from their wonted haunts.

There was a moderate sea at the time; and the moon, newly

risen and near to being at its full, silvered the white spar-deck wherever not blotted by the clear-cut shadows horizontally thrown of fixtures and moving men. On either side of the quarter-deck, the marine guard under arms was drawn up; and Captain Vere standing in his place surrounded by all the ward-room officers, addressed his men. In so doing his manner showed neither more nor less than that properly pertaining to his supreme position aboard his own ship. In clear terms and concise he told them what had taken place in the cabin; that the Master-at-arms was dead; that he who had killed him had been already tried by a summary court and condemned to death; and that the execution would take place in the early morning watch. The word *mutiny* was not named in what he said. He refrained too from making the occasion an opportunity for any preachment as to the maintenance of discipline, thinking perhaps that under existing circumstances in the navy the consequence of violating discipline should be made to speak for itself.

Their Captain's announcement was listened to by the throng of standing sailors in a dumbness like that of a seated congregation of believers in hell listening to the clergyman's announcement of his Calvinistic text.

At the close, however, a confused murmur went up. It began to wax. All but instantly, then, at a sign, it was pierced and suppressed by shrill whistles of the Boatswain and his Mates piping down one watch.

To be prepared for burial Claggart's body was delivered to certain petty-officers of his mess. And here, not to clog the sequel with lateral matters, it may be added that at a suitable hour, the Master-at-arms was committed to the sea with every funeral honor properly belonging to his naval grade.

In this proceeding as in every public one growing out of the tragedy, strict adherence to usage was observed. Nor in any point could it have been at all deviated from, either with respect to Claggart or Billy Budd, without begetting undesirable speculations in the ship's company, sailors, and more particularly men-of-war's-men, being of all men the greatest sticklers for usage.

For similar cause, all communication between Captain Vere

and the condemned one ended with the closeted interview already given, the latter being now surrendered to the ordinary routine preliminary to the end. This transfer under guard from the Captain's quarters was effected without unusual precautions—at least no visible ones.

If possible, not to let the men so much as surmise that their officers anticipate aught amiss from them is the tacit rule in a military ship. And the more that some sort of trouble should really be apprehended the more do the officers keep that apprehension to themselves; tho' not the less unostentatious vigilance may be augmented.

In the present instance the sentry placed over the prisoner had strict orders to let no one have communication with him but the Chaplain. And certain unobtrusive measures were taken absolutely to insure this point.

25

In a seventy-four of the old order the deck known as the upper gun deck was the one covered over by the spar-deck which last though not without its armament was for the most part exposed to the weather. In general it was at all hours free from hammocks; those of the crew swinging on the lower gun deck, and berth-deck, the latter being not only a dormitory but also the place for the stowing of the sailors' bags, and on both sides lined with the large chests or movable pantries of the many messes of the men.

On the starboard side of the *Indomitable's* upper gun deck, behold Billy Budd under sentry, lying prone in irons, in one of the bays formed by the regular spacing of the guns comprising the batteries on either side. All these pieces were of the heavier calibre of that period. Mounted on lumbering wooden carriages they were hampered with cumbersome harness of breechen and strong side-tackles for running them out. Guns and carriages, together with the long rammers and shorter lintstocks lodged in loops overhead—all these, as customary, were painted black; and the heavy hempen breechens, tarred to the same tint, wore the like livery of the undertakers. In contrast with the funereal hue of these surroundings the prone sailor's exterior apparel, white *jumper* and white duck trousers, each more or less soiled, dimly glimmered in the obscure light of the bay like a patch of discolored snow in early April lingering at some upland cave's black mouth. In effect he is already in his shroud or the garments that shall serve him in lieu of one. Over him, but scarce illuminating him, two battle-lanterns swing from two massive beams of the deck above. Fed with the oil supplied by the war-contractors (whose gains, honest or otherwise, are in every land an anticipated portion of the harvest of death), with flickering splashes of dirty yellow light they pollute the pale moonshine all but ineffectually struggling in obstructed flecks thro' the open ports from which the tompioned cannon protrude. Other lanterns at intervals serve but to bring out somewhat the obscurer bays which, like small confessionals or side-chapels in a cathedral, branch from the long dim-vistaed broad aisle between the two batteries of that covered tier.

Such was the deck where now lay the Handsome Sailor. Through the rose-tan of his complexion, no pallor could have shown. It would have taken days of sequestration from the winds and the sun to have brought about the effacement of that. But the skeleton in the cheekbone at the point of its angle was just beginning delicately to be defined under the warm-tinted skin. In fervid hearts self-contained, some brief experiences devour our human tissue as secret fire in a ship's hold consumes cotton in the bale.

But now lying between the two guns, as nipped in the vice of fate, Billy's agony, mainly proceeding from a generous young heart's virgin experience of the diabolical incarnate and effective in some men—the tension of that agony was over now. It survived not the something healing in the closeted interview with Captain Vere. Without movement, he lay as in a trance. That adolescent expression previously noted as his, taking on something akin to the look of a slumbering child in the cradle when the warm hearth-glow of the still chamber at night plays on the dimples that at whiles mysteriously form in the cheek, silently coming and going there. For now and then in the gyved one's trance a serene happy light born of some wandering reminiscence or dream would diffuse itself over his face, and then wane away only anew to return.

The Chaplain coming to see him and finding him thus, and perceiving no sign that he was conscious of his presence, attentively regarded him for a space, then slipping aside, withdrew for the time, peradventure feeling that even he the minister of Christ, tho' receiving his stipend from Mars, had no consolation to proffer which could result in a peace transcending that which he beheld. But in the small hours he came again. And the prisoner, now awake to his surroundings, noticed his approach, and civilly, all but cheerfully, welcomed him. But it was to little purpose that in the interview following the good man sought to bring Billy Budd to some godly understanding that he must die, and at dawn. True, Billy himself freely referred to his death as a thing close at hand; but it was something in the way that children will refer to death in general, who yet among their other sports will play a funeral with hearse and mourners.

Not that like children Billy was incapable of conceiving what death really is. No, but he was wholly without irrational fear of it, a fear more prevalent in highly civilized communities than those so-called barbarous ones which in all respects stand nearer to unadulterate Nature. And, as elsewhere said, a barbarian Billy radically was; as much so, for all the costume, as his countrymen the British captives, living trophies, made to march in the Roman triumph of Germanicus. Quite as much so as those later barbarians, young men probably, and picked specimens among the earlier British converts to Christianity, at least nominally such, and taken to Rome (as to-day converts from lesser isles of the sea may be taken to London), of whom the Pope of that time, admiring the strangeness of their personal beauty so unlike the Italian stamp, their clear ruddy complexion and curled flaxen locks, exclaimed, "Angles—" (meaning *English* the modern derivative) "Angles do you call them? And is it because they look so like angels?" Had it been later in time one would think that the Pope had in mind Fra Angelico's seraphs some of whom, plucking apples in gardens of the Hesperides, have the faint rose-bud complexion of the more beautiful English girls.

If in vain the good Chaplain sought to impress the young barbarian with ideas of death akin to those conveyed in the skull, dial, and cross-bones on old tombstones; equally futile to all appearance were his efforts to bring home to him the thought of salvation and a Saviour. Billy listened, but less out of awe or reverence perhaps than from a certain natural politeness; doubtless at bottom regarding all that in much the same way that most mariners of his class take any discourse abstract or out of the common tone of the work-a-day world. And this sailor-way of taking clerical discourse is not wholly unlike the way in which the pioneer of Christianity full of transcendent miracles was received long ago on tropic isles by any superior *savage* so called—a Tahitian say of Captain Cook's time or shortly after that time. Out of natural courtesy he received, but did not appropriate. It was like a gift placed in the palm of an outreached hand upon which the fingers do not close.

But the *Indomitable's* Chaplain was a discreet man possessing the good sense of a good heart. So he insisted not in his vocation here. At the instance of Captain Vere, a lieutenant had apprised him of pretty much everything as to Billy; and since he felt that innocence was even a better thing than religion wherewith to go to Judgement, he reluctantly withdrew; but in his emotion not without first performing an act strange enough in an Englishman, and under the circumstances yet more so in any regular priest. Stooping over, he kissed on the fair cheek his fellow-man, a felon in martial law, one who though on the confines of death he felt he could never convert to a dogma; nor for all that did he fear for his future.

Marvel not that having been made acquainted with the young sailor's essential innocence (an irruption of heretic thought hard to suppress) the worthy man lifted not a finger to avert the doom of such a martyr to martial discipline. So to do would not only have been as idle as invoking the desert, but would also have been an audacious transgression of the bounds of his function, one as exactly prescribed to him by military law as that of the boatswain or any other naval officer. Bluntly put, a chaplain is the minister of the Prince of Peace serving in the host of the God of War—Mars. As such, he is as incongruous as a musket would be on the altar at Christmas. Why then is he there? Because he indirectly subserves the purpose attested by the cannon; because too he lends the sanction of the religion of the meek to that which practically is the abrogation of everything but brute Force.

26

The night, so luminous on the spar-deck, but otherwise on the cavernous ones below, levels so like the tiered galleries in a coal-mine—the luminous night passed away. But, like the prophet in the chariot disappearing in heaven and dropping his mantle to Elisha, the withdrawing night transferred its pale robe to the breaking day. A meek shy light appeared in the East, where stretched a diaphanous fleece of white furrowed vapor. That light slowly waxed. Suddenly *eight bells* was struck aft, responded to by one louder metallic stroke from forward. It was four o'clock in the morning. Instantly the silver whistles were heard summoning all hands to witness punishment. Up through the great hatchways rimmed with racks of heavy shot, the watch below came pouring, overspreading with the watch already on deck the space between the main-mast and fore-mast including that occupied by the capacious *launch* and the black booms tiered on either side of it, boat and booms making a summit of observation for the powder-boys and younger tars. A different group comprising one watch of topmen leaned over the rail of that sea-balcony, no small one in a seventy-four, looking down on the crowd below. Man or boy, none spake but in whisper, and few spake at all. Captain Vere—as before, the central figure among the assembled commissioned officers—stood nigh the break of the poop-deck facing forward. Just below him on the quarter-deck the marines in full equipment were drawn up much as at the scene of the promulgated sentence.

At sea in the old time, the execution by halter of a military sailor was generally from the fore-yard. In the present instance, for special reasons the main-yard was assigned. Under an arm of that lee-yard the prisoner was presently brought up, the Chaplain attending him. It was noted at the time and remarked upon afterwards, that in this final scene the good man evinced little or nothing of the perfunctory. Brief speech indeed he had with the condemned one, but the genuine Gospel was less on his tongue than in his aspect and manner towards him. The final preparations personal to the latter being speedily brought to an end by two boatswain's-mates, the consummation impended. Billy stood facing aft. At the penultimate moment, his words, his only ones, words wholly unobstructed in the utterance were these—"God bless Captain Vere!" Syllables so unanticipated coming from one with the ignominious hemp about his neck—a conventional felon's benediction directed aft towards the quarters of honor; syllables too delivered in the clear melody of a singing-bird on the point of launching from the twig, had a phenomenal effect, not unenhanced by the rare personal beauty of the young sailor spiritualized now thro' late experiences so poignantly profound.

Without volition as it were, as if indeed the ship's populace were but the vehicles of some vocal current electric, with one voice from alow and aloft came a resonant sympathetic echo—"God bless Captain Vere!" And yet at that instant Billy alone must have been in their hearts, even as he was in their eyes.

At the pronounced words and the spontaneous echo that voluminously rebounded them, Captain Vere, either thro' stoic self-control or a sort of momentary paralysis induced by emotional shock, stood erectly rigid as a musket in the ship-armorer's rack.

The hull deliberately recovering from the periodic roll to leeward was just regaining an even keel, when the last signal, a preconcerted dumb one, was given. At the same moment it chanced that the vapory fleece hanging low in the East, was shot thro' with a soft glory as of the fleece of the Lamb of God seen in mystical vision, and simultaneously therewith, watched by the wedged mass of upturned faces, Billy ascended; and, ascending, took the full rose of the dawn.

In the pinioned figure, arrived at the yard-end, to the wonder of all no motion was apparent, none save that created by the ship's motion, in moderate weather so majestic in a great ship ponderously cannoned.

27

A DIGRESSION

When some days afterward in reference to the singularity just mentioned, the Purser, a rather ruddy rotund person more accurate as an accountant than profound as a philosopher, said at mess to the Surgeon, "What testimony to the force lodged in will-power," the latter—saturnine, spare and tall, one in whom a discreet causticity went along with a manner less genial than polite, replied, "Your pardon, Mr. Purser. In a hanging scientifically conducted—and under special orders I myself directed how Budd's was to be effected—any movement following the completed suspension and originating in the body suspended, such movement indicates mechanical spasm in the muscular system. Hence the absence of that is no more attributable to will-power as you call it than to horsepower—begging your pardon."

"But this muscular spasm you speak of, is not that in a degree more or less invariable in these cases?"

"Assuredly so, Mr. Purser."

"How then, my good sir, do you account for its absence in this instance?"

"Mr. Purser, it is clear that your sense of the singularity in this matter equals not mine. You account for it by what you call will-power, a term not yet included in the lexicon of science. For me I do not, with my present knowledge, pretend to account for it at all. Even should we assume the hypothesis that at the first touch of the halyards the action of Budd's heart, intensified by extraordinary emotion at its climax, abruptly stopt—much like a watch when in carelessly winding it up you strain at the finish, thus snapping the chain—even under that hypothesis, how account for the phenomenon that followed?"

"You admit then that the absence of spasmodic movement was phenomenal."

"It was phenomenal, Mr. Purser, in the sense that it was an appearance the cause of which is not immediately to be assigned."

"But tell me, my dear Sir," pertinaciously continued the other, "was the man's death effected by the halter, or was it a species of euthanasia?"

"*Euthanasia*, Mr. Purser, is something like your *will-power:* I doubt its authenticity as a scientific term—begging your pardon again. It is at once imaginative and metaphysical,—in short, Greek. But," abruptly changing his tone, "there is a case in the sick-bay that I do not care to leave to my assistants. Beg your pardon, but excuse me." And rising from the mess he formally withdrew.

28

The silence at the moment of execution and for a moment or two continuing thereafter, a silence but emphasized by the regular wash of the sea against the hull or the flutter of a sail caused by the helmsman's eyes being tempted astray, this emphasized silence was gradually disturbed by a sound not easily to be verbally rendered. Whoever has heard the freshet-wave of a torrent suddenly swelled by pouring showers in tropical mountains, showers not shared by the plain; whoever has heard the first muffled murmur of its sloping advance through precipitous woods, may form some conception of the sound now heard. The seeming remoteness of its source was because of its murmurous indistinctness since it came from close-by, even from the men massed on the ship's open deck. Being inarticulate, it was dubious in significance further than it seemed to indicate some capricious revulsion of thought or feeling such as mobs ashore are liable to, in the present instance possibly implying a sullen revocation on the men's part of their involuntary echoing of Billy's benediction. But ere the murmur had time to wax into clamour it was met by a strategic command, the more telling that it came with abrupt unexpectedness.

"Pipe down the starboard watch, Boatswain, and see that they go."

Shrill as the shriek of the sea-hawk the whistles of the Boatswain and his Mates pierced that ominous low sound, dissipating it; and yielding to the mechanism of discipline, the throng was thinned by one half. For the remainder most of them were set to temporary employments connected with trimming the yards and so forth, business readily to be got up to serve occasion by any officer-of-the-deck.

Now each proceeding that follows a mortal sentence pronounced at sea by a drum-head court is characterised by promptitude not perceptibly merging into hurry, tho' bordering that. The hammock, the one which had been Billy's bed when alive, having already been ballasted with shot and otherwise prepared to serve for his canvas coffin, the last offices of the sea-undertakers, the Sail-Maker's Mates, were now speedily completed. When everything was in readiness a second call for all hands made necessary by the strategic movement before mentioned was sounded and now to witness burial.

The details of this closing formality it needs not to give. But when the tilted plank let slide its freight into the sea, a second strange human murmur was heard, blended now with another inarticulate sound proceeding from certain larger sea-fowl, whose attention having been attracted by the peculiar commotion in the water resulting from the heavy sloped dive of the shotted hammock into the sea, flew screaming to the spot. So near the hull did they come, that the stridor or bony creak of their gaunt double-jointed pinions was audible. As the ship under light airs passed on, leaving the burial-spot astern, they still kept circling it low down with the moving shadow of their outstretched wings and the croaked requiem of their cries.

Upon sailors as superstitious as those of the age preceding ours, men-of-war's-men too who had just beheld the prodigy of repose in the form suspended in air and now foundering in the deeps; to such mariners the action of the sea-fowl, tho' dictated by mere animal greed for prey, was big with no prosaic significance. An uncertain movement began among them, in which some encroachment was made. It was tolerated but for a moment. For suddenly the drum beat to quarters, which familiar sound happening at least twice every day, had upon the present occasion a signal peremptoriness in it. True martial discipline long continued superinduces in average man a sort of impulse of docility whose operation at the official sound of command much resembles in its promptitude the effect of an instinct.

The drum-beat dissolved the multitude, distributing most of them along the batteries of the two covered gun decks. There, as wont, the guns' crews stood by their respective cannon erect and silent. In due course the First Officer, sword under arm and standing in his place on the quarter-deck, formally received the successive reports of the sworded Lieutenants commanding the sections of batteries below; the last of which reports being made, the summed report he delivered with the customary salute to the Commander. All this occupied time, which in the present case, was the object of beating to quarters at an hour prior to the customary one. That such variance from usage was authorized by an officer like Captain Vere, a martinet as some deemed him, was evidence of the necessity for unusual action implied in what he deemed to be temporarily the mood of his men. "With mankind," he would say, "forms, measured forms are everything; and that is the import couched in the story of Orpheus with his lyre spell-binding the wild denizens of the wood." And this he once applied to the disruption of forms going on across the Channel and the consequences thereof.

At this unwonted muster at quarters, all proceeded as at the regular hour. The band on the quarter-deck played a sacred air. After which the Chaplain went thro' the customary morning service. That done, the drum beat the retreat, and toned by music and religious rites subserving the discipline and purpose of war, the men in their wonted orderly manner, dispersed to the places allotted them when not at the guns.

And now it was full day. The fleece of low-hanging vapor had vanished, licked up by the sun that late had so glorified it. And the circumambient air in the clearness of its serenity was like smooth marble in the polished block not yet removed from the marble-dealer's yard.

~ 29 ~

The symmetry of form attainable in pure fiction can not so readily be achieved in a narration essentially having less to do with fable than with fact. Truth uncompromisingly told will always have its ragged edges; hence the conclusion of such a narration is apt to be less finished than an architectural finial.

How it fared with the Handsome Sailor during the year of the Great Mutiny has been faithfully given. But tho' properly the story ends with his life, something in way of sequel will not be amiss. Three brief chapters will suffice.

In the general re-christening under the Directory of the craft originally forming the navy of the French monarchy, the *St. Louis* line-of-battle ship was named the *Athéiste.* Such a name, like some other substituted ones in the Revolutionary fleet, while proclaiming the infidel audacity of the ruling power was yet, tho' not so intended to be, the aptest name, if one consider it, ever given to a war-ship; far more so indeed than the *Devastation,* the *Erebus* (the *Hell*) and similar names bestowed upon fighting-ships.

On the return-passage to the English fleet from the detached cruise during which occurred the events already recorded, the *Indomitable* fell in with the *Athéiste.* An engagement ensued; during which Captain Vere, in the act of putting his ship alongside the enemy with a view of throwing his boarders across her bulwarks, was hit by a musket-ball from a port-hole of the enemy's main cabin. More than disabled he dropped to the deck and was carried below to the same cock-pit where some of his men already lay. The senior Lieutenant took command. Under him the enemy was finally captured and though much crippled was by rare good fortune successfully taken into Gibraltar, an English port not very distant from the scene of the fight. There, Captain Vere with the rest of the wounded was put ashore. He lingered for some days, but the end came. Unhappily he was cut off too early for the Nile and Trafalgar. The spirit that spite its philosophic austerity may yet have indulged in the most secret of all passions, ambition, never attained to the fulness of fame.

Not long before death, while lying under the influence of that magical drug which soothing the physical frame mysteriously operates on the subtler element in man, he was heard to murmur words inexplicable to his attendant—"Billy Budd, Billy Budd." That these were not the accents of remorse, would seem clear from what the attendant said to the *Indomitable's* senior officer of marines who, as the most reluctant to condemn of the members of the drum-head court, too well knew, tho' here he kept the knowledge to himself, who Billy Budd was.

30

Some few weeks after the execution, among other matters under the head of *News from the Mediterranean*, there appeared in a naval chronicle of the time, an authorized weekly publication, an account of the affair. It was doubtless for the most part written in good faith, tho' the medium, partly rumor, through which the facts must have reached the writer, served to deflect and in part falsify them. The account was as follows:—

"On the tenth of the last month a deplorable occurrence took place on board H.M.S. *Indomitable*. John Claggart, the ship's Master-at-arms, discovering that some sort of plot was incipient among an inferior section of the ship's company, and that the ringleader was one William Budd; he, Claggart, in the act of arraigning the man before the Captain was vindictively stabbed to the heart by the suddenly drawn sheath-knife of Budd.

"The deed and the implement employed, sufficiently suggest that tho' mustered into the service under an English name the assassin was no Englishman, but one of those aliens adopting English cognomens whom the present extraordinary necessities of the Service have caused to be admitted into it in considerable numbers.

"The enormity of the crime and the extreme depravity of the criminal, appear the greater in view of the character of the victim, a middle-aged man respectable and discreet, belonging to that official grade, the petty-officers, upon whom, as none know better than the commissioned gentlemen, the efficiency of His Majesty's

Navy so largely depends. His function was a responsible one, at once onerous & thankless, and his fidelity in it the greater because of his strong patriotic impulse. In this instance as in so many other instances in these days, the character of this unfortunate man signally refutes, if refutation were needed, that peevish saying attributed to the late Dr. Johnson, that patriotism is the last refuge of a scoundrel.

"The criminal paid the penalty of his crime. The promptitude of the punishment has proved salutary. Nothing amiss is now apprehended aboard H.M.S. *Indomitable.*"

The above, appearing in a publication now long ago superannuated and forgotten, is all that hitherto has stood in human record to attest what manner of men respectively were John Claggart and Billy Budd.

31

Everything is for a term remarkable in navies. Any tangible object associated with some striking incident of the service is converted into a monument. The spar from which the Foretopman was suspended, was for some few years kept trace of by the blue-jackets. Their knowledge followed it from ship to dock-yard and again from dock-yard to ship, still pursuing it even when at last reduced to a mere dock-yard boom. To them a chip of it was as a piece of the Cross. Ignorant tho' they were of the secret facts of the tragedy, and not thinking but that the penalty was somehow unavoidably inflicted from the naval point of view, for all that they instinctively felt that Billy was a sort of man as incapable of mutiny as of wilful murder. They recalled the fresh young image of the Handsome Sailor, that face never deformed by a sneer or subtler vile freak of the heart within. Their impression of him was doubtless deepened by the fact that he was gone, and in a measure mysteriously gone. At the time, on the gun decks of the *Indomitable,* the general estimate of his nature and its unconscious simplicity eventually found rude utterance from another foretopman, one of his own watch, gifted, as some sailors are, with an artless poetic temperament; the tarry hands made some lines which after circulating among the shipboard crew for a while, finally got rudely printed at Portsmouth as a ballad. The title given to it was the sailor's.

BILLY IN THE DARBIES

Good of the Chaplain to enter Lone Bay
And down on his marrow-bones here and pray
For the likes just o' me, Billy Budd.—But look:
Through the port comes the moon-shine astray!
It tips the guard's cutlas and silvers this nook;
But 'twill die in the dawning of Billy's last day.
A jewel-block they'll make of me to-morrow,
Pendant pearl from the yard-arm-end
Like the ear-drop I gave to Bristol Molly—
O, 'tis me, not the sentence they'll suspend.
Ay, Ay, all is up; and I must up too
Early in the morning, aloft from alow.
On an empty stomach, now, never it would do.
They'll give me a nibble—bit o' biscuit ere I go.
Sure, a messmate will reach me the last parting cup;
But, turning heads away from the hoist and the belay,
Heaven knows who will have the running of me up!
No pipe to those halyards.—But aren't it all sham?
A blur's in my eyes; it is dreaming that I am.
A hatchet to my hawser? all adrift to go?
The drum roll to grog, and Billy never know?
But Donald he has promised to stand by the plank;
So I'll shake a friendly hand ere I sink.
But—no! It is dead then I'll be, come to think.—
I remember Taff the Welshman when he sank.
And his cheek it was like the budding pink.
But me they'll lash me in hammock, drop me deep.
Fathoms down, fathoms down, how I'll dream fast asleep.
I feel it stealing now. Sentry, are you there?
Just ease this darbies at the wrist, and roll me over fair,
I am sleepy, and the oozy weeds about me twist.

Benito Cereno

IN THE YEAR 1799, Captain Amasa Delano, of Duxbury, in Massachusetts, commanding a large sealer and general trader, lay at anchor, with a valuable cargo, in the harbour of St. Maria—a small, desert, uninhabited island towards the southern extremity of the long coast of Chili. There he had touched for water.

On the second day, not long after dawn, while lying in his berth, his mate came below, informing him that a strange sail was coming into the bay. Ships were then not so plenty in those waters as now. He rose, dressed, and went on deck.

The morning was one peculiar to that coast. Everything was mute and calm; everything grey. The sea, though undulated into long roods of swells, seemed fixed, and was sleeked at the surface like waved lead that has cooled and set in the smelter's mould. The sky seemed a grey mantle. Flights of troubled grey fowl, kith and kin with flights of troubled grey vapours among which they were mixed, skimmed low and fitfully over the waters, as swallows over meadows before storms. Shadows present, foreshadowing deeper shadows to come.

To Captain Delano's surprise, the stranger, viewed through the glass, showed no colours; though to do so upon entering a haven, however uninhabited in its shores, where but a single other ship might be lying, was the custom among peaceful seamen of all nations. Considering the lawlessness and loneliness of the spot, and the sort of stories, at that day, associated with those seas, Captain Delano's surprise might have deepened into some uneasiness had he not been a person of a singularly undistrustful good nature, not liable, except on extraordinary and repeated excitement, and hardly then, to indulge in personal alarms, any way involving the imputation of malign evil in man. Whether, in view of what humanity is capable, such a trait implies, along with a benevolent heart, more than ordinary quickness and accuracy of intellectual perception, may be left to the wise to determine.

But whatever misgivings might have obtruded on first seeing the stranger would almost, in any seaman's mind, have been dissipated by observing that the ship, in navigating into the harbour, was drawing too near the land, for her own safety's sake, owing to a sunken reef making out off her bow. This seemed to prove her a stranger, indeed, not only to the sealer, but the island; consequently, she could be no wonted freebooter on that ocean. With no small interest, Captain Delano continued to watch her—a proceeding not much facilitated by the vapours partly mantling the hull, through which the far matin light from her cabin streamed equivocally enough; much like the sun—by this time crescented on the rim of the horizon, and apparently, in company with the strange ship, entering the harbour—which, wimpled by the same low, creeping clouds, showed not unlike a Lima intriguante's one sinister eye peering across the Plaza from the Indian loop-hole of her dusk *saya-y-manta.*

It might have been but a deception of the vapours, but, the longer the stranger was watched, the more singular appeared her manoeuvres. Ere long it seemed hard to decide whether she meant to come in or no—what she wanted, or what she was about. The wind, which had breezed up a little during the night, was now extremely light and baffling, which the more increased the apparent uncertainty of her movements.

Surmising, at last, that it might be a ship in distress, Captain Delano ordered his whale-boat to be dropped, and, much to the wary opposition of his mate, prepared to board her, and, at the least, pilot her in. On the night previous, a fishing-party of the seamen had gone a long distance to some detached rocks out of sight from the sealer, and, an hour or two before day-break, had returned, having met with no small success. Presuming that the stranger might have been long off soundings, the good captain put several baskets of the fish, for presents, into his boat, and so pulled away. From her continuing too near the sunken reef, deeming her in danger, calling to his men, he made all haste to apprise those on board of their situation. But, some time ere the boat came up, the wind, light though it was, having shifted, had headed the vessel off, as well as partly broken the vapours from about her.

Upon gaining a less remote view, the ship, when made signally visible on the verge of the leaden-hued swells, with the shreds of fog here and there raggedly furring her, appeared like a white-washed monastery after a thunder-storm, seen perched upon some dun cliff among the Pyrenees. But it was no purely fanciful resemblance which now, for a moment, almost led Captain Delano to think that nothing less than a ship-load of monks was before him. Peering over the bulwarks were what really seemed, in the hazy distance, throngs of dark cowls; while, fitfully revealed through the open port-holes, other dark moving figures were dimly descried, as of Black Friars pacing the cloisters.

Upon a still nigher approach, this appearance was modified, and the true character of the vessel was plain—a Spanish merchantman of the first class; carrying Negro slaves, amongst other valuable freight, from one colonial port to another. A very large, and, in its time, a very fine vessel, such as in those days were at intervals encountered along that main; sometimes superseded Acapulco treasure-ships, or retired frigates of the Spanish king's navy, which, like superannuated Italian palaces, still, under a decline of masters, preserved signs of former state.

As the whale-boat drew more and more nigh, the cause of the peculiar pipe-clayed aspect of the stranger was seen in the slovenly neglect pervading her. The spars, ropes, and great part of the bulwarks looked woolly, from long unacquaintance with the scraper, tar, and the brush. Her keel seemed laid, her ribs put together, and she launched, from Ezekiel's Valley of Dry Bones.

In the present business in which she was engaged, the ship's general model and rig appeared to have undergone no material change from their original warlike and Froissart pattern. However, no guns were seen.

The tops were large, and were railed about with what had

once been octagonal net-work, all now in sad disrepair. These tops hung overhead like three ruinous aviaries, in one of which was seen perched, on a ratlin, a white noddy, a strange fowl, so called from its lethargic somnambulistic character, being frequently caught by hand at sea. Battered and mouldy, the castellated forecastle seemed some ancient turret, long ago taken by assault, and then left to decay. Towards the stern, two high-raised quarter galleries—the balustrades here and there covered with dry, tindery sea-moss—opening out from the unoccupied state-cabin, whose dead lights, for all the mild weather, were hermetically closed and caulked—these tenantless balconies hung over the sea as if it were the grand Venetian canal. But the principal relic of faded grandeur was the ample oval of the shield-like stern-piece, intricately carved with the arms of Castile and Leon, medallioned about by groups of mythological or symbolical devices; uppermost and central of which was a dark satyr in a mask, holding his foot on the prostrate neck of a writhing figure, likewise masked.

Whether the ship had a figure-head, or only a plain beak, was not quite certain, owing to canvas wrapped about that part, either to protect it while undergoing a refurbishing, or else decently to hide its decay. Rudely painted or chalked, as in a sailor freak, along the forward side of a sort of pedestal below the canvas, was the sentence, "*Seguid vuestro jefe*" (follow your leader); while upon the tarnished head-boards, near by, appeared, in stately capitals, once gilt, the ship's name, "SAN DOMINICK," each letter streakingly corroded with tricklings of copper-spike rust; while, like mourning weeds, dark festoons of sea-grass slimily swept to and fro over the name, with every hearse-like roll of the hull.

As at last the boat was hooked from the bow along toward the gangway amidship, its keel, while yet some inches separated from the hull, harshly grated as on a sunken coral reef. It proved a huge bunch of conglobated barnacles adhering below the water to the side like a wen; a token of baffling airs and long calms passed somewhere in those seas.

Climbing the side, the visitor was at once surrounded by a

clamorous throng of whites and blacks, but the latter outnumbering the former more than could have been expected, Negro transportation-ship as the stranger in port was. But, in one language, and as with one voice, all poured out a common tale of suffering; in which the Negresses, of whom there were not a few, exceeded the others in their dolorous vehemence. The scurvy, together with a fever, had swept off a great part of their number, more especially the Spaniards. Off Cape Horn, they had narrowly escaped shipwreck; then, for days together, they had lain tranced without wind; their provisions were low; their water next to none; their lips that moment were baked.

While Captain Delano was thus made the mark of all eager tongues, his one eager glance took in all the faces, with every other object about him.

Always upon first boarding a large and populous ship at sea, especially a foreign one, with a nondescript crew such as Lascars or Manilla men, the impression varies in a peculiar way from that produced by first entering a strange house with strange inmates in a strange land. Both house and ship, the one by its walls and blinds, the other by its high bulwarks like ramparts, hoard from view their interiors till the last moment; but in the case of the ship there is this addition: that the living spectacle it contains, upon its sudden and complete disclosure, has, in contrast with the blank ocean which zones it, something of the effect of enchantment. The ship seems unreal; these strange costumes, gestures, and faces, but a shadowy tableau just emerged from the deep, which directly must receive back what it gave.

Perhaps it was some such influence as above is attempted to be described which, in Captain Delano's mind, heightened whatever, upon a staid scrutiny, might have seemed unusual; especially the conspicuous figures of four elderly grizzled Negroes, their heads like black, doddered willow tops, who, in venerable contrast to the tumult below them, were couched sphynx-like, one on the starboard cat-head, another on the larboard, and the remaining pair face to face on the opposite bulwarks above the main-chains. They each had bits of unstranded old junk in their hands, and, with a sort of stoical self-content, were picking the junk into oakum, a small heap of which lay by their sides. They accompanied the task with a continuous, low, monotonous chant; droning and drooling away like so many grey-headed bag-pipers playing a funeral march.

The quarter-deck rose into an ample elevated poop, upon the forward verge of which, lifted, like the oakum-pickers, some eight feet above the general throng, sat along in a row, separated by regular spaces, the cross-legged figures of six other blacks; each with a rusty hatchet in his hand, which, with a bit of brick and a rag, he was engaged like a scullion in scouring; while between each two was a small stack of hatchets, their rusted edges turned forward awaiting a like operation. Though occasionally the four oakum-pickers would briefly address some person or persons in the crowd below, yet the six hatchet-polishers neither spoke to others, nor breathed a whisper among themselves, but sat intent upon their task, except at intervals, when, with the peculiar love in Negroes of uniting industry with pastime, two-and-two they sideways clashed their hatchets together, like cymbals, with a barbarous din. All six, unlike the generality, had the raw aspect of unsophisticated Africans.

But the first comprehensive glance which took in those ten figures, with scores less conspicuous, rested but an instant upon them, as, impatient of the hubbub of voices, the visitor turned in quest of whomsoever it might be that commanded the ship.

But as if not unwilling to let nature make known her own case among his suffering charge, or else in despair of restraining it for the time, the Spanish captain, a gentlemanly, reserved-looking, and rather young man to a stranger's eye, dressed with singular richness, but bearing plain traces of recent sleepless cares and disquietudes, stood passively by, leaning against the main-mast, at one moment casting a dreary, spiritless look upon his excited people, at the next an unhappy glance toward his visitor. By his side stood a black of small stature, in whose rude face, as occasionally, like a shepherd's dog, he mutely turned it up into the Spaniard's, sorrow and affection were equally blended.

Struggling through the throng, the American advanced to the Spaniard, assuring him of his sympathies, and offering to render whatever assistance might be in his power. To which the Spaniard returned, for the present, but grave and ceremonious acknowledgments, his national formality dusked by the saturnine mood of ill health.

But losing no time in mere compliments, Captain Delano returning to the gangway, had his baskets of fish brought up; and as the wind still continued light, so that some hours at least must elapse ere the ship could be brought to the anchorage, he bade his men return to the sealer, and fetch back as much water as the whaleboat could carry, with whatever soft bread the steward might have, all the remaining pumpkins on board, with a box of sugar, and a dozen of his private bottles of cider.

Not many minutes after the boat's pushing off, to the vexation of all, the wind entirely died away, and the tide turning, began drifting back the ship helplessly seaward. But trusting this would not last, Captain Delano sought with good hopes to cheer up the strangers, feeling no small satisfaction that, with persons in their condition he could—thanks to his frequent voyages along the Spanish main—converse with some freedom in their native tongue.

While left alone with them, he was not long in observing some things tending to heighten his first impressions; but surprise was lost in pity, both for the Spaniards and blacks, alike evidently reduced from scarcity of water and provisions; while long-continued suffering seemed to have brought out the less good-natured qualities of the Negroes, besides, at the same time, impairing the Spaniard's authority over them. But, under the circumstances, precisely this condition of things was to have been anticipated. In armies, navies, cities, or families—in nature herself—nothing more relaxes good order than misery. Still, Captain Delano was not without the idea, that had Benito Cereno been a man of greater energy, misrule would hardly have come to the present pass. But the debility, constitutional or induced by the hardships, bodily and mental, of the Spanish captain, was too obvious to be overlooked. A prey to settled dejection, as if long mocked with hope he would not now indulge it, even when it had ceased to be a mock, the prospect of that day or evening at furthest, lying at anchor, with plenty of water for his people, and a brother captain to counsel and befriend, seemed in no perceptible degree to encourage him. His mind appeared unstrung, if not still more seriously affected. Shut up in these oaken walls, chained to one dull round of command, whose unconditionality cloyed him, like some hypochondriac abbot he moved slowly about, at times suddenly pausing, starting, or staring, biting his lip, biting his finger-nail, flushing, paling, twitching his beard, with other symptoms of an absent or moody mind. This distempered spirit was lodged, as before hinted, in as distempered a frame. He was rather tall, but seemed never to have been robust, and now with nervous suffering was almost worn to a skeleton. A tendency to some pulmonary complaint appeared to have been lately confirmed. His voice was like that of one with lungs half gone, hoarsely suppressed, a husky whisper. No wonder that, as in this state he tottered about, his private servant apprehensively followed him. Sometimes the Negro gave his master his arm, or took his handkerchief out of his pocket for him; performing these and similar offices with that affectionate zeal which transmutes into something filial or fraternal acts in themselves but menial; and which has gained for the Negro the repute of making the most pleasing body-servant in the world; one, too, whom a master need be on no stiffly superior terms with, but may treat with familiar trust; less a servant than a devoted companion.

Marking the noisy indocility of the blacks in general, as well as what seemed the sullen inefficiency of the whites, it was not without humane satisfaction that Captain Delano witnessed the steady good conduct of Babo.

But the good conduct of Babo, hardly more than the ill-behaviour of others, seemed to withdraw the half-lunatic Don Benito from his cloudy languor. Not that such precisely was the impression made by the Spaniard on the mind of his visitor. The Spaniard's individual unrest was, for the present, but noted as a conspicuous feature in the ship's general affliction. Still, Captain Delano was not a little concerned at what he could not help taking for the time to be Don Benito's unfriendly indifference toward himself. The Spaniard's manner, too, conveyed a sort of sour and gloomy disdain, which he seemed at no pains to disguise. But this the American in charity ascribed to the harassing effects of sickness, since, in former instances, he had noted that there are peculiar natures on whom prolonged physical suffering seems to cancel every social instinct of kindness; as if forced to black bread themselves, they deemed it but equity that each person coming nigh them should, indirectly, by some slight or affront, be made to partake of their fare.

But ere long Captain Delano bethought him that, indulgent as he was at the first, in judging the Spaniard, he might not, after all, have exercised charity enough. At bottom it was Don Benito's reserve which displeased him; but the same reserve was shown toward all but his personal attendant. Even the formal reports which, according to sea-usage, were at stated times made to him by some petty underling (either a white, mulatto or black), he hardly had patience enough to listen to, without betraying contemptuous aversion. His manner upon such occasions was, in its degree, not unlike that which might be supposed to have been his imperial countryman's, Charles V., just previous to the anchoritish retirement of that monarch from the throne.

This splenetic disrelish of his place was evinced in almost every function pertaining to it. Proud as he was moody, he condescended to no personal mandate. Whatever special orders were necessary, their delivery was delegated to his body-servant, who in turn transferred them to their ultimate destination, through runners, alert Spanish boys or slave boys, like pages or pilot-fish within easy call continually hovering round Don Benito. So that to have beheld this undemonstrative invalid gliding about, apathetic and mute, no landsman could have dreamed that in him was lodged a dictatorship beyond which, while at sea, there was no earthly appeal.

Thus, the Spaniard, regarded in his reserve, seemed as the involuntary victim of mental disorder. But, in fact, his reserve might, in some degree, have proceeded from design. If so, then in Don Benito was evinced the unhealthy climax of that icy though conscientious policy, more or less adopted by all commanders of large ships, which, except in signal emergencies, obliterates alike the manifestation of sway with every trace of sociality; transforming the man into a block, or rather into a loaded cannon, which, until there is call for thunder, has nothing to say.

Viewing him in this light, it seemed but a natural token of the perverse habit induced by a long course of such hard self-restraint, that, notwithstanding the present condition of his ship, the Spaniard should still persist in a demeanour, which, however harmless—or it may be, appropriate—in a well-appointed vessel, such as the *San Dominick* might have been at the outset of the voyage, was anything but judicious now. But the Spaniard perhaps thought that it was with captains as with gods: reserve, under all events, must still be their cue. But more probably this appearance of slumbering dominion might have been but an attempted disguise to conscious imbecility—not deep policy, but shallow device. But be all this as it might, whether Don Benito's manner was designed or not, the more Captain Delano noted its pervading reserve, the less he felt uneasiness at any particular manifestation of that reserve toward himself.

Neither were his thoughts taken up by the captain alone. Wonted to the quiet orderliness of the sealer's comfortable family of a crew, the noisy confusion of the *San Dominick's* suffering host repeatedly challenged his eye. Some prominent breaches not only of discipline but of decency were observed. These Captain Delano could not but ascribe, in the main, to the absence of those subordinate deck-officers to whom, along with higher duties, is entrusted what may be styled the police department of a populous ship. True, the old oakum-pickers appeared at times to act the part of monitorial constables to their countrymen, the blacks; but though occasionally succeeding in allaying trifling outbreaks now and then between man and man, they could do little or nothing toward establishing general quiet. The *San Dominick* was in the condition of a transatlantic emigrant ship, among whose multitude of living freight are some individuals, doubtless, as little troublesome as crates and bales; but the friendly remonstrances of such with their ruder companions are of not so much avail as the unfriendly arm of the mate.

What the *San Dominick* wanted was, what the emigrant ship has, stern superior officers. But on these decks not so much as a fourth mate was to be seen.

The visitor's curiosity was roused to learn the particulars of those mishaps which had brought about such absenteeism, with its consequences; because, though deriving some inkling of the voyage from the wails which at the first moment had greeted him, yet of the details no clear understanding had been had. The best account would, doubtless, be given by the captain. Yet at first the visitor was loth to ask it, unwilling to provoke some distant rebuff. But plucking up courage, he at last accosted Don Benito, renewing the expression of his benevolent interest, adding, that did he (Captain Delano) but know the particulars of the ship's misfortunes, he would, perhaps, be better able in the end to relieve them. Would Don Benito favour him with the whole story?

Don Benito faltered; then, like some somnambulist suddenly interfered with, vacantly stared at his visitor, and ended by looking down on the deck. He maintained this posture so long, that Captain Delano, almost equally disconcerted, and involuntarily almost as rude, turned suddenly from him, walking forward to accost one of the Spanish seamen for the desired information. But he had hardly gone five paces, when with a sort of eagerness Don Benito invited him back, regretting his momentary absence of mind, and professing readiness to gratify him.

While most part of the story was being given, the two captains stood on the after part of the main-deck, a privileged spot, no one being near but the servant.

"It is now a hundred and ninety days," began the Spaniard, in his husky whisper, "that this ship, well officered and well manned, with several cabin passengers—some fifty Spaniards in all—sailed from Buenos Ayres bound to Lima, with a general cargo, Paraguay tea and the like—and," pointing forward, "that parcel of Negroes, now not more than a hundred and fifty, as you see, but then numbering over three hundred souls. Off Cape Horn we had heavy gales. In one moment, by night, three of my best officers, with fifteen sailors, were lost, with the main-yard; the spar snapping under them in the slings, as they sought, with heavers, to beat down the icy sail. To lighten the hull, the heavier sacks of mata were thrown into the sea, with most of the water-pipes lashed on deck at the time. And this last necessity it was, combined with the prolonged detentions afterwards experienced, which eventually brought about our chief causes of suffering. When—"

Here there was a sudden fainting attack of his cough, brought on, no doubt, by his mental distress. His servant sustained him, and drawing a cordial from his pocket placed it to his lips. He a little revived. But unwilling to leave him unsupported while yet imperfectly restored, the black with one arm still encircled his master, at the same time keeping his eye fixed on his face, as if to watch for the first sign of complete restoration, or relapse, as the event might prove.

The Spaniard proceeded, but brokenly and obscurely, as one in a dream.

—"Oh, my God! rather than pass through what I have, with joy I would have hailed the most terrible gales; but—"

His cough returned and with increased violence; this subsiding, with reddened lips and closed eyes he fell heavily against his supporter.

"His mind wanders. He was thinking of the plague that followed the gales," plaintively sighed the servant; "my poor, poor master!" wringing one hand, and with the other wiping the mouth. "But be patient, Señor," again turning to Captain Delano, "these fits do not last long; master will soon be himself."

Don Benito reviving, went on; but as this portion of the story was very brokenly delivered, the substance only will here be set down.

It appeared that after the ship had been many days tossed in storms off the Cape, the scurvy broke out, carrying off numbers of the whites and blacks. When at last they had worked round into the Pacific, their spars and sails were so damaged, and so inadequately handled by the surviving mariners, most of whom were become invalids, that, unable to lay her northerly course by the wind, which was powerful, the unmanageable ship for successive days and nights was blown northwestward, where the breeze suddenly deserted her, in unknown waters, to sultry calms. The absence of the water-pipes now proved as fatal to life as before their presence had menaced it. Induced, or at least aggravated, by the more than scanty allowance of water, a malignant fever followed the scurvy; with the excessive heat of the lengthened calm, making such short work of it as to sweep away, as by billows, whole families of the Africans, and a yet larger number, proportionally, of the Spaniards, including, by a luckless fatality, every officer on board. Consequently, in the smart west winds eventually following the calm, the already rent sails having to be simply dropped, not furled, at need, had been gradually reduced to the beggar's rags they were now. To procure substitutes for his lost sailors, as well as supplies of water and sails, the captain at the earliest opportunity had made for Baldivia, the southermost civilized port of Chili and South America; but upon nearing the coast the thick weather had prevented him from so much as sighting that harbour. Since which period, almost without a crew, and almost without canvas and almost without water, and at intervals giving its added dead to the sea, the *San Dominick* had been battle-dored about by contrary winds, inveigled by currents, or grown weedy in calms. Like a man lost in woods, more than once she had doubled upon her own track.

"But throughout these calamities," huskily continued Don Benito, painfully turning in the half embrace of his servant, "I have to thank those Negroes you see, who, though to your inexperienced eyes appearing unruly, have, indeed, conducted themselves with less of restlessness than even their owner could have thought possible under such circumstances."

Here he again fell faintly back. Again his mind wandered: but he rallied, and less obscurely proceeded.

"Yes, their owner was quite right in assuring me that no fetters would be needed with his blacks; so that while, as is wont in this transportation, those Negroes have always remained upon deck—not thrust below, as in the Guineamen—they have, also, from the beginning, been freely permitted to range within given bounds at their pleasure."

Once more the faintness returned—his mind roved—but, recovering, he resumed:

"But it is Babo here to whom, under God, I owe not only my own preservation, but likewise to him, chiefly, the merit is due, of pacifying his more ignorant brethren, when at intervals tempted to murmurings."

"Ah, master," sighed the black, bowing his face, "don't speak of me; Babo is nothing; what Babo has done was but duty."

"Faithful fellow!" cried Captain Delano. "Don Benito, I envy you such a friend; slave I cannot call him."

As master and man stood before him, the black upholding the white, Captain Delano could not but bethink him of the beauty of that relationship which could present such a spectacle of fidelity on the one hand and confidence on the other. The scene was heightened by the contrast in dress, denoting their relative positions. The Spaniard wore a loose Chili jacket of dark velvet; white small clothes and stockings, with silver buckles at the knee and instep; a high-crowned sombrero, of fine grass; a slender sword, silver mounted, hung from a knot in his sash; the last being an almost invariable adjunct, more for utility than ornament, of a South American gentleman's dress to this hour. Excepting when his occasional nervous contortions brought about disarray, there was a certain precision in his attire, curiously at variance with the unsightly disorder around; especially in the belittered Ghetto, forward of the main-mast, wholly occupied by the blacks.

The servant wore nothing but wide trousers, apparently, from their coarseness and patches, made out of some old top-sail; they were clean, and confined at the waist by a bit of unstranded rope, which, with his composed, deprecatory air at times, made him look something like a begging friar of St. Francis.

However unsuitable for the time and place, at least in the blunt-thinking American's eyes, and however strangely surviving in the midst of all his afflictions, the toilette of Don Benito might not, in fashion at least, have gone beyond the style of the day among South Americans of his class. Though on the present voyage sailing from Buenos Ayres, he had avowed himself a native and resident of Chili, whose inhabitants had not so generally adopted the plain coat and once plebeian pantaloons; but, with a becoming modification, adhered to their provincial costume, picturesque as any in the world. Still, relatively to the pale history of the voyage, and his own pale face, there seemed something so incongruous in the Spaniard's apparel, as almost to suggest the image of an invalid courtier tottering about London streets in the time of the plague.

The portion of the narrative which, perhaps, most excited interest, as well as some surprise, considering the latitudes in question, was the long calms spoken of, and more particularly the ship's so long drifting about. Without communicating the opinion, of course, the American could not but impute at least part of the detentions both to clumsy seamanship and faulty navigation. Eyeing Don Benito's small, yellow hands, he easily inferred that the young captain had not got into command at the hawse-hole but the cabin-window, and if so, why wonder at incompetence, in youth, sickness, and aristocracy united? Such was his democratic conclusion.

But drowning criticism in compassion, after a fresh repetition of his sympathies, Captain Delano having heard out his story, not only engaged, as in the first place, to see Don Benito and his people supplied in their immediate bodily needs, but, also, now further promised to assist him in procuring a large permanent supply of water, as well as some sails and rigging; and, though it would involve no small embarrassment to himself, yet he would spare three of his best seamen for temporary deck officers; so that without delay the ship might proceed to Concepcion, there fully to refit for Lima, her destined port.

Such generosity was not without its effect, even upon the invalid. His face lighted up; eager and hectic, he met the honest glance of his visitor. With gratitude he seemed overcome.

"This excitement is bad for master," whispered the servant, taking his arm, and with soothing words gently drawing him aside.

When Don Benito returned, the American was pained to observe that his hopefulness, like the sudden kindling in his cheek, was but febrile and transient.

Ere long, with a joyless mien, looking up toward the poop, the host invited his guest to accompany him there, for the benefit of what little breath of wind might be stirring.

As during the telling of the story, Captain Delano had once or twice started at the occasional cymballing of the hatchet-polishers, wondering why such an interruption should be allowed, especially in that part of the ship, and in the ears of an invalid; and, moreover, as the hatchets had anything but an attractive look, and the handlers of them still less so, it was, therefore, to tell the truth, not without some lurking reluctance, or even shrinking, it may be, that Captain Delano, with apparent complaisance, acquiesced in his host's invitation. The more so, since with an untimely caprice of punctilio, rendered distressing by his cadaverous aspect, Don Benito, with Castilian bows, solemnly insisted upon his guest's preceding him up the ladder leading to the elevation; where, one on each side of the last step, sat four armorial supporters and sentries, two of the ominous file. Gingerly enough stepped good Captain Delano between them, and in the instant of leaving them behind, like one running the gauntlet, he felt an apprehensive twitch in the calves of his legs.

But when, facing about, he saw the whole file, like so many organ-grinders, still stupidly intent on their work, unmindful of everything beside, he could not but smile at his late fidgeting panic.

Presently, while standing with Don Benito, looking forward upon the decks below, he was struck by one of those instances of insubordination previously alluded to. Three black boys, with two Spanish boys, were sitting together on the hatches, scraping a rude wooden platter, in which some scanty mess had recently been cooked. Suddenly, one of the black boys, enraged at a word dropped by one of his white companions, seized a knife, and thougn called to forbear by one of the oakum-pickers, struck the lad over the head, inflicting a gash from which blood flowed.

In amazement, Captain Delano inquired what this meant. To which the pale Benito dully muttered, that it was merely the sport of the lad.

"Pretty serious sport, truly," rejoined Captain Delano. "Had such a thing happened on board the *Bachelor's Delight*, instant punishment would have followed."

At these words the Spaniard turned upon the American one of his sudden, staring, half-lunatic looks; then, relapsing into his torpor, answered, "Doubtless, doubtless, Señor."

Is it, thought Captain Delano, that this helpless man is one of those paper captains I've known, who by policy wink at what by power they cannot put down? I know no sadder sight than a commander who has little of command but the name.

"I should think, Don Benito," he now said, glancing toward the oakum-picker who had sought to interfere with the boys, "that you would find it advantageous to keep all your blacks employed, especially the younger ones, no matter at what useless task, and no matter what happens to the ship. Why, even with my little band, I find such a course indispensable. I once kept a crew on my quarter-deck thrumming mats for my cabin, when, for three days, I had given up my ship—mats, men, and all—for a speedy loss, owing to the violence of a gale in which we could do nothing but helplessly drive before it."

"Doubtless, doubtless," muttered Don Benito.

"But," continued Captain Delano, again glancing upon the oakum-pickers and then at the hatchet-polishers, near by, "I see you keep some at least of your host employed."

"Yes," was again the vacant response.

"Those old men there, shaking their pows from their pulpits," continued Captain Delano, pointing to the oakum-pickers, "seem to act the part of old dominies to the rest, little heeded as their admonitions are at times. Is this voluntary on their part, Don Benito, or have you appointed them shepherds to your flock of black sheep?"

"What posts they fill, I appointed them," rejoined the Spaniard in an acrid tone, as if resenting some supposed satiric reflection.

"And these others, these Ashantee conjurors here," continued Captain Delano, rather uneasily eyeing the brandished steel of the hatchet-polishers, where in spots it had been brought to a shine, "this seems a curious business they are at, Don Benito?"

"In the gales we met," answered the Spaniard, "what of our

general cargo was not thrown overboard was much damaged by the brine. Since coming into calm weather, I have had several cases of knives and hatchets daily brought up for overhauling and cleaning."

"A prudent idea, Don Benito. You are part owner of ship and cargo, I presume; but not of the slaves, perhaps?"

"I am owner of all you see," impatiently returned Don Benito, "except the main company of blacks, who belonged to my late friend, Alexandro Aranda."

As he mentioned this name, his air was heart-broken, his knees shook; his servant supported him.

Thinking he divined the cause of such unusual emotion, to confirm his surmise, Captain Delano, after a pause, said, "And may I ask, Don Benito, whether—since awhile ago you spoke of some cabin passengers—the friend, whose loss so afflicts you, at the outset of the voyage accompanied his blacks?"

"Yes."

"But died of the fever?"

"Died of the fever.—Oh, could I but—"

Again quivering, the Spaniard paused.

"Pardon me," said Captain Delano slowly, "but I think that, by a sympathetic experience, I conjecture, Don Benito, what it is that gives the keener edge to your grief. It was once my hard fortune to lose at sea a dear friend, my own brother, then supercargo. Assured of the welfare of his spirit, its departure I could have borne like a man; but that honest eye, that honest hand—both of which had so often met mine—and that warm heart; all, all—like scraps to the dogs—to throw all to the sharks! It was then I vowed never to have for fellow-voyager a man I loved, unless, unbeknown to him, I had provided every requisite, in case of a fatality, for embalming his mortal part for interment on shore. Were your friend's remains now on board this ship, Don Benito, not thus strangely would the mention of his name affect you."

"On board this ship?" echoed the Spaniard. Then, with horrified gestures, as directed against some spectre, he unconsciously fell into the ready arms of his attendant, who, with a silent appeal toward Captain Delano, seemed beseeching him not again to broach a theme so unspeakably distressing to his master.

This poor fellow now, thought the pained American, is the victim of that sad superstition which associates goblins with the deserted body of man, as ghosts with an abandoned house. How unlike are we made! What to me, in like case, would have been a solemn satisfaction, the bare suggestion, even, terrifies the Spaniard into this trance. Poor Alexandro Aranda! what would you say could you see your friend—who, on former voyages, when you for months were left behind, has, I dare say, often longed, and longed, for one peep at you—now transported with terror at the least thought of having you anyway nigh him.

At this moment, with a dreary graveyard toll, betokening a flaw, the ship's forecastle bell, smote by one of the grizzled oakum-pickers, proclaimed ten o'clock through the leaden calm; when Captain Delano's attention was caught by the moving figure of a gigantic black, emerging from the general crowd below, and slowly advancing toward the elevated poop. An iron collar was about his neck, from which depended a chain, thrice wound round his body; the terminating links padlocked together at a broad band of iron, his girdle.

"How like a mute Atufal moves," murmured the servant.

The black mounted the steps of the poop, and, like a brave prisoner, brought up to receive sentence, stood in unquailing muteness before Don Benito, now recovered from his attack.

At the first glimpse of his approach, Don Benito had started, a resentful shadow swept over his face; and, as with the sudden memory of bootless rage, his white lips glued together.

This is some mulish mutineer, thought Captain Delano, surveying, not without a mixture of admiration, the colossal form of the Negro.

"See, he waits your question, master," said the servant.

Thus reminded, Don Benito, nervously averting his glance, as if shunning, by anticipation, some rebellious response, in a disconcerted voice, thus spoke:

"Atufal, will you ask my pardon now?"

The black was silent.

"Again, master," murmured the servant, with bitter upbraiding eyeing his countryman. "Again, master; he will bend to master yet."

"Answer," said Don Benito, still averting his glance, "say but the one word *pardon*, and your chains shall be off."

Upon this, the black, slowly raising both arms, let them lifelessly fall, his links clanking, his head bowed; as much as to say, "No, I am content."

"Go," said Don Benito, with inkept and unknown emotion.

Deliberately as he had come, the black obeyed.

"Excuse me, Don Benito," said Captain Delano, "but this scene surprises me; what means it, pray?"

"It means that that Negro alone, of all the band, has given me peculiar cause of offence. I have put him in chains; I—"

Here he paused; his hand to his head, as if there were a swimming there, or a sudden bewilderment of memory had come over him; but meeting his servant's kindly glance seemed reassured, and proceeded:

"I could not scourge such a form. But I told him he must ask my pardon. As yet he has not. At my command, every two hours he stands before me."

"And how long has this been?"

"Some sixty days."

"And obedient in all else? And respectful?"

"Yes."

"Upon my conscience, then," exclaimed Captain Delano, impulsively, "he has a royal spirit in him, this fellow."

"He may have some right to it," bitterly returned Don Benito; "he says he was king in his own land."

"Yes," said the servant, entering a word, "those slits in Atufal's ears once held wedges of gold; but poor Babo here, in his own land, was only a poor slave; a black man's slave was Babo, who now is the white's."

Somewhat annoyed by these conversational familiarities, Captain Delano turned curiously upon the attendant, then glanced inquiringly at his master; but, as if long wonted to these little informalities, neither master nor man seemed to understand him.

"What, pray, was Atufal's offence, Don Benito?" asked Captain Delano; "if it was not something very serious, take a fool's advice, and, in view of his general docility, as well as in some natural respect for his spirit, remit his penalty."

"No, no, master never will do that," here murmured the servant to himself, "proud Atufal must first ask master's pardon. The slave there carries the padlock, but master here carries the key."

His attention thus directed, Captain Delano now noticed for the first time that, suspended by a slender silken cord, from Don Benito's neck hung a key. At once, from the servant's muttered syllables divining the key's purpose, he smiled and said: "So, Don Benito—padlock and key—significant symbols, truly."

Biting his lip, Don Benito faltered.

Though the remark of Captain Delano, a man of such native simplicity as to be incapable of satire or irony, had been dropped in playful allusion to the Spaniard's singularly evidenced lordship over the black; yet the hypochondriac seemed in some way to have taken it as a malicious reflection upon his confessed inability thus far to break down, at least, on a verbal summons, the entrenched will of the slave. Deploring this supposed misconception, yet despairing of correcting it, Captain Delano shifted the subject; but finding his companion more than ever withdrawn, as if still slowly digesting the lees of the presumed affront above-mentioned, by-and-by Captain Delano likewise became less talkative, oppressed, against his own will, by what seemed the secret vindictiveness of the morbidly sensitive Spaniard. But the good sailor himself, of a quite contrary disposition, refrained, on his part, alike from the appearance as from the feeling of resentment, and if silent, was only so from contagion.

Presently the Spaniard, assisted by his servant, somewhat discourteously crossed over from Captain Delano; a procedure which, sensibly enough, might have been allowed to pass for idle caprice of ill-humour, had not master and man, lingering round the corner of the elevated skylight, begun whispering together in low voices.

This was unpleasing. And more: the moody air of the Spaniard, which at times had not been without a sort of valetudinarian stateliness, now seemed anything but dignified; while the menial familiarity of the servant lost its original charm of simple-hearted attachment.

In his embarrassment, the visitor turned his face to the other side of the ship. By so doing, his glance accidentally fell on a young Spanish sailor, a coil of rope in his hand, just stepped from the deck to the first round of the mizzen-rigging. Perhaps the man would not have been particularly noticed, were it not that, during his ascent to one of the yards, he, with a sort of covert intentness, kept his eye fixed on Captain Delano, from whom, presently, it passed, as if by a natural sequence, to the two whisperers.

His own attention thus redirected to that quarter, Captain Delano gave a slight start. From something in Don Benito's manner just then, it seemed as if the visitor had, at least partly, been the subject of the withdrawn consultation going on—a conjecture as little agreeable to the guest as it was little flattering to the host.

The singular alternations of courtesy and ill-breeding in the Spanish captain were unaccountable, except on one of two suppositions—innocent lunacy, or wicked imposture.

But the first idea, though it might naturally have occurred to an indifferent observer, and, in some respects, had not hitherto been wholly a stranger to Captain Delano's mind, yet, now that, in an incipient way, he began to regard the stranger's conduct something in the light of an intentional affront, of course the idea of lunacy was virtually vacated. But if not a lunatic, what then? Under the circumstances, would a gentleman, nay, any honest boor, act the part now acted by his host? The man was an impostor. Some low-born adventurer, masquerading as an oceanic grandee; yet so ignorant of the first requisites of mere gentlemanhood as to be betrayed into the present remarkable indecorum. That strange ceremoniousness, too, at other times evinced, seemed not uncharacteristic of one playing a part above his real level. Benito Cereno—Don Benito Cereno—a sounding name. One, too, at that period, not unknown, in the surname, to supercargoes and sea captains trading along the Spanish Main, as belonging to one of the most enterprising and extensive mercantile families in all those provinces; several members of it having titles; a sort of Castilian Rothschild, with a noble brother, or cousin, in every great trading town of South America. The alleged Don Benito was in early manhood, about twenty-nine or thirty. To assume a sort of roving cadetship in the maritime affairs of such a house, what more likely scheme for a young knave of talent and spirit? But the Spaniard was a pale invalid. Never mind. For even to the degree of simulating mortal disease, the craft of some tricksters had been known to attain. To think that, under the aspect of infantile weakness, the most savage energies might be couched—those velvets of the Spaniard but the velvet paw to his fangs.

From no train of thought did these fancies come; not from within, but from without; suddenly, too, and in one throng, like hoar frost; yet as soon to vanish as the mild sun of Captain Delano's good-nature regained its meridian.

Glancing over once again toward Don Benito—whose side-face, revealed above the skylight, was now turned toward him—Captain Delano was struck by the profile, whose clearness of cut was refined by the thinness incident to ill-health, as well as ennobled about the chin by the beard. Away with suspicion. He was a true off-shoot of a true hidalgo Cereno.

Relieved by these and other better thoughts, the visitor, lightly humming a tune, now began indifferently pacing the poop, so as not to betray to Don Benito that he had at all mistrusted incivility, much less duplicity; for such mistrust would yet be proved illusory, and by the event; though, for the present, the circumstance which had provoked that distrust remained unexplained. But when that little mystery should have been cleared up, Captain Delano thought he might extremely regret it, did he allow Don Benito to become aware that he had indulged in ungenerous surmises. In short, to the Spaniard's black-letter text, it was best, for a while, to leave open margin.

Presently, his pale face twitching and overcast, the Spaniard, still supported by his attendant, moved over toward his guest, when, with even more than usual embarrassment, and a strange sort of intriguing intonation in his husky whisper, the following conversation began:

"Señor, may I ask how long you have lain at this isle?"

"Oh, but a day or two, Don Benito."

"And from what port are you last?"

"Canton."

"And there, Señor, you exchanged your seal-skins for teas and silks, I think you said?"

"Yes. Silks, mostly."

"And the balance you took in specie, perhaps?"

Captain Delano, fidgeting a little, answered—

"Yes; some silver; not a very great deal, though."

"Ah—well. May I ask how many men have you on board, Señor?"

Captain Delano slightly started, but answered:

"About five-and-twenty, all told."

"And at present, Señor, all on board, I suppose?"

"All on board, Don Benito," replied the captain now with satisfaction.

"And will be to-night, Señor?"

At this last question, following so many pertinacious ones, for the soul of him Captain Delano could not but look very earnestly at the questioner, who, instead of meeting the glance, with every token of craven discomposure dropped his eyes to the deck; presenting an unworthy contrast to his servant, who, just then, was kneeling at his feet adjusting a loose shoe-buckle; his disengaged face meantime, with humble curiosity, turned openly up into his master's downcast one.

The Spaniard, still with a guilty shuffle, repeated his question:

"And—and will be to-night, Señor?"

"Yes, for aught I know," returned Captain Delano,—"but nay," rallying himself into fearless truth, "some of them talked of going off on another fishing party about midnight."

"Your ships generally go—go more or less armed, I believe, Señor?"

"Oh, a six-pounder or two, in case of emergency," was the intrepidly indifferent reply, "with a small stock of muskets, sealing-spears, and cutlasses, you know."

As he thus responded, Captain Delano again glanced at Don Benito, but the latter's eyes were averted; while abruptly and awkwardly shifting the subject, he made some peevish allusion to the calm, and then, without apology, once more, with his attendant, withdrew to the opposite bulwarks, where the whispering was resumed.

At this moment, and ere Captain Delano could cast a cool thought upon what had just passed, the young Spanish sailor before mentioned was seen descending from the rigging. In act of stooping over to spring inboard to the deck, his voluminous, unconfined frock, or shirt, of coarse woollen, much spotted with tar, opened out far down the chest, revealing a soiled under-garment of what seemed the finest linen, edged, about the neck, with a narrow blue ribbon, sadly faded and worn. At this moment the young sailor's eye was again fixed on the whisperers, and Captain Delano thought he observed a lurking significance in it, as if silent signs of some freemason sort had that instant been interchanged.

This once more impelled his own glance in the direction of Don Benito, and, as before, he could not but infer that himself formed the subject of the conference. He paused. The sound of the hatchet-polishing fell on his ears. He cast another swift side-look at the two. They had the air of conspirators. In connection with the late questionings, and the incident of the young sailor, these things now begat such return of involuntary suspicion, that the singular guilelessness of the American could not endure it. Plucking up a gay and humorous expression, he crossed over to the two rapidly, saying: "Ha, Don Benito, your black here seems high in your trust; a sort of privy-counsellor, in fact."

Upon this, the servant looked up with a good-natured grin, but the master started as from a venomous bite. It was a moment or two before the Spaniard sufficiently recovered himself to reply; which he did, at last, with cold constraint: "Yes, Señor, I have trust in Babo."

Here Babo, changing his previous grin of mere animal humour into an intelligent smile, not ungratefully eyed his master.

Finding that the Spaniard now stood silent and reserved, as if involuntarily, or purposely giving hint that his guest's proximity was inconvenient just then, Captain Delano, unwilling to appear uncivil even to incivility itself, made some trivial remark and moved off; again and again turning over in his mind the mysterious demeanour of Don Benito Cereno.

He had descended from the poop, and, wrapped in thought, was passing near a dark hatchway, leading down into the steerage, when, perceiving motion there, he looked to see what moved. The same instant there was a sparkle in the shadowy hatchway, and he saw one of the Spanish sailors, prowling there, hurriedly placing his hand in the bosom of his frock, as if hiding something. Before the man could have been certain who it was that was passing, he slunk below out of sight. But enough was seen of him to make it sure that he was the same young sailor before noticed in the rigging.

What was that which so sparkled? thought Captain Delano. It was no lamp—no match—no live coal. Could it have been a jewel? But how come sailors with jewels?—or with silk-trimmed undershirts either? Has he been robbing the trunks of the dead cabin passengers? But if so, he would hardly wear one of the stolen articles on board ship here. Ah, ah—if now that was, indeed, a secret sign I saw passing between this suspicious fellow and his captain awhile since; if I could only be certain that in my uneasiness my senses did not deceive me, then—

Here, passing from one suspicious thing to another, his mind revolved the point of the strange questions put to him concerning his ship.

By a curious coincidence, as each point was recalled, the black wizards of Ashantee would strike up with their hatchets, as in ominous comment on the white stranger's thoughts. Pressed by such enigmas and portents, it would have been almost against nature, had not, even into the least distrustful heart, some ugly misgivings obtruded.

Observing the ship now helplessly fallen into a current, with enchanted sails, drifting with increased rapidity seaward; and noting that, from a lately intercepted projection of the land, the sealer was hidden, the stout mariner began to quake at thoughts which he barely durst confess to himself. Above all, he began to feel a ghostly dread of Don Benito. And yet when he roused himself, dilated his chest, felt himself strong on his legs, and coolly considered it—what did all these phantoms amount to?

Had the Spaniard any sinister scheme, it must have reference not so much to him (Captain Delano) as to his ship (the *Bachelor's Delight*). Hence the present drifting away of the one ship from the other, instead of favouring any such possible scheme, was, for the time at least, opposed to it. Clearly any suspicion, combining such contradictions, must need be delusive. Beside, was it not absurd to think of a vessel in distress—a vessel by sickness almost dismanned of her crew—a vessel whose inmates were parched for water—was it not a thousand times absurd that such a craft should, at present, be of a piratical character; or her commander, either for himself or those under him, cherish any desire but for speedy relief and refreshment? But then, might not general distress, and thirst in particular, be affected? And might not that same undiminished Spanish crew, alleged to have perished off to a remnant, be at that very moment lurking in the hold? On heart-broken pretence of entreating a cup of cold water, fiends in human form had got into lonely dwellings, nor retired until a dark deed had been done. And among the Malay pirates, it was no unusual thing to lure ships after them into their treacherous harbours, or entice boarders from a declared enemy at sea, by the spectacle of thinly manned or vacant decks, beneath which prowled a hundred spears with yellow arms ready to upthrust them through the mats. Not that Captain Delano had entirely credited such things. He had heard of them—and now, as stories, they recurred. The present destination of the ship was the anchorage. There she would be near his own vessel. Upon gaining that vicinity, might not the *San Dominick*, like a slumbering volcano, suddenly let loose energies now hid?

He recalled the Spaniard's manner while telling his story. There was a gloomy hesitancy and subterfuge about it. It was just the manner of one making up his tale for evil purposes, as he goes. But if that story was not true, what was the truth? That the ship had unlawfully come into the Spaniard's possession? But in many of its details, especially in reference to the more calamitous parts, such as the fatalities among the seamen, the consequent prolonged beating about, the past sufferings from obstinate calms, and still continued suffering from thirst; in all these points, as well as others, Don Benito's story had been corroborated not only by the wailing ejaculations of the indiscriminate multitude, white and black, but likewise—what seemed impossible to be counterfeit—by the very expression and play of every human feature, which Captain Delano saw. If Don Benito's story was throughout an invention, then every soul on board, down to the youngest Negress, was his carefully drilled recruit in the plot: an incredible inference. And yet, if there was ground for mistrusting the Spanish captain's veracity, that inference was a legitimate one.

In short, scarce an uneasiness entered the honest sailor's mind but, by a subsequent spontaneous act of good sense, it was ejected. At last he began to laugh at these forebodings; and laugh at the strange ship for, in its aspect someway siding with them, as it were; and laugh, too, at the odd-looking blacks, particularly those old scissors-grinders, the Ashantees; and those bed-ridden old knitting-women, the oakum-pickers; and, in a human way, he almost began to laugh at the dark Spaniard himself, the central hobgoblin of all.

For the rest, whatever in a serious way seemed enigmatical, was now good-naturedly explained away by the thought that, for the most part, the poor invalid scarcely knew what he was about; either sulking in black vapours, or putting random questions without sense or object. Evidently, for the present, the man was not fit to be entrusted with the ship. On some benevolent plea withdrawing the command from him, Captain Delano would yet have to send her to Concepcion in charge of his second mate, a worthy person and good navigator—a plan which would prove no wiser for the *San Dominick* than for Don Benito; for—relieved from all anxiety, keeping wholly to his cabin—the sick man, under the good nursing of his servant, would probably, by the end of the passage, be in a measure restored to health and with that he should also be restored to authority.

Such were the American's thoughts. They were tranquillizing. There was a difference between the idea of Don Benito's darkly pre-ordaining Captain Delano's fate, and Captain Delano's lightly arranging Don Benito's. Nevertheless, it was not without something of relief that the good seaman presently perceived his whale-boat in the distance. Its absence had been prolonged by unexpected detention at the sealer's side, as well as its returning trip lengthened by the continual recession of the goal.

The advancing speck was observed by the blacks. Their shouts attracted the attention of Don Benito, who, with a return of courtesy, approaching Captain Delano, expressed satisfaction at the coming of some supplies, slight and temporary as they must necessarily prove.

Captain Delano responded; but while doing so, his attention was drawn to something passing on the deck below: among the crowd climbing the landward bulwarks, anxiously watching the coming boat, two blacks, to all appearances accidentally incommoded by one of the sailors, flew out against him with horrible curses, which the sailor someway resenting, the two blacks dashed him to the deck and jumped upon him, despite the earnest cries of the oakum-pickers.

"Don Benito," said Captain Delano quickly, "do you see what is going on there? Look!"

But, seized by his cough, the Spaniard staggered, with both hands to his face, on the point of falling. Captain Delano would have supported him, but the servant was more alert, who, with one hand sustaining his master, with the other applied the cordial. Don Benito, restored, the black withdrew his support, slipping aside a little, but dutifully remaining within call of a whisper. Such discretion was here evinced as quite wiped away, in the visitor's eyes, any blemish of impropriety which might have attached to the attendant, from the indecorous conferences before mentioned; showing, too, that if the servant were to blame, it might be more the master's fault than his own, since when left to himself he could conduct thus well.

His glance thus called away from the spectacle of disorder to the more pleasing one before him, Captain Delano could not avoid again congratulating Don Benito upon possessing such a servant, who, though perhaps a little too forward now and then, must upon the whole be invaluable to one in the invalid's situation.

"Tell me, Don Benito," he added, with a smile—"I should like to have your man here myself—what will you take for him? Would fifty doubloons be any object?"

"Master wouldn't part with Babo for a thousand doubloons," murmured the black, overhearing the offer, and taking it in earnest, and, with the strange vanity of a faithful slave appreciated by his master, scorning to hear so paltry a valuation put upon him by a stranger. But Don Benito, apparently hardly yet completely restored, and again interrupted by his cough, made but some broken reply.

Soon his physical distress became so great, affecting his mind, too, apparently, that, as if to screen the sad spectacle, the servant gently conducted his master below.

Left to himself, the American, to while away the time till his boat should arrive, would have pleasantly accosted some one of the few Spanish seamen he saw; but recalling something that Don Benito had said touching their ill conduct, he refrained, as a shipmaster indisposed to countenance cowardice or unfaithfulness in seamen.

While, with these thoughts, standing with eye directed forward toward that handful of sailors—suddenly he thought that some of them returned the glance and with a sort of meaning. He rubbed his eyes, and looked again; but again seemed to see the same thing. Under a new form, but more obscure than any previous one, the old suspicions recurred, but, in the absence of Don Benito, with less of panic than before. Despite the bad account given of the sailors, Captain Delano resolved forthwith to accost one of them. Descending the poop, he made his way through the blacks, his movement drawing a queer cry from the oakum-pickers, prompted by whom the Negroes, twitching each other aside, divided before him; but, as if curious to see what was the object of this deliberate visit to their Ghetto, closing in behind, in tolerable order, followed the white stranger up. His progress thus proclaimed as by mounted kings-at-arms, and escorted as by a Caffre guard of honour, Captain Delano, assuming a good-humoured, off-hand air, continued to advance; now and then saying a blithe word to the Negroes, and his eye curiously surveying the white faces, here and there sparsely mixed in with the blacks, like stray white pawns venturously involved in the ranks of the chessmen opposed.

While thinking which of them to select for his purpose, he chanced to observe a sailor seated on the deck engaged in tarring the strap of a large block, with a circle of blacks squatted round him inquisitively eyeing the process.

The mean employment of the man was in contrast with something superior in his figure. His hand, black with continually thrusting it into the tar-pot held for him by a Negro, seemed not naturally allied to his face, a face which would have been a very fine one but for its haggardness. Whether this haggardness had aught to do with criminality could not be determined; since, as intense heat and cold, though unlike, produce like sensations, so innocence and guilt, when, through casual association with mental pain, stamping any visible impress, use one seal—a hacked one.

Not again that this reflection occurred to Captain Delano at the time, charitable man as he was. Rather another idea. Because observing so singular a haggardness to be combined with a dark eye, averted as in trouble and shame, and then, however illogically, uniting in his mind his own private suspicions of the crew with the confessed ill-opinion on the part of their captain, he was insensibly operated upon by certain general notions, which, while disconnecting pain and abashment from virtue, as invariably link them with vice.

If, indeed, there be any wickedness on board this ship, thought

Captain Delano, be sure that man there has fouled his hand in it, even as now he fouls it in the pitch. I don't like to accost him. I will speak to this other, this old Jack here on the windlass.

He advanced to an old Barcelona tar, in ragged red breeches and dirty night-cap, cheeks trenched and bronzed, whiskers dense as thorn hedges. Seated between two sleepy-looking Africans, this mariner, like his younger shipmate, was employed upon some rigging—splicing a cable—the sleepy-looking blacks performing the inferior function of holding the outer parts of the ropes for him.

Upon Captain Delano's approach, the man at once hung his head below its previous level; the one necessary for business. It appeared as if he desired to be thought absorbed, with more than common fidelity, in his task. Being addressed, he glanced up, but with what seemed a furtive, diffident air, which sat strangely enough on his weather-beaten visage, much as if a grizzly bear, instead of growling and biting, should simper and cast sheep's eyes. He was asked several questions concerning the voyage—questions purposely referring to several particulars in Don Benito's narrative—not previously corroborated by those impulsive cries greeting the visitor on first coming on board. The questions were briefly answered, confirming all that remained to be confirmed of the story. The Negroes about the windlass joined in with the old sailor, but, as they became talkative, he by degrees became mute, and at length quite glum, seemed morosely unwilling to answer more questions, and yet, all the while, this ursine air was somehow mixed with his sheepish one.

Despairing of getting into unembarrassed talk with such a centaur, Captain Delano, after glancing round for a more promising countenance, but seeing none, spoke pleasantly to the blacks to make way for him; and so, amid various grins and grimaces, returned to the poop, feeling a little strange at first, he could hardly tell why, but upon the whole with regained confidence in Benito Cereno.

How plainly, thought he, did that old whiskerando yonder betray a consciousness of ill-desert. No doubt, when he saw me coming, he dreaded lest I, apprised by his captain of the crew's general misbehaviour, came with sharp words for him, and so down with his head. And yet—and yet, now that I think of it, that very old fellow, if I err not, was one of those who seemed so earnestly eyeing me here awhile since. Ah, these currents spin one's head round almost as much as they do the ship. Ha, there now's a pleasant sort of sunny sight; quite sociable, too.

His attention had been drawn to a slumbering Negress, partly disclosed through the lace-work of some rigging, lying, with youthful limbs carelessly disposed, under the lee of the bulwarks, like a doe in the shade of a woodland rock. Sprawling at her lapped breasts was her wide-awake fawn, stark naked, its black little body half lifted from the deck, crosswise with its dam's; its hands, like two paws, clambering upon her; its mouth and nose ineffectually rooting to get at the mark; and meantime giving a vexatious half-grunt, blending with the composed snore of the Negress.

The uncommon vigour of the child at length roused the mother. She started up, at distance facing Captain Delano. But, as if not at all concerned at the attitude in which she had been caught, delightedly she caught the child up, with maternal transports, covering it with kisses.

There's naked nature, now; pure tenderness and love, thought Captain Delano, well pleased.

This incident prompted him to remark the other Negresses more particularly than before. He was gratified with their manners; like most uncivilized women, they seemed at once tender of heart and tough of constitution; equally ready to die for their infants or fight for them. Unsophisticated as leopardesses; loving as doves. Ah! thought Captain Delano, these perhaps are some of the very women whom Mungo Park saw in Africa, and gave such a noble account of.

These natural sights somehow insensibly deepened his confidence and ease. At last he looked to see how his boat was getting on; but it was still pretty remote. He turned to see if Don Benito had returned; but he had not.

To change the scene, as well as to please himself with a leisurely observation of the coming boat, stepping over into the mizzen-chains he clambered his way into the starboard quarter-galley; one of those abandoned Venetian-looking water-balconies previously mentioned; retreats cut off from the deck. As his foot pressed the half-damp, half-dry sea-mosses matting the place, and a chance phantom cat's-paw—an islet of breeze, unheralded, unfollowed—as this ghostly cat's-paw came fanning his cheek, his glance fell upon the row of small, round dead-lights, all closed like coppered eyes of the coffined, and the state-cabin door, once connecting with the gallery, even as the dead-lights had once looked out upon it, but now caulked fast like a sarcophagus lid, to a purple-black, tarred-over panel, threshold, and post; and he bethought him of the time, when that state-cabin and this state-balcony had heard the voices of the Spanish king's officers, and the forms of the Lima viceroy's daughters had perhaps leaned where he stood—as these and other images flitted through his mind, as the cat's-paw through the calm, gradually he felt rising a dreamy inquietude, like that of one who alone on the prairie feels unrest from the repose of the noon.

He leaned against the carved balustrade, again looking off toward his boat; but found his eye falling upon the ribboned grass, trailing along the ship's water-line, straight as a border of green box; and parterres of sea-weed, broad ovals and crescents, floating nigh and far, with what seemed long formal alleys between, crossing the terraces of swells, and sweeping round as if leading to the grottoes below. And overhanging all was the balustrade by his arm, which, partly stained with pitch and partly embossed with moss, seemed the charred ruin of some summer-house in a grand garden long running to waste.

Trying to break one charm, he was but becharmed anew. Though upon the wide sea, he seemed in some far inland country; prisoner in some deserted château, left to stare at empty grounds, and peer out at vague roads, where never wagon or wayfarer passed.

But these enchantments were a little disenchanted as his eye fell on the corroded main-chains. Of an ancient style, massy and rusty in link, shackle and bolt, they seemed even more fit for the ship's present business than the one for which probably she had been built.

Presently he thought something moved nigh the chains. He rubbed his eyes, and looked hard. Groves of rigging were about the chains; and there, peering from behind a great stay, like an Indian from behind a hemlock, a Spanish sailor, a marlingspike in his hand, was seen, who made what seemed an imperfect gesture toward the balcony—but immediately, as if alarmed by some advancing step along the deck within, vanished into the recesses of the hempen forest, like a poacher.

What meant this? Something the man had sought to communicate, unbeknown to any one, even to his captain? Did the secret involve aught unfavourable to his captain? Were those previous misgivings of Captain Delano's about to be verified? Or, in his haunted mood at the moment, had some random, unintentional motion of the man, while busy with the stay, as if repairing it, been mistaken for a significant beckoning?

Not unbewildered, again he gazed off for his boat. But it was temporarily hidden by a rocky spur of the isle. As with some eagerness he bent forward, watching for the first shooting view of its beak, the balustrade gave way before him like charcoal. Had he not clutched an outreaching rope he would have fallen into the sea. The crash, though feeble, and the fall, though hollow, of the rotten fragments, must have been overheard. He glanced up. With sober curiosity peering down upon him was one of the old oakum-pickers, slipped from his perch to an outside boom; while below the old Negro—and, invisible to him, reconnoitring from a port-hole like a fox from the mouth of its den—crouched the Spanish sailor again. From something suddenly suggested by the man's air, the mad idea now darted into Captain Delano's mind: that Don Benito's plea of indisposition, in withdrawing below, was but a pretence: that he was engaged there maturing some plot, of which the sailor, by some means gaining an inkling, had a mind to warn the stranger against; incited, it may be, by gratitude for a kind word on first boarding the ship. Was it from foreseeing some possible interference like this, that Don Benito had, beforehand, given such a bad character of his sailors, while praising the Negroes; though, indeed, the former seemed as docile as the latter the contrary? The whites, too, by nature, were the shrewder race. A man with some evil design, would not he be likely to speak well of that stupidity which was blind to his depravity, and malign that intelligence from which it might not be hidden? Not unlikely, perhaps. But if the whites had dark secrets concerning Don Benito, could then Don Benito be any way in complicity with the blacks? But they were too stupid. Besides, who ever heard of a white so far a renegade as to apostatize from his very species almost, by leaguing in against it with Negroes? These difficulties recalled former ones. Lost in their mazes, Captain Delano, who had now regained the deck, was uneasily advancing along it, when he observed a new face: an aged sailor seated cross-legged near the main hatchway. His skin was shrunk up with wrinkles like a pelican's empty pouch; his hair frosted; his countenance grave and composed. His hands were full of ropes, which he was working into a large knot. Some blacks were about him obligingly dipping the strands for him, here and there, as the exigencies of the operation demanded.

Captain Delano crossed over to him, and stood in silence surveying the knot; his mind, by a not uncongenial transition, passing from its own entanglements to those of the hemp. For intricacy such a knot he had never seen in an American ship, or indeed any other. The old man looked like an Egyptian priest, making Gordian knots for the temple of Ammon. The knot seemed a combination of double-bowline-knot, treble-crown-knot, back-handed-well-knot, knot-in-and-out-knot, and jamming-knot.

At last, puzzled to comprehend the meaning of such a knot, Captain Delano, addressed the knotter:—

"What are you knotting there, my man?"

"The knot," was the brief reply, without looking up.

"So it seems; but what is it for?"

"For some one else to undo," muttered back the old man, plying his fingers harder than ever, the knot being now nearly completed.

While Captain Delano stood watching him, suddenly the old

man threw the knot toward him, and said in broken English,—the first heard in the ship,—something to this effect—"Undo it, cut it, quick." It was said lowly, but with such condensation of rapidity, that the long, slow words in Spanish, which had preceded and followed, almost operated as covers to the brief English between.

For a moment, knot in hand, and knot in head, Captain Delano stood mute; while, without further heeding him, the old man was now intent upon other ropes. Presently there was a slight stir behind Captain Delano. Turning, he saw the chained Negro, Atufal, standing quietly there. The next moment the old sailor rose, muttering, and, followed by his subordinate Negroes, removed to the forward part of the ship, where in the crowd he disappeared.

An elderly Negro, in a clout like an infant's, and with a pepper and salt head, and a kind of attorney air, now approached Captain Delano. In tolerable Spanish, and with a good-natured, knowing wink, he informed him that the old knotter was simple-witted, but harmless; often playing his old tricks. The Negro concluded by begging the knot, for of course the stranger would not care to be troubled with it. Unconsciously, it was handed to him. With a sort of congé, the Negro received it, and turning his back ferreted into it like a detective Custom House officer after smuggled laces. Soon, with some African word, equivalent to pshaw, he tossed the knot overboard.

All this is very queer now, thought Captain Delano, with a qualmish sort of emotion; but as one feeling incipient seasickness, he strove, by ignoring the symptoms, to get rid of the malady. Once more he looked off for his boat. To his delight, it was now again in view, leaving the rocky spur astern.

The sensation here experienced, after at first relieving his uneasiness, with unforeseen efficiency, soon began to remove it. The less distant sight of that well-known boat—showing it, not as before, half blended with the haze, but with outline defined, so that its individuality, like a man's, was manifest; that boat, *Rover* by name, which, though now in strange seas, had often pressed the beach of Captain Delano's home, and, brought to its threshold for repairs, had familiarly lain there, as a Newfoundland dog; the sight of that household boat evoked a thousand trustful associations, which, contrasted with previous suspicions, filled him not only with lightsome confidence, but somehow with half humorous self-reproaches at his former lack of it.

"What, I, Amasa Delano—Jack of the Beach, as they called me when a lad—I, Amasa; the same that, duck-satchel in hand, used to paddle along the waterside to the schoolhouse made from the old hulk;—I, little Jack of the Beach, that used to go berrying with cousin Nat and the rest; I to be murdered here at the ends of the earth, on board a haunted pirate-ship by a horrible Spaniard?—Too nonsensical to think of! Who would murder Amasa Delano? His conscience is clean. There is some one above. Fie, fie, Jack of the Beach! you are a child indeed; a child of the second childhood, old boy; you are beginning to dote and drool, I'm afraid."

Light of heart and foot, he stepped aft, and there was met by Don Benito's servant, who, with a pleasing expression, responsive to his own present feelings, informed him that his master had recovered from the effects of his coughing fit, and had just ordered him to go present his compliments to his good guest, Don Amasa, and say that he (Don Benito) would soon have the happiness to rejoin him.

There now, do you mark that? again thought Captain Delano, walking the poop. What a donkey I was. This kind gentleman who here sends me his kind compliments, he, but ten minutes ago, dark-lantern in hand, was dodging round some old grind-stone in the hold, sharpening a hatchet for me, I thought. Well, well; these long calms have a morbid effect on the mind, I've often heard, though I never believed it before. Ha! glancing toward the boat; there's *Rover;* a good dog; a white bone in her mouth. A pretty big bone though, seems to me.—What? Yes, she has fallen afoul of the bubbling tide-rip there. It sets her the other way, too, for the time. Patience.

It was now about noon, though, from the greyness of everything, it seemed to be getting toward dusk.

The calm was confirmed. In the far distance, away from the influence of land, the leaden ocean seemed laid out and leaded up, its

course finished, soul gone, defunct. But the current from landward, where the ship was, increased; silently sweeping her further and further toward the tranced waters beyond.

Still, from his knowledge of those latitudes, cherishing hopes of a breeze, and a fair and fresh one, at any moment, Captain Delano, despite present prospects, buoyantly counted upon bringing the *San Dominick* safely to anchor ere night. The distance swept over was nothing; since, with a good wind, ten minutes' sailing would retrace more than sixty minutes' drifting. Meantime, one moment turning to mark *Rover* fighting the tide-rip, and the next to see Don Benito approaching, he continued walking the poop.

Gradually he felt a vexation arising from the delay of his boat; this soon merged into uneasiness; and at last, his eye falling continually, as from a stage-box into the pit, upon the strange crowd before and below him, and by-and-by recognizing there the face—now composed to indifference—of the Spanish sailor who had seemed to beckon from the main-chains, something of his old trepidations returned.

Ah, thought he—gravely enough—this is like the ague: because it went off, it follows not that it won't come back.

Though ashamed of the relapse, he could not altogether subdue it; and so, exerting his good nature to the utmost, insensibly he came to a compromise.

Yes, this is a strange craft; a strange history, too, and strange folks on board. But—nothing more.

By way of keeping his mind out of mischief till the boat should arrive, he tried to occupy it with turning over and over, in a purely speculative sort of way, some lesser peculiarities of the captain and crew. Among others, four curious points recurred.

First, the affair of the Spanish lad assailed with a knife by the slave boy; an act winked at by Don Benito. Second, the tyranny in Don Benito's treatment of Atufal, the black; as if a child should lead a bull of the Nile by the ring in his nose. Third, the trampling of the sailor by the two Negroes; a piece of insolence passed over without so much as a reprimand. Fourth, the cringing submission to their master of all the ship's underlings, mostly blacks; as if by the least inadvertence they feared to draw down his despotic displeasure.

Coupling these points, they seemed somewhat contradictory. But what then, thought Captain Delano, glancing toward his now nearing boat,—what then? Why, this Don Benito is a very capricious commander. But he is not the first of the sort I have seen; though it's true he rather exceeds any other. But as a nation—continued he in his reveries—these Spaniards are all an odd set; the very word Spaniard has a curious, conspirator, Guy-Fawkish twang to it. And yet, I dare say, Spaniards in the main are as good folks as any in Duxbury, Massachusetts. Ah, good! At last *Rover* has come.

As, with its welcome freight, the boat touched the side, the oakum-pickers, with venerable gestures, sought to restrain the blacks, who, at the sight of three gurried water-casks in its bottom, and a pile of wilted pumpkins in its bow, hung over the bulwarks in disorderly raptures.

Don Benito with his servant now appeared; his coming, perhaps, hastened by hearing the noise. Of him Captain Delano sought permission to serve out the water, so that all might share alike, and none injure themselves by unfair excess. But sensible, and, on Don Benito's account, kind as this offer was, it was received with what seemed impatience; as if aware that he lacked energy as a commander, Don Benito, with the true jealousy of weakness, resented as an affront any interference. So, at least, Captain Delano inferred.

In another moment the casks were being hoisted in, when some of the eager Negroes accidentally jostled Captain Delano, where he stood by the gangway; so that, unmindful of Don Benito, yielding to the impulse of the moment, with good-natured authority he bade the blacks stand back; to enforce his words making use of a half-mirthful, half-menacing gesture. Instantly the blacks paused, just where they were, each Negro and Negress suspended in his or her posture, exactly as the word had found them—for a few seconds continuing so—while, as between the responsive posts of a telegraph, an unknown syllable ran from man to man among the perched oakum-pickers. While Captain Delano's attention was fixed by this scene, suddenly the hatchet-polishers half rose, and a rapid cry came from Don Benito.

Thinking that at the signal of the Spaniard he was about to be massacred, Captain Delano would have sprung for his boat, but paused, as the oakum-pickers, dropping down into the crowd with earnest exclamations, forced every white and every Negro back, at the same moment, with gestures friendly and familiar, almost jocose, bidding him, in substance, not be a fool. Simultaneously the hatchet-polishers resumed their seats, quietly as so many tailors, and at once, as if nothing had happened, the work of hoisting in the casks was resumed, whites and blacks singing at the tackle.

Captain Delano glanced toward Don Benito. As he saw his meagre form in the act of recovering itself from reclining in the servant's arms, into which the agitated invalid had fallen, he could not but marvel at the panic by which himself had been surprised on the darting supposition that such a commander, who upon a legitimate occasion, so trivial, too, as it now appeared, could lose all self-command, was, with energetic iniquity, going to bring about his murder.

The casks being on deck, Captain Delano was handed a number of jars and cups by one of the steward's aides, who, in the name of Don Benito, entreated him to do as he had proposed: dole out the water. He complied, with republican impartiality as to this republican element, which always seeks one level, serving the oldest white no better than the youngest black; excepting, indeed, poor Don Benito, whose condition, if not rank, demanded an extra allowance. To him, in the first place, Captain Delano presented a fair pitcher of the fluid; but, thirsting as he was for fresh water, Don Benito quaffed not a drop until after several grave bows and salutes: a reciprocation of courtesies which the sight-loving Africans hailed with clapping of hands.

Two of the less wilted pumpkins being reserved for the cabin table, the residue were minced up on the spot for the general regalement. But the soft bread, sugar, and bottled cider, Captain Delano would have given the Spaniards alone, and in chief Don Benito;

but the latter objected; which disinterestedness, on his part, not a little pleased the American; and so mouthfuls all around were given alike to whites and blacks; excepting one bottle of cider, which Babo insisted upon setting aside for his master.

Here it may be observed that as, on the first visit of the boat, the American had not permitted his men to board the ship, neither did he now; being unwilling to add to the confusion of the decks.

Not uninfluenced by the peculiar good humour at present prevailing, and for the time oblivious of any but benevolent thoughts, Captain Delano, who from recent indications counted upon a breeze within an hour or two at furthest, despatched the boat back to the sealer with orders for all the hands that could be spared immediately to set about rafting casks to the watering-place and filling them. Likewise he bade word be carried to his chief officer, that if against present expectation the ship was not brought to anchor by sunset, he need be under no concern, for as there was to be a full moon that night, he (Captain Delano) would remain on board ready to play the pilot, should the wind come soon or late.

As the two captains stood together, observing the departing boat—the servant as it happened having just spied a spot on his master's velvet sleeve, and silently engaged rubbing it out—the American expressed his regrets that the *San Dominick* had no boats; none, at least, but the unseaworthy old hulk of the long-boat, which, warped as a camel's skeleton in the desert, and almost as bleached, lay pot-wise inverted amidships, one side a little tipped, furnishing a subterrraneous sort of den for family groups of the blacks, mostly women and small children; who, squatting on old mats below, or perched above in the dark dome, on the elevated seats, were descried, some distance within, like a social circle of bats, sheltering in some friendly cave; at intervals, ebon flights of naked boys and girls, three or four years old, darting in and out of the den's mouth.

"Had you three or four boats now, Don Benito," said Captain Delano, "I think that, by tugging at the oars, your Negroes here might help along matters some.—Did you sail from port without boats, Don Benito?"

"They were stove in the gales, Señor."

"That was bad. Many men, too, you lost then. Boats and men. —Those must have been hard gales, Don Benito."

"Past all speech," cringed the Spaniard.

"Tell me, Don Benito," continued his companion with increased interest, "tell me, were these gales immediately off the pitch of Cape Horn?"

"Cape Horn?—who spoke of Cape Horn?"

"Yourself did, when giving me an account of your voyage," answered Captain Delano with almost equal astonishment at this eating of his own words, even as he ever seemed eating his own heart, on the part of the Spaniard. "You yourself, Don Benito, spoke of Cape Horn," he emphatically repeated.

The Spaniard turned, in a sort of stooping posture, pausing an instant, as one about to make a plunging exchange of elements, as from air to water.

At this moment a messenger-boy, a white, hurried by, in the regular performance of his function carrying the last expired half-hour forward to the forecastle, from the cabin time-piece, to have it struck at the ship's large bell.

"Master," said the servant, discontinuing his work on the coat sleeve, and addressing the rapt Spaniard with a sort of timid apprehensiveness, as one charged with a duty, the discharge of which, it was foreseen, would prove irksome to the very person who had imposed it, and for whose benefit it was intended, "master told me never mind where he was, or how engaged, always to remind him, to a minute, when shaving-time comes. Miguel has gone to strike the half-hour after noon. It is *now*, master. Will master go into the cuddy?"

"Ah—yes," answered the Spaniard, starting, somewhat as from dreams into realities; then turning upon Captain Delano, he said that ere long he would resume the conversation.

"Then if master means to talk more to Don Amasa," said the servant, "why not let Don Amasa sit by master in the cuddy, and master can talk, and Don Amasa can listen, while Babo here lathers and strops."

"Yes," said Captain Delano, not unpleased with this sociable plan, "yes, Don Benito, unless you had rather not, I will go with you."

"Be it so, Señor."

As the three passed aft, the American could not but think it another strange instance of his host's capriciousness, this being shaved with such uncommon punctuality in the middle of the day. But he deemed it more than likely that the servant's anxious fidelity had something to do with the matter; inasmuch as the timely interruption served to rally his master from the mood which had evidently been coming upon him.

The place called the cuddy was a light deck-cabin formed by the poop, a sort of attic to the large cabin below. Part of it had formerly been the quarters of the officers; but since their death all the partitionings had been thrown down, and the whole interior converted into one spacious and airy marine hall; for absence of fine furniture and picturesque disarray, of odd appurtenances, somewhat answering to the wide, cluttered hall of some eccentric bachelor squire in the country, who hangs his shooting-jacket and tobacco-pouch on deer antlers, and keeps his fishing-rod, tongs, and walking-stick in the same corner.

The similitude was heightened, if not originally suggested, by glimpses of the surrounding sea; since, in one aspect, the country and the ocean seem cousins-german.

The floor of the cuddy was matted. Overhead, four or five old muskets were stuck into horizontal holes along the beams. On one side was a claw-footed old table lashed to the deck; a thumbed missal on it, and over it a small, meagre crucifix attached to the bulkhead. Under the table lay a dented cutlass or two, with a hacked harpoon, among some melancholy old rigging, like a heap of poor friar's girdles. There were also two long, sharp-ribbed settees of malacca cane, black with age, and uncomfortable to look at as inquisitors' racks, with a large, misshapen arm-chair, which, furnished with a rude barber's crutch at the back, working with a screw, seemed some grotesque Middle Age engine of torment. A flag locker was in one corner, exposing various coloured bunting, some rolled up, others half unrolled, still others tumbled. Opposite was a cumbrous washstand, of black mahogany, all of one block, with a pedestal, like a font, and over it a railed shelf, containing combs, brushes, and other implements of the toilet. A torn hammock of stained grass swung near; the sheets tossed, and the pillow wrinkled up like a brow, as if whoever slept here slept but illy, with alternate visitations of sad thoughts and bad dreams.

The further extremity of the cuddy, overhanging the ship's stern, was pierced with three openings, windows or port-holes, according as men or cannon might peer, socially or unsocially, out of them. At present neither men nor cannon were seen, though huge ring-bolts and other rusty iron fixtures of the wood-work hinted of twenty-four-pounders.

Glancing toward the hammock as he entered, Captain Delano said, "You sleep here, Don Benito?"

"Yes, Señor, since we got into mild weather."

"This seems a sort of dormitory, sitting-room, sail-loft, chapel, armoury, and private closet together, Don Benito," added Captain Delano, looking around.

"Yes, Señor; events have not been favourable to much order in my arrangements."

Here the servant, napkin on arm, made a motion as if waiting his master's good pleasure. Don Benito signified his readiness, when, seating him in the malacca arm-chair, and for the guest's convenience drawing opposite it one of the settees, the servant commenced operations by throwing back his master's collar and loosening his cravat.

There is something in the Negro which, in a peculiar way, fits him for avocations about one's person. Most Negroes are natural valets and hair-dressers; taking to the comb and brush congenially as to the castanets, and flourishing them apparently with almost equal satisfaction. There is, too, a smooth tact about them in this employment, with a marvellous, noiseless, gliding briskness, not ungraceful in its way, singularly pleasing to behold, and still more so to be the manipulated subject of. And above all is the great gift of good humour. Not the mere grin or laugh is here meant. Those were unsuitable. But a certain easy cheerfulness, harmonious in every glance and gesture; as though God had set the whole Negro to some pleasant tune.

When to all this is added the docility arising from the unaspiring contentment of a limited mind, and that susceptibility of blind attachment sometimes inhering in indisputable inferiors, one readily perceives why those hypochondriacs, Johnson and Byron—it may be something like the hypochondriac, Benito Cereno—took to their hearts, almost to the exclusion of the entire white race, their serving men, the Negroes, Barber and Fletcher. But if there be that in the Negro which exempts him from the inflicted sourness of the morbid or cynical mind, how, in his most prepossessing aspects, must he appear to a benevolent one? When at ease with respect to exterior things, Captain Delano's nature was not only benign, but familiarly and humorously so. At home, he had often taken rare satisfaction in sitting in his door, watching some free man of colour at his work or play. If on a voyage he chanced to have a black sailor, invariably he was on chatty, and half-gamesome terms with him. In fact, like most men of a good, blithe heart, Captain Delano took to Negroes, not philanthropically, but genially, just as other men to Newfoundland dogs.

Hitherto the circumstances in which he found the *San Dominick* had repressed the tendency. But in the cuddy, relieved from his former uneasiness, and, for various reasons, more sociably inclined than at any previous period of the day, and seeing the coloured servant, napkin on arm, so debonair about his master, in a business so familiar as that of shaving, too, all his old weakness for Negroes returned.

Among other things, he was amused with an odd instance ot the African love of bright colours and fine shows, in the black's informally taking from the flag-locker a great piece of bunting of all hues, and lavishly tucking it under his master's chin for an apron.

The mode of shaving among the Spaniards is a little different from what it is with other nations. They have a basin, specially called a barber's basin, which on one side is scooped out, so as accurately to receive the chin, against which it is closely held in lathering; which is done, not with a brush, but with soap dipped in the water of the basin and rubbed on the face.

In the present instance salt-water was used for lack of better; and the parts lathered were only the upper lip, and low down under the throat, all the rest being cultivated beard.

These preliminaries being somewhat novel to Captain Delano he sat curiously eyeing them, so that no conversation took place, nor for the present did Don Benito appear disposed to renew any.

Setting down his basin, the Negro searched among the razors, as for the sharpest, and having found it, gave it an additional edge by expertly stropping it on the firm, smooth, oily skin of his open palm; he then made a gesture as if to begin, but midway stood suspended for an instant, one hand elevating the razor, the other professionally dabbling among the bubbling suds on the Spaniard's lank neck. Not unaffected by the close sight of the gleaming steel, Don Benito nervously shuddered, his usual ghastliness was heightened by the lather, which lather, again, was intensified in its hue by the sootiness of the Negro's body. Altogether the scene was somewhat peculiar, at least to Captain Delano, nor, as he saw the two thus postured, could he resist the vagary, that in the black he saw a headsman, and in the white, a man at the block. But this was one of those antic conceits, appearing and vanishing in a breath, from which, perhaps, the best regulated mind is not free.

Meantime the agitation of the Spaniard had a little loosened the bunting from around him, so that one broad fold swept curtain-like over the chair-arm to the floor, revealing, amid a profusion of armorial bars and ground-colours—black, blue and yellow—a closed castle in a blood-red field diagonal with a lion rampant in a white.

"The castle and the lion," exclaimed Captain Delano—"why, Don Benito, this is the flag of Spain you use here. It's well it's only I, and not the King, that sees this," he added with a smile, "but"—turning toward the black,—"it's all one, I suppose, so the colours be gay," which playful remark did not fail somewhat to tickle the Negro.

"Now, master," he said, readjusting the flag, and pressing the head gently further back into the crotch of the chair; "now master," and the steel glanced nigh the throat.

Again Don Benito faintly shuddered.

"You must not shake so, master.—See, Don Amasa, master always shakes when I shave him. And yet master knows I never yet have drawn blood, though it's true, if master will shake so, I may some of these times. Now, master," he continued. "And now, Don Amasa, please go on with your talk about the gale, and all that, master can hear, and between times master can answer."

"Ah yes, these gales," said Captain Delano; "but the more I think of your voyage, Don Benito, the more I wonder, not at the gales, terrible as they must have been, but at the disastrous interval following them. For here, by your account, have you been these two months and more getting from Cape Horn to St. Maria, a distance which I myself, with a good wind, have sailed in a few days. True, you had calms, and long ones, but to be becalmed for two months, that is, at least, unusual. Why, Don Benito, had almost any other gentleman told me such a story, I should have been half disposed to a little incredulity."

Here an involuntary expression came over the Spaniard, similar to that just before on the deck, and whether it was the start he gave, or a sudden gawky roll of the hull in the calm, or a momentary unsteadiness of the servant's hand; however it was, just then the razor drew blood, spots of which stained the creamy lather under the throat; immediately the black barber drew back his steel, and remaining in his professional attitude, back to Captain Delano, and face to Don Benito, held up the trickling razor, saying, with a sort of half humorous sorrow, "See, master,—you shook so—here's Babo's first blood."

No sword drawn before James the First of England, no assassination in that timid King's presence, could have produced a more terrified aspect than was now presented by Don Benito.

Poor fellow, thought Captain Delano, so nervous he can't even bear the sight of barber's blood; and this unstrung, sick man, is it credible that I should have imagined he meant to spill all my blood, who can't endure the sight of one little drop of his own? Surely,

Amasa Delano, you have been beside yourself this day. Tell it not when you get home, sappy Amasa. Well, well, he looks like a murderer, doesn't he? More like as if himself were to be done for. Well, well, this day's experience shall be a good lesson.

Meantime, while these things were running through the honest seaman's mind, the servant had taken the napkin from his arm, and to Don Benito had said: "But answer Don Amasa, please, master, while I wipe this ugly stuff off the razor, and strop it again."

As he said the words, his face was turned half round, so as to be alike visible to the Spaniard and the American, and seemed by its expression to hint, that he was desirous, by getting his master to go on with the conversation, considerately to withdraw his attention from the recent annoying accident. As if glad to snatch the offered relief, Don Benito resumed, rehearsing to Captain Delano, that not only were the calms of unusual duration, but the ship had fallen in with obstinate currents and other things he added, some of which were but repetitions of former statements, to explain how it came to pass that the passage from Cape Horn to St. Maria had been so exceedingly long, now and then mingling with his words, incidental praises, less qualified than before, to the blacks, for their general good conduct.

These particulars were not given consecutively, the servant now and then using his razor, and so, between the intervals of shaving, the story and panegyric went on with more than usual huskiness.

To Captain Delano's imagination, now again not wholly at rest, there was something so hollow in the Spaniard's manner, with apparently some reciprocal hollowness in the servant's dusky comment of silence, that the idea flashed across him, that possibly master and man, for some unknown purpose, were acting out, both in word and deed, nay, to the very tremor of Don Benito's limbs, some juggling play before him. Neither did the suspicion of collusion lack apparent support, from the fact of those whispered conferences before mentioned. But then, what could be the object of enacting this play of the barber before him? At last, regarding the notion as a whimsy, insensibly suggested, perhaps, by the theatrical aspect of Don Benito in his harlequin ensign, Captain Delano speedily banished it.

The shaving over, the servant bestirred himself with a small bottle of scented waters, pouring a few drops on the head, and then diligently rubbing; the vehemence of the exercise causing the muscles of his face to twitch rather strangely.

His next operation was with comb, scissors and brush; going round and round, smoothing a curl here, clipping an unruly whisker-hair there, giving a graceful sweep to the temple-lock, with other impromptu touches evincing the hand of a master; while, like any resigned gentleman in barber's hands, Don Benito bore all, much less uneasily, at least, than he had done the razoring; indeed, he sat so pale and rigid now, that the Negro seemed a Nubian sculptor finishing off a white statue-head.

All being over at last, the standard of Spain removed, tumbled up, and tossed back into the flag-locker, the Negro's warm breath blowing away any stray hair which might have lodged down his master's neck; collar and cravat readjusted; a speck of lint whisked off the velvet lapel; all this being done; backing off a little space, and pausing with an expression of subdued self-complacency, the servant for a moment surveyed his master, as, in toilet at least, the creature of his own tasteful hands.

Captain Delano playfully complimented him upon his achievement; at the same time congratulating Don Benito.

But neither sweet waters, nor shampooing, nor fidelity, nor sociality, delighted the Spaniard. Seeing him relapsing into forbidding gloom, and still remaining seated, Captain Delano, thinking that his presence was undesired just then, withdrew, on pretence of seeing whether, as he had prophesied, any signs of a breeze were visible.

Walking forward to the mainmast, he stood awhile thinking over the scene, and not without some undefined misgivings, when he heard a noise near the cuddy, and turning, saw the Negro, his hand to his cheek. Advancing, Captain Delano perceived that the cheek was bleeding. He was about to ask the cause, when the Negro's wailing soliloquy enlightened him.

"Ah, when will master get better from his sickness; only the sour heart that sour sickness breeds made him serve Babo so; cutting Babo with the razor, because, only by accident, Babo had given master one little scratch; and for the first time in so many a day, too. Ah, ah, ah," holding his hand to his face.

Is it possible, thought Captain Delano; was it to wreak in private his Spanish spite against this poor friend of his, that Don Benito, by his sullen manner, impelled me to withdraw? Ah, this slavery breeds ugly passions in man! Poor fellow!

He was about to speak in sympathy to the Negro, but with a timid reluctance he now re-entered the cuddy.

Presently master and man came forth; Don Benito leaning on his servant as if nothing had happened.

But a sort of love-quarrel, after all, thought Captain Delano.

He accosted Don Benito, and they slowly walked together. They had gone but a few paces, when the steward—a tall, rajah-looking mulatto, orientally set off with a pagoda turban formed by three or four Madras handkerchiefs wound about his head, tier on tier—approaching with a salaam, announced lunch in the cabin.

On their way thither, the two captains were preceded by the mulatto, who, turning round as he advanced, with continual smiles and bows, ushered them in, a display of elegance which quite completed the insignificance of the small bare-headed Babo, who, as if not unconscious of inferiority, eyed askance the graceful steward. But in part, Captain Delano imputed his jealous watchfulness to that peculiar feeling which the full-blooded African entertains for the adulterated one. As for the steward, his manner, if not bespeaking much dignity of self-respect, yet evidenced his extreme desire to please; which is doubly meritorious, as at once Christian and Chesterfieldian.

Captain Delano observed with interest that while the complexion of the mulatto was hybrid, his physiognomy was European; classically so.

"Don Benito," whispered he, "I am glad to see this usher-of-the-golden-rod of yours; the sight refutes an ugly remark once made to me by a Barbados planter that when a mulatto has a regular European face, look out for him; he is a devil. But see, your steward here has features more regular than King George's of England; and yet there he nods, and bows, and smiles; a king, indeed—the king of kind hearts and polite fellows. What a pleasant voice he has, too?"

"He has, Señor."

"But, tell me, has he not, so far as you have known him, always proved a good, worthy fellow?" said Captain Delano, pausing, while with a final genuflexion the steward disappeared into the cabin; "come, for the reason just mentioned, I am curious to know."

"Francesco is a good man," rather sluggishly responded Don Benito, like a phlegmatic appreciator, who would neither find fault nor flatter.

"Ah, I thought so. For it were strange indeed, and not very creditable to us white-skins, if a little of our blood mixed with the African's, should, far from improving the latter's quality, have the sad effect of pouring vitriolic acid into black broth; improving the hue, perhaps, but not the wholesomeness."

"Doubtless, doubtless, Señor, but"—glancing at Babo—"not to speak of Negroes, your planter's remark I have heard applied to the Spanish and Indian intermixtures in our provinces. But I know nothing about the matter," he listlessly added.

And here they entered the cabin.

The lunch was a frugal one. Some of Captain Delano's fresh fish and pumpkins, biscuit and salt beef, the reserved bottle of cider, and the *San Dominick's* last bottle of Canary.

As they entered, Francesco, with two or three coloured aides, was hovering over the table giving the last adjustments. Upon perceiving their master they withdrew, Francesco making a smiling congé, and the Spaniard, without condescending to notice it, fastidiously remarking to his companion that he relished not superfluous attendance.

Without companions, host and guest sat down, like a childless married couple, at opposite ends of the table, Don Benito waving Captain Delano to his place, and, weak as he was, insisting upon that gentleman being seated before himself.

The Negro placed a rug under Don Benito's feet, and a cushion behind his back, and then stood behind, not his master's chair, but Captain Delano's. At first, this a little surprised the latter. But it was soon evident that, in taking his position, the black was still true to his master; since by facing him he could the more readily anticipate his slightest want.

"This is an uncommonly intelligent fellow of yours, Don Benito," whispered Captain Delano across the table.

"You say true, Señor."

During the repast, the guest again reverted to parts of Don Benito's story, begging further particulars here and there. He inquired how it was that the scurvy and fever should have committed such wholesale havoc upon the whites, while destroying less than half of the blacks. As if this question reproduced the whole scene of plague before the Spaniard's eyes, miserably reminding him of his solitude in a cabin where before he had had so many friends and officers round him, his hand shook, his face became hueless, broken words escaped; but directly the sane memory of the past seemed replaced by insane terrors of the present. With starting eyes he stared before him at vacancy. For nothing was to be seen but the hand of his servant pushing the Canary over towards him. At length a few sips served partially to restore him. He made random reference to the different constitutions of races, enabling one to offer more resistance to certain maladies than another. The thought was new to his companion.

Presently Captain Delano, intending to say something to his host concerning the pecuniary part of the business he had undertaken for him, especially—since he was strictly accountable to his owners—with reference to the new suit of sails, and other things of that sort; and naturally preferring to conduct such affairs in private, was desirous that the servant should withdraw; imagining that Don Benito for a few minutes could dispense with his attendance. He, however, waited awhile; thinking that, as the conversation proceeded, Don Benito, without being prompted, would perceive the propriety of the step.

But it was otherwise. At last catching his host's eye, Captain

Delano, with a slight backward gesture of his thumb, whispered, "Don Benito, pardon me, but there is an interference with the full expression of what I have to say to you."

Upon this the Spaniard changed countenance; which was imputed to his resenting the hint, as in some way a reflection upon his servant. After a moment's pause, he assured his guest that the black's remaining with them could be of no disservice; because since losing his officers he had made Babo (whose original office, it now appeared, had been captain of the slaves) not only his constant attendant and companion, but in all things his confidant.

After this, nothing more could be said; though, indeed, Captain Delano could hardly avoid some little tinge of irritation upon being left ungratified in so inconsiderable a wish, by one, too, for whom he intended such solid services. But it is only his querulousness, thought he; and so filling his glass he proceeded to business.

The price of the sails and other matters was fixed upon. But while this was being done, the American observed that, though his original offer of assistance had been hailed with hectic animation, yet now when it was reduced to a business transaction, indifference and apathy were betrayed. Don Benito, in fact, appeared to submit to hearing the details more out of regard to common propriety, than from any impression that weighty benefit to himself and his voyage was involved.

Soon, his manner became still more reserved. The effort was vain to seek to draw him into social talk. Gnawed by his splenetic mood, he sat twitching his beard, while to little purpose the hand of his servant, mute as that on the wall, slowly pushed over the Canary.

Lunch being over, they sat down on the cushioned transom; the servant placing a pillow behind his master. The long continuance of the calm had now affected the atmosphere. Don Benito sighed heavily, as if for breath.

"Why not adjourn to the cuddy," said Captain Delano; "there is more air there." But the host sat silent and motionless.

Meantime his servant knelt before him, with a large fan of feathers. And Francesco, coming in on tiptoes, handed the Negro a little cup of aromatic waters, with which at intervals he chafed his master's brow, smoothing the hair along the temples as a nurse does a child's. He spoke no word. He only rested his eye on his master's, as if, amid all Don Benito's distress, a little to refresh his spirit by the silent sight of fidelity.

Presently the ship's bell sounded two o'clock; and through the cabin-windows a slight rippling of the sea was discerned; and from the desired direction.

"There," exclaimed Captain Delano, "I told you so, Don Benito, look!"

He had risen to his feet, speaking in a very animated tone, with a view the more to rouse his companion. But though the crimson curtain of the stern-window near him that moment fluttered against his pale cheek, Don Benito seemed to have even less welcome for the breeze than the calm.

Poor fellow, thought Captain Delano, bitter experience has taught him that one ripple does not make a wind, any more than one swallow a summer. But he is mistaken for once. I will get his ship in for him, and prove it.

Briefly alluding to his weak condition, he urged his host to remain quietly where he was, since he (Captain Delano) would with pleasure take upon himself the responsibility of making the best use of the wind.

Upon gaining the deck, Captain Delano started at the unexpected figure of Atufal, monumentally fixed at the threshold, like one of those sculptured porters of black marble guarding the porches of Egyptian tombs.

But this time the start was, perhaps, purely physical. Atufal's presence, singularly attesting docility even in sullenness, was contrasted with that of the hatchet-polishers, who in patience evinced their industry; while both spectacles showed, that lax as Don Benito's general authority might be, still, whenever he chose to exert it, no man so savage or colossal but must, more or less, bow.

Snatching a trumpet which hung from the bulwarks, with a free step Captain Delano advanced to the forward edge of the poop, issuing his orders in his best Spanish. The few sailors and many Negroes, all equally pleased, obediently set about heading the ship toward the harbour.

While giving some directions about setting a lower stu'n'-sail, suddenly Captain Delano heard a voice faithfully repeating his orders. Turning, he saw Babo, now for the time acting, under the pilot, his original part of captain of the slaves. This assistance proved valuable. Tattered sails and warped yards were soon brought into some trim. And no brace or halyard was pulled but to the blithe songs of the inspirited Negroes.

Good fellows, thought Captain Delano, a little training would make fine sailors of them. Why see, the very women pull and sing, too. These must be some of those Ashantee Negresses that make such capital soldiers, I've heard. But who's at the helm? I must have a good hand there.

He went to see.

The *San Dominick* steered with a cumbrous tiller, with large horizontal pulleys attached. At each pulley-end stood a subordinate black, and between them, at the tiller-head, the responsible post, a Spanish seaman, whose countenance evinced his due share in the general hopefulness and confidence at the coming of the breeze.

He proved the same man who had behaved with so shame-faced an air on the windlass.

"Ah,—it is you, my man," exclaimed Captain Delano—"well, no more sheep's-eyes now;—look straight forward and keep the ship so. Good hand, I trust? And want to get into the harbour, don't you?"

"Si Señor," assented the man with an inward chuckle, grasping the tiller-head firmly. Upon this, unperceived by the American, the two blacks eyed the sailor askance.

Finding all right at the helm, the pilot went forward to the forecastle, to see how matters stood there.

The ship now had way enough to breast the current. With the approach of evening, the breeze would be sure to freshen.

Having done all that was needed for the present, Captain Delano, giving his last orders to the sailors, turned aft to report affairs to Don Benito in the cabin; perhaps additionally incited to rejoin him by the hope of snatching a moment's private chat while his servant was engaged upon deck.

From opposite sides, there were, beneath the poop, two approaches to the cabin; one further forward than the other, and consequently communicating with a longer passage. Marking the servant still above, Captain Delano, taking the nighest entrance—the one last named, and at whose porch Atufal still stood—hurried on his way, till, arrived at the cabin threshold, he paused an instant, a little to recover from his eagerness. Then, with the words of his intended business upon his lips, he entered. As he advanced toward the Spaniard, on the transom, he heard another footstep, keeping time with his. From the opposite door, a salver in hand, the servant was likewise advancing.

"Confound the faithful fellow," thought Captain Delano; "what a vexatious coincidence."

Possibly, the vexation might have been something different, were it not for the buoyant confidence inspired by the breeze. But even as it was, he felt a slight twinge, from a sudden involuntary association in his mind of Babo with Atufal.

"Don Benito," said he, "I give you joy; the breeze will hold, and will increase. By the way, your tall man and time-piece, Atufal, stands without. By your order, of course?"

Don Benito recoiled, as if at some bland satirical touch, delivered with such adroit garnish of apparent good-breeding as to present no handle for retort.

He is like one flayed alive, thought Captain Delano; where may one touch him without causing a shrink?

The servant moved before his master, adjusting a cushion; recalled to civility, the Spaniard stiffly replied: "You are right. The slave appears where you saw him, according to my command; which is, that if at the given hour I am below, he must take his stand and abide my coming."

"Ah now, pardon me, but that is treating the poor fellow like an ex-king denied. Ah, Don Benito," smiling, "for all the license you permit in some things, I fear lest, at bottom, you are a bitter hard master."

Again Don Benito shrank; and this time, as the good sailor thought, from a genuine twinge of his conscience.

Conversation now became constrained. In vain Captain Delano called attention to the now perceptible motion of the keel gently cleaving the sea; with lack-lustre eye, Don Benito returned words few and reserved.

By-and-by, the wind having steadily risen, and still blowing right into the harbour, bore the *San Dominick* swiftly on. Rounding a point of land, the sealer at distance came into open view.

Meantime Captain Delano had again repaired to the deck, remaining there some time. Having at last altered the ship's course, so as to give the reef a wide berth, he returned for a few moments below.

I will cheer up my poor friend, this time, thought he.

"Better and better, Don Benito," he cried as he blithely reentered; "there will soon be an end to your cares, at least for awhile. For when, after a long, sad voyage, you know, the anchor drops into the haven, all its vast weight seems lifted from the captain's heart. We are getting on famously, Don Benito. My ship is in sight. Look through this side-light here; there she is; all a-taunt-o! The *Bachelor's Delight*, my good friend. Ah, how this wind braces one up. Come, you must take a cup of coffee with me this evening. My old steward will give you as fine a cup as ever any sultan tasted. What say you, Don Benito, will you?"

At first, the Spaniard glanced feverishly up, casting a longing look toward the sealer, while with mute concern his servant gazed into his face. Suddenly the old ague of coldness returned, and dropping back to his cushions he was silent.

"You do not answer. Come, all day you have been my host; would you have hospitality all on one side?"

"I cannot go," was the response.

"What? it will not fatigue you. The ships will lie together as near as they can, without swinging foul. It will be little more than stepping from deck to deck; which is but as from room to room. Come, come, you must not refuse me."

"I cannot go," decisively and repulsively repeated Don Benito.

Renouncing all but the last appearance of courtesy, with a sort of cadaverous sullenness, and biting his thin nails to the quick, he glanced, almost glared, at his guest; as if impatient that a stranger's presence should interfere with the full indulgence of his morbid hour. Meantime the sound of the parted waters came more and more gurglingly and merrily in at the windows; as reproaching him for his dark spleen; as telling him that, sulk as he might, and go mad with it, nature cared not a jot; since, whose fault was it, pray? But the foul mood was now at its depth, as the fair wind at its height.

There was something in the man so far beyond any mere unsociality or sourness previously evinced, that even the forbearing good-nature of his guest could no longer endure it. Wholly at a loss to account for such demeanour, and deeming sickness with eccentricity, however extreme, no adequate excuse, well satisfied, too, that nothing in his own conduct could justify it, Captain Delano's pride began to be roused. Himself became reserved. But all seemed one to the Spaniard. Quitting him, therefore, Captain Delano once more went to the deck.

The ship was now within less than two miles of the sealer. The whale-boat was seen darting over the interval.

To be brief, the two vessels, thanks to the pilot's skill, ere long in neighbourly style lay anchored together.

Before returning to his own vessel, Captain Delano had intended communicating to Don Benito the practical details of the proposed services to be rendered. But, as it was, unwilling anew to subject himself to rebuffs, he resolved, now that he had seen the *San Dominick* safely moored, immediately to quit her, without further allusion to hospitality or business. Indefinitely postponing his ulterior plans, he would regulate his future actions according to future circumstances. His boat was ready to receive him; but his host still tarried below. Well, thought Captain Delano, if he has little breeding, the more need to show mine. He descended to the cabin to bid a ceremonious, and, it may be, tacitly rebukeful adieu. But to his great satisfaction, Don Benito, as if he began to feel the weight of that treatment with which his slighted guest had, not indecorously, retaliated upon him, now supported by his servant, rose to his feet, and grasping Captain Delano's hand, stood tremulous; too much agitated to speak. But the good augury hence drawn was suddenly dashed, by his resuming all his previous reserve, with augmented gloom, as, with half-averted eyes, he silently reseated himself on his cushions. With a corresponding return of his own chilled feelings, Captain Delano bowed and withdrew.

He was hardly midway in the narrow corridor, dim as a tunnel, leading from the cabin to the stairs, when a sound, as of the tolling for execution in some jail-yard, fell on his ears. It was the echo of the ship's flawed bell, striking the hour, drearily reverberated in this subterranean vault. Instantly, by a fatality not to be withstood, his mind, responsive to the portent, swarmed with superstitious suspicions. He paused. In images far swifter than these sentences, the minutest details of all his former distrusts swept through him.

Hitherto, credulous good-nature had been too ready to furnish excuses for reasonable fears. Why was the Spaniard, so superfluously punctilious at times, now heedless of common propriety in not accompanying to the side his departing guest? Did indisposition forbid? Indisposition had not forbidden more irksome exertion that day. His last equivocal demeanour recurred. He had risen to his feet, grasped his guest's hand, motioned toward his hat; then, in an instant, all was eclipsed in sinister muteness and gloom. Did this imply one brief, repentant relenting at the final moment, from some iniquitous plot, followed by remorseless return to it? His last glance seemed to express a calamitous, yet acquiescent farewell to Captain Delano for ever. Why decline the invitation to visit the sealer that evening? Or was the Spaniard less hardened than the Jew, who refrained not from supping at the board of him whom the same night he meant to betray? What imported all those day-long enigmas and contradictions, except they were intended to mystify, preliminary to some stealthy blow? Atufal, the pretended rebel, but punctual shadow, that moment lurked by the threshold without. He seemed a sentry, and more. Who, by his own confession, had stationed him there? Was the Negro now lying in wait?

The Spaniard behind—his creature before: to rush from darkness to light was the involuntary choice.

The next moment, with clenched jaw and hand, he passed Atufal, and stood unarmed in the light. As he saw his trim ship lying peacefully at her anchor, and almost within ordinary call; as he saw his household boat, with familiar faces in it, patiently rising and falling on the short waves by the *San Dominick's* side; and then, glancing about the decks where he stood, saw the oakum-pickers still gravely plying their fingers; and heard the low, buzzing whistle and industrious hum of the hatchet-polishers, still bestirring themselves over their endless occupation; and more than all, as he saw the benign aspect of Nature, taking her innocent repose in the evening; the screened sun in the quiet camp of the west shining out like the mild light from Abraham's tent; as his charmed eye and ear took in all these, with the chained figure of the black, the clenched jaw and hand relaxed. Once again he smiled at the phantoms which had mocked him, and felt something like a tinge of remorse, that, by indulging them even for a moment, he should, by implication, have betrayed an almost atheistic doubt of the ever-watchful Providence above.

There was a few minutes' delay, while, in obedience to his orders, the boat was being hooked along to the gangway. During this interval, a sort of saddened satisfaction stole over Captain Delano, at thinking of the kindly offices he had that day discharged for a stranger. Ah, thought he, after good actions one's conscience is never ungrateful, however much so the benefited party may be.

Presently, his foot, in the first act of descent into the boat, pressed the first round of the side-ladder, his face presented inward upon the deck. In the same moment, he heard his name courteously sounded; and, to his pleased surprise, saw Don Benito advancing—an unwonted energy in his air, as if, at the last moment, intent upon making amends for his recent discourtesy. With instinctive good feeling, Captain Delano, revoking his foot, turned and reciprocally advanced. As he did so, the Spaniard's nervous eagerness increased, but his vital energy failed; so that, the better to support him, the servant, placing his master's hand on his naked shoulder, and gently holding it there, formed himself into a sort of crutch.

When the two captains met, the Spaniard again fervently took the hand of the American, at the same time casting an earnest glance into his eyes, but, as before, too much overcome to speak.

I have done him wrong, self-reproachfully thought Captain Delano; his apparent coldness has deceived me; in no instance has he meant to offend.

Meantime, as if fearful that the continuance of the scene might too much unstring his master, the servant seemed anxious to terminate it. And so, still presenting himself as a crutch, and walking between the two captains, he advanced with them toward the gangway; while still, as if full of kindly contrition, Don Benito would not let go the hand of Captain Delano, but retained it in his, across the black's body.

Soon they were standing by the side, looking over into the boat, whose crew turned up their curious eyes. Waiting a moment for the Spaniard to relinquish his hold, the now embarrassed Captain Delano lifted his foot, to overstep the threshold of the open gangway; but still Don Benito would not let go his hand. And yet, with an agitated tone, he said, "I can go no further; here I must bid you adieu. Adieu, my dear, dear Don Amasa. Go—go!" suddenly tearing his hand loose, "go, and God guard you better than me, my best friend."

Not unaffected, Captain Delano would now have lingered; but catching the meekly admonitory eye of the servant, with a hasty farewell he descended into his boat, followed by the continual adieus of Don Benito, standing rooted in the gangway.

Seating himself in the stern, Captain Delano, making a last salute, ordered the boat shoved off. The crew had their oars on end. The bowsman pushed the boat a sufficient distance for the oars to be lengthwise dropped. The instant that was done, Don Benito sprang over the bulwarks, falling at the feet of Captain Delano; at the same time, calling towards his ship, but in tones so frenzied, that none in the boat could understand him. But, as if not equally obtuse, three Spanish sailors, from three different and distant parts of the ship, splashed into the sea, swimming after their captain, as if intent upon his rescue.

The dismayed officer of the boat eagerly asked what this meant. To which, Captain Delano, turning a disdainful smile upon the unaccountable Benito Cereno, answered that, for his part, he neither knew nor cared; but it seemed as if the Spaniard had taken it into his head to produce the impression among his people that the boat wanted to kidnap him. "Or else—give way for your lives," he wildly added, starting at a clattering hubbub in the ship, above which rang the tocsin of the hatchet-polishers; and seizing Don Benito by the throat he added, "this plotting pirate means murder!" Here, in apparent verification of the words, the servant, a dagger in his hand, was seen on the rail overhead, poised, in the act of leaping, as if with desperate fidelity to befriend his master to the last; while, seemingly to aid the black, the three Spanish sailors were trying to clamber into the hampered bow. Meantime, the whole host of Negroes, as if inflamed at the sight of their jeopardized captain, impended in one sooty avalanche over the bulwarks.

All this, with what preceded, and what followed, occurred with such involutions of rapidity, that past, present, and future seemed one.

Seeing the Negro coming, Captain Delano had flung the Spaniard aside, almost in the very act of clutching him, and, by the unconscious recoil, shifting his place, with arms thrown up, so promptly grappled the servant in his descent, that with dagger presented at Captain Delano's heart, the black seemed of purpose to have leaped there as to his mark. But the weapon was wrenched away, and the assailant dashed down into the bottom of the boat, which now, with disentangled oars, began to speed through the sea.

At this juncture, the left hand of Captain Delano, on one side, again clutched the half-reclined Don Benito, heedless that he was in a speechless faint, while his right foot, on the other side, ground the prostrate Negro; and his right arm pressed for added speed on the after oar, his eye bent forward, encouraging his men to their utmost.

But here, the officer of the boat, who had at last succeeded in beating off the towing Spanish sailors, and was now, with face turned aft, assisting the bowsman at his oar, suddenly called to Captain Delano, to see what the black was about; while a Portuguese oarsman shouted to him to give heed to what the Spaniard was saying.

Glancing down at his feet, Captain Delano saw the freed hand of the servant aiming with a second dagger—a small one, before concealed in his wool—with this he was snakishly writhing up from the boat's bottom, at the heart of his master, his countenance lividly vindictive, expressing the centred purpose of his soul; while the Spaniard, half-choked, was vainly shrinking away, with husky words, incoherent to all but the Portuguese.

That moment, across the long benighted mind of Captain Delano, a flash of revelation swept, illuminating in unanticipated clearness Benito Cereno's whole mysterious demeanour, with every enigmatic event of the day, as well as the entire past voyage of the *San Dominick*. He smote Babo's hand down, but his own heart smote him harder. With infinite pity he withdrew his hold from Don Benito. Not Captain Delano, but Don Benito, the black, in leaping into the boat, had intended to stab.

Both the black's hands were held, as, glancing up toward the *San Dominick*, Captain Delano, now with the scales dropped from his eyes, saw the Negroes, not in misrule, not in tumult, not as if frantically concerned for Don Benito, but with mask torn away, flourishing hatchets and knives, in ferocious piratical revolt. Like delirious black dervishes, the six Ashantees danced on the poop. Prevented by their foes from springing into the water, the Spanish boys were hurrying up to the topmost spars, while such of the few Spanish sailors, not already in the sea, less alert, were descried, helplessly mixed in, on deck, with the blacks.

Meantime Captain Delano hailed his own vessel, ordering the ports up, and the guns run out. But by this time the cable of the *San Dominick* had been cut; and the fag-end, in lashing out, whipped away the canvas shroud about the beak, suddenly revealing, as the bleached hull swung round toward the open ocean, death for the figurehead, in a human skeleton; chalky comment on the chalked words below, "*Follow your leader.*"

At the sight, Don Benito, covering his face, wailed out: " 'Tis he, Aranda! my murdered, unburied friend!"

Upon reaching the sealer, calling for ropes, Captain Delano bound the Negro, who made no resistance, and had him hoisted to the deck. He would then have assisted the now almost helpless Don Benito up the side; but Don Benito, wan as he was, refused to move, or be moved, until the Negro should have been first put below out of view. When, presently assured that it was done, he no more shrank from the ascent.

The boat was immediately despatched back to pick up the three swimming sailors. Meantime, the guns were in readiness, though, owing to the *San Dominick* having glided somewhat astern of the sealer, only the aftermost one could be brought to bear. With this, they fired six times; thinking to cripple the fugitive ship by bringing down her spars. But only a few inconsiderable ropes were shot away. Soon the ship was beyond the guns' range, steering broad out of the bay; the blacks thickly clustering round the bowsprit, one moment with taunting cries toward the whites, the next with upthrown gestures hailing the now dusky expanse of ocean—cawing crows escaped from the hand of the fowler.

The first impulse was to slip the cables and give chase. But, upon second thought, to pursue with whale-boat and yawl seemed more promising.

Upon inquiring of Don Benito what firearms they had on board the *San Dominick*, Captain Delano was answered that they had none that could be used; because, in the earlier stages of the mutiny, a cabin-passenger, since dead, had secretly put out of order the locks of what few muskets there were. But with all his remaining strength, Don Benito entreated the American not to give chase, either with ship or boat; for the Negroes had already proved themselves such desperadoes, that, in case of a present assault, nothing but a total massacre of the whites could be looked for. But, regarding this warning as coming from one whose spirit had been crushed by misery, the American did not give up his design.

The boats were got ready and armed. Captain Delano ordered twenty-five men into them. He was going himself when Don Benito grasped his arm. "What! have you saved my life, Señor, and are you now going to throw away your own?"

The officers also, for reasons connected with their interests and those of the voyage, and a duty owing to the owners, strongly objected against their commander's going. Weighing their remonstrances a moment, Captain Delano felt bound to remain; appointing his chief mate—an athletic and resolute man, who had been a privateer's man, and, as his enemies whispered, a pirate—to head the party. The more to encourage the sailors, they were told, that the Spanish captain considered his ship as good as lost; that she and her cargo, including some gold and silver, were worth upwards of ten thousand doubloons. Take her, and no small part should be theirs. The sailors replied with a shout.

The fugitives had now almost gained an offing. It was nearly night; but the moon was rising. After hard, prolonged pulling, the boats came up on the ship's quarters, at a suitable distance laying upon their oars to discharge their muskets. Having no bullets to return, the Negroes sent their yells. But, upon the second volley, Indian-like, they hurtled their hatchets. One took off a sailor's fingers. Another struck the whale-boat's bow, cutting off the rope there, and remaining stuck in the gunwale, like a woodman's axe. Snatching it, quivering from its lodgment, the mate hurled it back. The returned gauntlet now stuck in the ship's broken quarter-gallery, and so remained.

The Negroes giving too hot a reception, the whites kept a more respectful distance. Hovering now just out of reach of the hurtling hatchets, they, with a view to the close encounter which must soon come, sought to decoy the blacks into entirely disarming themselves of their most murderous weapons in a hand-to-hand fight, by foolishly flinging them, as missiles, short of the mark, into the sea. But ere long perceiving the stratagem, the Negroes desisted, though not before many of them had to replace their lost hatchets with handspikes; an exchange which, as counted upon, proved in the end favourable to the assailants.

Meantime, with a strong wind, the ship still clove the water; the boats alternately falling behind, and pulling up, to discharge fresh volleys.

The fire was mostly directed toward the stern, since there, chiefly, the Negroes, at present, were clustering. But to kill or maim the Negroes was not the object. To take them, with the ship, was the object. To do it, the ship must be boarded; which could not be done by boats while she was sailing so fast.

A thought now struck the mate. Observing the Spanish boys still aloft, high as they could get, he called to them to descend to the yards, and cut adrift the sails. It was done. About this time, owing to causes hereafter to be shown, two Spaniards, in the dress of sailors and conspicuously showing themselves, were killed; not by volleys, but by deliberate marksman's shots; while, as it afterwards appeared, during one of the general discharges, Atufal, the black, and the Spaniard at the helm likewise were killed. What now, with the loss of the sails, and loss of leaders, the ship became unmanageable to the Negroes.

With creaking masts she came heavily round to the wind; the prow slowly swinging into view of the boats, its skeleton gleaming in the horizontal moonlight, and casting a gigantic ribbed shadow upon the water. One extended arm of the ghost seemed beckoning the whites to avenge it.

"Follow your leader!" cried the mate; and, one on each bow, the boats boarded. Sealing-spears and cutlasses crossed hatchets and handspikes. Huddled upon the long-boat amidships, the Negresses raised a wailing chant, whose chorus was the clash of the steel.

For a time, the attack wavered; the Negroes wedging themselves to beat it back; the half-repelled sailors, as yet unable to gain a footing, fighting as troopers in the saddle, one leg sideways flung over the bulwarks, and one without, plying their cutlasses like carters' whips. But in vain. They were almost overborne, when, rallying themselves into a squad as one man, with a huzza, they sprang inboard; where, entangled, they involuntarily separated again. For a few breaths' space there was a vague, muffled, inner sound as of submerged sword-fish rushing hither and thither through shoals of black-fish. Soon, in a reunited band, and joined by the Spanish seamen, the whites came to the surface, irresistibly driving the Negroes toward the stern. But a barricade of casks and sacks, from side to side, had been thrown up by the mainmast. Here the Negroes faced about, and though scorning peace or truce, yet fain would have had a respite. But, without pause, overleaping the barrier, the unflagging sailors again closed. Exhausted, the blacks now fought in despair. Their red tongues lolled, wolf-like, from their black mouths. But the pale sailors' teeth were set; not a word was spoken; and, in five minutes more, the ship was won.

Nearly a score of the Negroes were killed. Exclusive of those by the balls, many were mangled; their wounds—mostly inflicted by the long-edged sealing-spears—resembling those shaven ones of the English at Preston Pans, made by the poled scythes of the Highlanders. On the other side, none were killed, though several were wounded; some severely, including the mate. The surviving Negroes were temporarily secured, and the ship, towed back into the harbour at midnight, once more lay anchored.

Omitting the incidents and arrangements ensuing, suffice it that, after two days spent in refitting, the two ships sailed in company for Concepcion in Chili, and thence for Lima in Peru; where, before the vice-regal courts, the whole affair, from the beginning, underwent investigation.

Though, midway on the passage, the ill-fated Spaniard, relaxed from constraint, showed some signs of regaining health with free-will; yet, agreeably to his own foreboding, shortly before arriving at Lima, he relapsed, finally becoming so reduced as to be carried ashore in arms. Hearing of his story and plight, one of the many religious institutions of the City of Kings opened an hospitable refuge to him, where both physician and priest were his nurses, and a member of the order volunteered to be his one special guardian and consoler, by night and by day.

The following extracts, translated from one of the official Spanish documents, will, it is hoped, shed light on the preceding narrative, as well as, in the first place, reveal the true port of departure and true history of the *San Dominick's* voyage, down to the time of her touching at the island of Santa Maria.

But, ere the extracts come, it may be well to preface them with a remark.

The document selected, from among many others, for partial translation, contains the deposition of Benito Cereno; the first taken in the case. Some disclosures therein were, at the time, held dubious for both learned and natural reasons. The tribunal inclined to the opinion that the deponent, not undisturbed in his mind by recent events, raved of some things which could never have happened. But subsequent depositions of the surviving sailors, bearing out the revelations of their captain in several of the strangest particulars, gave credence to the rest. So that the tribunal, in its final decision, rested its capital sentences upon statements which, had they lacked confirmation, it would have deemed it but duty to reject.

⚓ ⚓ ⚓ ⚓ ⚓

I, DON JOSÉ DE ABOS AND PADILLA, His Majesty's Notary for the Royal Revenue, and Register of this Province, and Notary Public of the Holy Crusade of this Bishopric, etc.

Do certify and declare, as much as is requisite in law, that, in the criminal cause commenced the twenty-fourth of the month of September, in the year seventeen hundred and ninety-nine, against the Senegal Negroes of the ship *San Dominick*, the following declaration before me was made.

Declaration of the first witness, DON BENITO CERENO.

The same day, and month, and year, His Honour, Doctor Juan Martinez de Dozas, Councillor of the Royal Audience of this Kingdom, and learned in the law of this Intendancy, ordered the captain of the ship *San Dominick*, Don Benito Cereno, to appear; which he did in his litter, attended by the monk Infelez; of whom he received, before Don José de Abos and Padilla, Notary Public of the Holy Crusade, the oath, which he took by God, our Lord, and a sign of the Cross; under which he promised to tell the truth of whatever he should know and should be asked;—and being interrogated agreeably to the tenor of the act commencing the process, he said, that on the twentieth of May last, he set sail with his ship from the port of Valparaiso, bound to that of Callao; loaded with the produce of the country and one hundred and sixty blacks, of both sexes, mostly belonging to Don Alexandro Aranda, gentleman, of the city of Mendoza; that the crew of the ship consisted of thirty-six men, beside the persons who went as passengers; that the Negroes were in part as follows:

[*Here, in the original, follows a list of some fifty names, descriptions, and ages, compiled from certain recovered documents of Aranda's, and also from recollections of the deponent, from which portions only are extracted.*]

—One, from about eighteen to nineteen years, named José, and this was the man that waited upon his master, Don Alexandro, and who speaks well the Spanish, having served him four or five years; . . . a mulatto, named Francesco, the cabin steward, of a good person and voice, having sung in the Valparaiso churches, native of the province of Buenos Ayres, aged about thirty-five years. . . . A smart Negro, named Dago, who had been for many years a grave-digger among the Spaniards, aged forty-six years. . . . Four old Negroes, born in Africa, from sixty to seventy, but sound, caulkers by trade, whose names are as follows:—the first was named Muri, and he was killed (as was also his son named Diamelo); the second, Nacta; the third, Yola, likewise killed; the fourth, Ghofan; and six full-grown Negroes, aged from thirty to forty-five, all raw, and born among the Ashantees—Martinqui, Yan, Lecbe, Mapenda, Yambaio, Akim; four of whom were killed; . . . a powerful Negro named Atufal, who, being supposed to have been a chief in Africa, his owners set great store by him. . . . And a small Negro of Senegal, but some years among the Spaniards, aged about thirty, which Negro's name was Babo; . . . that he does not remember the names of the others, but that still expecting the residue of Don Alexandro's papers will be found, will then take due account of them all, and remit to the court; . . . and thirty-nine women and children of all ages.

[*After the catalogue, the deposition goes on as follows:*]

. . . That all the Negroes slept upon deck, as is customary in this navigation, and none wore fetters, because the owner, his friend Aranda, told him that they were all tractable; . . . that on the seventh day after leaving port, at three o'clock in the morning, all the Spaniards being asleep except the two officers on the watch, who were the boatswain, Juan Robles, and the carpenter, Juan Bautista Gayete, and the helmsman and his boy, the Negroes revolted suddenly, wounded dangerously the boatswain and the carpenter, and successively killed eighteen men of those who were sleeping upon deck, some with handspikes and hatchets, and others by throwing them alive overboard, after tying them; that of the Spaniards upon deck, they left about seven, as he thinks, alive and tied, to manoeuvre the ship, and three or four more who hid themselves remained also alive. Although in the act of revolt the Negroes made themselves masters of the hatchway, six or seven wounded went through it to the cockpit, without any hindrance on their part; that in the act of revolt, the mate and another person, whose name he does not recollect, attempted to come up through the hatchway, but having been wounded at the onset, they were obliged to return to the cabin; that the deponent resolved at break of day to come up the companionway, where the Negro Babo was, being the ringleader, and Atufal, who assisted him, and having spoken to them, exhorted them to cease committing such atrocities, asking them, at the same time, what they wanted and intended to do, offering, himself, to obey their commands; that, notwithstanding this, they threw, in his presence, three men, alive and tied, overboard; that they told the deponent to come up, and that they would not kill him; which having done, the Negro Babo asked him whether there were in those seas any Negro countries where they might be carried, and he answered them, No, that the Negro Babo afterwards told him to carry them to Senegal, or to the neighbouring islands of St. Nicholas; and he answered, that this was impossible, on account of the great distance, the necessity involved of rounding Cape Horn, the bad condition of the vessel, the want of provisions, sails, and water; but that the Negro Babo replied to him he must carry them in any way; that they would do and conform themselves to everything the deponent should require as to eating and drinking; that after a long conference, being absolutely compelled to please them, for they threatened him to kill all the whites if they were not, at all events, carried to Senegal, he told them that what was most wanting for the voyage was water; that they would go near the coast to take it, and hence they would proceed on their course; that the Negro Babo agreed to it; and the deponent steered toward the intermediate ports, hoping to meet some Spanish or foreign vessel that would save them; that within ten or eleven days they saw the land, and continued their course by it in the vicinity of Nasca; that the deponent observed that the Negroes were now restless and mutinous, because he did not effect the taking in of water, the Negro Babo having required, with threats, that it should be done, without fail, the following day; he told him he saw plainly that the coast was steep, and the rivers designated in the maps were not be found, with other reasons suitable to the circumstances; that the best way would be to go to the island of Santa Maria, where they might water and victual easily, it being a desert island, as the foreigners did; that the deponent did not go to Pisco, that was near, nor make any other port of the coast, because the Negro Babo had intimated to him several times, that he would kill all the whites the very moment he should perceive any city, town, or settlement of any kind on the shores to which they should be carried; that having determined to go to the island of Santa Maria, as the deponent had planned, for the purpose of trying whether, in the passage or in the island itself, they could find any vessel that should favour them, or whether he could escape from it in a boat to the neighbouring coast of Arruco; to adopt the necessary means he immediately changed his course, steering for the island; that the Negroes Babo and Atufal held daily conferences, in which they discussed what was necessary for their design of returning to Senegal, whether they were to kill all the Spaniards, and particularly the deponent; that eight days after parting from the coast of Nasca, the deponent being on the watch a little after day-break, and soon after the Negroes had their meeting, the Negro Babo came to the place where the deponent was, and told him that he had determined to kill his master, Don Alexandro Aranda, both because he and his companions could not otherwise be sure of their liberty, and that, to keep the seamen in subjection, he wanted to prepare a warning of what road they should be made to take did they or any of them oppose him; and that, by means of the death of Don Alexandro, that warning would best be given; but, that what this last meant, the deponent did not at the time comprehend, nor could not, further than that the death of Don Alexandro was intended; and moreover, the Negro Babo proposed to the deponent to call the mate Raneds, who was sleeping in the cabin, before the thing was done, for fear, as the deponent understood it, that the mate, who was a good navigator, should be killed with Don Alexandro and the rest; that the deponent, who was the friend, from youth of Don Alexandro, prayed and conjured, but all was useless; for the Negro Babo answered him that the thing could not be prevented, and that all the Spaniards risked their death if they should attempt to frustrate his will in this matter, or any other; that, in this conflict, the deponent called the mate, Raneds, who was forced to go apart, and immediately the Negro Babo commanded the Ashantee Martinqui and the Ashantee Lecbe to go and commit the murder; that those two went down with hatchets to the berth of Don Alexandro; that, yet half alive and mangled, they dragged him on deck; that they were going to throw him overboard in that state, but the Negro Babo stopped them, bidding the murder be completed on the deck before him, which was done, when, by his orders, the body was carried below, forward; that nothing more was seen of it by the deponent for three days; . . . that Don Alonzo Sidonia, an old man, long resident at Valparaiso, and lately appointed to a civil office in Peru, whither he had taken passage, was at the time sleeping in the berth opposite Don Alexandro's; that, awakening at his cries, surprised by them, and at the sight of the Negroes with their bloody hatchets in their hands, he threw himself into the sea through a window which was near him, and was drowned, without it being in the power of the deponent to assist or take him up; . . . that, a short time after killing Aranda, they brought upon deck his german-cousin, of middle-age, Don Francisco Masa, of Mendoza, and the young Don Joaquin, Marques de Aramboalaza, then lately from Spain, with his Spanish servant Ponce, and the three young clerks of Aranda, José Mozairi, Lorenzo Bargas, and Hermenegildo Gandix, all of Cadiz; that Don Joaquin and Hermenegildo Gandix, the Negro Babo for purposes hereafter to appear, preserved alive; but Don Francisco Masa, José Mozairi, and Lorenzo Bargas, with Ponce, the servant, beside the boatswain, Juan Robles, the boatswain's mates, Manuel Viscaya and Roderigo Hurta, and four of the sailors, the Negro Babo ordered to be thrown alive into the sea, although they made no resistance, nor begged for anything else but mercy; that the boatswain, Juan Robles, who knew how to swim, kept the longest above water, making acts of contrition, and, in the last words he uttered, charged this deponent to cause mass to be said for his soul to our Lady of Succour; . . . that, during the three days which followed, the deponent, uncertain what fate had befallen the remains of Don Alexandro, frequently asked the Negro Babo where they were, and, if still on board, whether they were to be preserved for interment ashore, entreating him so to order it; that the Negro Babo answered nothing till the fourth day, when at sunrise, the deponent coming on deck, the Negro Babo showed him a skeleton, which had been substituted for the ship's proper figure-head, the image of Christopher Colon, the discoverer of the New World; that the Negro Babo asked him whose skeleton that was, and whether, from its whiteness, he should not think it a white's; that, upon his covering his face, the Negro Babo, coming close, said words to this effect: "Keep faith with the blacks from here to Senegal, or you shall in spirit, as now in body, follow your leader," pointing to the prow; . . . that the same morning the Negro Babo took by succession each Spaniard forward, and asked him whose skeleton that was, and whether, from its whiteness, he should not think it a white's; that each Spaniard covered his face; that then to each the Negro Babo repeated the words in the first place said to the deponent; . . . that they (the Spaniards), being then assembled aft, the Negro Babo harangued them, saying that he had now done all; that the deponent (as navigator for the Negroes) might pursue his course, warning him and all of them that they should, soul and body, go the way of Don Alexandro if he saw them (the Spaniards) speak or plot anything against them (the Negroes)—a threat which was repeated every day; that, before the events last mentioned, they had tied the cook to throw him overboard, for it is not known what thing they heard him speak, but finally the Negro Babo spared his life, at the request of the deponent; that a few days after, the deponent, endeavouring not to omit any means to preserve the lives of the remaining whites, spoke to the Negroes peace and tranquillity, and agreed to draw up a paper, signed by the deponent and the sailors who could write, as also by the Negro Babo, for himself and all the blacks, in which the deponent obliged himself to carry them to Senegal, and they not to kill any more, and he formally to make over to them the ship, with the cargo, with which they were for that time satisfied and quieted. . . . But the next day, the more surely to guard against the sailors' escape, the Negro Babo commanded all the boats to be destroyed but the long-boat, which was unseaworthy, and another, a cutter in good condition, which, knowing it would yet be wanted for lowering the water casks, he had it lowered down into the hold.

[*Various particulars of the prolonged and perplexed navigation ensuing here follow, with incidents of a calamitous calm, from which portion one passage is extracted, to wit:*]

—That on the fifth day of the calm, all on board suffering much from the heat, and want of water, and five having died in fits, and mad, the Negroes became irritable, and for a chance gesture, which they deemed suspicious—though it was harmless—made by the mate, Raneds, to the deponent, in the act of handing a quadrant, they killed him; but that for this they afterwards were sorry, the mate being the only remaining navigator on board, except the deponent.

⚓ ⚓ ⚓ ⚓ ⚓

—That omitting other events, which daily happened, and which can only serve uselessly to recall past misfortunes and conflicts, after seventy-three days' navigation, reckoned from the time they sailed from Nasca, during which they navigated under a scanty allowance of water, and were afflicted with the calms before mentioned, they at last arrived at the island of Santa Maria, on the seventeenth of the month of August, at about six o'clock in the afternoon, at which hour they cast anchor very near the American ship, *Bachelor's Delight*, which lay in the same bay, commanded by the generous Captain Amasa Delano; but at six o'clock in the morning, they had already descried the port, and the Negroes became uneasy, as soon as at distance they saw the ship, not having expected to see one there; that the Negro Babo pacified them, assuring them that no fear need be had; that straightway he ordered the figure on the bow to be covered with canvas, as for repairs, and had the decks a little set in order; that for a time the Negro Babo and the Negro Atufal conferred; that the Negro Atufal was for sailing away, but the Negro Babo would not, and, by himself, cast about what to do; that at last he came to the deponent, proposing to him to say and do all that the deponent declares to have said and done to the American captain; . . . that the Negro Babo warned him that if he varied in the least, or uttered any word, or gave any look that should give the least intimation of the past events or present state, he would instantly kill him, with all his companions, showing a dagger, which he carried hid, saying something which, as he understood it, meant that that dagger would be alert as his eye; that the Negro Babo then announced the plan to all his companions, which pleased them; that he then, the better to disguise the truth, devised many expedients, in some of them uniting deceit and defence; that of this sort was the device of the six Ashantees before named, who were his bravos; that them he stationed on the break of the poop, as if to clean certain hatchets (in cases, which were part of the cargo), but in reality to use them, and distribute them at need, and at a given word he told them that, among other devices, was the device of presenting Atufal, his right-hand man, as chained, though in a moment the chains could be dropped; that in every particular he informed the deponent what part he was expected to enact in every device, and what story he was to tell on every occasion, always threatening him with instant death if he varied in the least; that, conscious that many of the Negroes would be turbulent, the Negro Babo appointed the four aged Negroes, who were caulkers, to keep what domestic order they could on the decks; that again and again he harangued the Spaniards and his companions, informing them of his intent, and of his devices, and of the invented story that this deponent was to tell, charging them lest any of them varied from that story; that these arrangements were made and matured during the interval of two or three hours, between their first sighting the ship and the arrival on board of Captain Amasa Delano; that this happened at about half-past seven in the morning, Captain Amasa Delano coming in his boat, and all gladly receiving him; that the deponent, as well as he could force himself, acting then the part of principal owner, and a free captain of the ship, told Captain Amasa Delano, when called upon, that he came from Buenos Ayres, bound to Lima, with three hundred Negroes; that off Cape Horn, and in a subsequent fever, many Negroes had died; that also, by similar casualties, all the sea officers and the greatest part of the crew had died.

⚓ ⚓ ⚓ ⚓ ⚓

[*And so the deposition goes on, circumstantially recounting the fictitious story dictated to the deponent by Babo, and through the deponent imposed upon Captain Delano; and also recounting the friendly offers of Captain Delano, with other things, but all of which is here omitted. After the fictitious, strange story, etc., the deposition proceeds:*]

—That the generous Captain Amasa Delano remained on board all the day, till he left the ship anchored at six o'clock in the evening, deponent speaking to him always of his pretended misfortunes, under the fore-mentioned principles, without having had it in his power to tell a single word, or give him the least hint, that he might know the truth and state of things; because the Negro Babo, performing the office of an officious servant with all the appearance of submission of the humble slave, did not leave the deponent one moment; that this was in order to observe the deponent's actions and words, for the Negro Babo understands well the Spanish; and besides, there were thereabout some others who were constantly on the watch, and likewise understood the Spanish; . . . that upon one occasion, while deponent was standing on the deck conversing with Amasa Delano, by a secret sign the Negro Babo drew him (the deponent) aside, the act appearing as if originating with the deponent; that then, he being drawn aside, the Negro Babo proposed to him to gain from Amasa Delano full particulars about his ship, and crew, and arms; that the deponent asked "For what?" that the Negro Babo answered he might conceive; that, grieved at the prospect of what might overtake the generous Captain Amasa Delano, the deponent at first refused to ask the desired questions, and used every argument to induce the Negro Babo to give up this new design; that the Negro Babo showed the point of his dagger; that, after the information had been obtained, the Negro Babo again drew him aside, telling him that that very night he (the deponent) would be captain of two ships instead of one, for that, great part of the American's ship's crew being to be absent fishing, the six Ashantees, without any one else, would easily take it; that at this time he said other things to the same purpose; that no entreaties availed; that before Amasa Delano's coming on board, no hint had been given touching the capture of the American ship; that to prevent this project the deponent was powerless; . . . —that in some things his memory is confused, he cannot distinctly recall every event; . . . —that as soon as they had cast anchor at six of the clock in the evening, as has before been stated, the American captain took leave to return to his vessel; that upon a sudden impulse, which the deponent believes to have come from God and his angels, he, after the farewell had been said, followed the generous Captain Amasa Delano as far as the gunwale, where he stayed, under the pretence of taking leave, until Amasa Delano should have been seated in his boat; that on shoving off, the deponent sprang from the gunwale, into the boat, and fell into it, he knows not how, God guarding him; that—

⚓ ⚓ ⚓ ⚓ ⚓

[*Here, in the original, follows the account of what further happened at the escape, and how the "San Dominick" was retaken, and of the passage to the coast; including in the recital many expressions of "eternal gratitude" to the "generous Captain Amasa Delano." The deposition then proceeds with recapitulatory remarks, and a partial renumeration of the Negroes, making record of their individual part in the past events, with a view to furnishing, according to command of the court, the data whereon to found the criminal sentences to be pronounced. From this portion is the following:*]

—That he believes that all the Negroes, though not in the first place knowing to the design of revolt, when it was accomplished, approved it. . . . That the Negro, José, eighteen years old, and in the personal service of Don Alexandro, was the one who communicated the information to the Negro Babo, about the state of things in the cabin, before the revolt; that this is known, because, in the preceding midnight, he used to come from his berth, which was under his master's, in the cabin, to the deck where the ringleader and his associates were, and had secret conversations with the Negro Babo, in which he was several times seen by the mate; that, one night, the mate drove him away twice; . . . that this same Negro José, was the one who, without being commanded to do so by the Negro Babo, as Lecbe and Martinqui were, stabbed his master, Don Alexandro, after he had been dragged half-lifeless to the deck; . . . that the mulatto steward, Francesco, was of the first band of revolters, that he was, in all things, the creature and tool of the Negro Babo; that, to make his court, he, just before a repast in the cabin, proposed, to the Negro Babo, poisoning a dish for the generous Captain Amasa Delano; this is known and believed, because the Negroes have said it; but that the Negro Babo, having another design, forbade Francesco; . . . that the Ashantee Lecbe was one of the worst of them; for that, on the day the ship was retaken, he assisted in the defence of her, with a hatchet in each hand, with one of which he wounded, in the breast, the chief mate of Amasa Delano, in the first act of boarding; this all knew; that, in sight of the deponent, Lecbe struck, with a hatchet, Don Francisco Masa when, by the Negro Babo's orders, he was carrying him to throw him overboard, alive; beside participating in the murder, before mentioned, of Don Alexandro Aranda, and others of the cabin-passengers; that, owing to the fury with which the Ashantees fought in the engagement with the boats, but this Lecbe and Yan survived; that Yan was bad as Lecbe; that Yan was the man who, by Babo's command, willingly prepared the skeleton of Don Alexandro, in a way the Negroes afterwards told the deponent, but which he, so long as reason is left him, can never divulge; that Yan and Lecbe were the two who, in a calm by night, riveted the skeleton to the bow; this also the Negroes told him; that the Negro Babo was he who traced the inscription below it; that the Negro Babo was the plotter from first to last; he ordered every murder, and was the helm and keel of the revolt; that Atufal was his lieutenant in all; but Atufal, with his own hand, committed no murder; nor did the Negro Babo; . . . that Atufal was shot, being killed in the fight with the boats, ere boarding; . . . that the Negresses, of age, were knowing to the revolt, and testified themselves satisfied at the death of their master, Don Alexandro; that, had the Negroes not restrained them, they would have tortured to death, instead of simply killing, the Spaniards slain by command of the Negro Babo; that the Negresses used their utmost influence to have the deponent made away with; that, in the various acts of murder, they sang songs and danced—not gaily, but solemnly; and before the engagement with the boats, as well as during the action, they sang melancholy songs to the Negroes, and that this melancholy tone was more inflaming than a different one would have been, and was so intended; that all this is believed, because the Negroes have said it.

—That of the thirty-six men of the crew—exclusive of the passengers (all of whom are now dead), which the deponent had knowledge of—six only remained alive, with four cabin-boys and ship-boys, not included with the crew; . . . —that the Negroes broke an arm of one of the cabin-boys and gave him strokes with hatchets.

[*Then follow various random disclosures referring to various periods of time. The following are extracted:*]

—That during the presence of Captain Amasa Delano on board, some attempts were made by the sailors, and one by Hermenegildo Gandix, to convey hints to him of the true state of affairs; but that these attempts were ineffectual, owing to fear of incurring death, and furthermore owing to the devices which offered contradictions to the true state of affairs; as well as owing to the generosity and piety of Amasa Delano, incapable of sounding such wickedness; . . . that Luys Galgo, a sailor about sixty years of age, and formerly of the king's navy, was one of those who sought to convey tokens to Captain Amasa Delano; but his intent, though undiscovered, being suspected, he was, on a pretence, made to retire out of sight, and at last into the hold, and there was made away with. This the Negroes have since said; . . . that one of the ship-boys feeling, from Captain Amasa Delano's presence, some hopes of release, and not having enough prudence, dropped some chance-word respecting his expectations, which being overheard and understood by a slave-boy with whom he was eating at the time, the latter struck him on the head with a knife, inflicting a bad wound, but of which the boy is now healing; that likewise, not long before the ship was brought to anchor, one of the seamen, steering at the time, endangered himself by letting the blacks remark a certain unconscious hopeful expression in his countenance, arising from some cause similar to the above; but this sailor, by his heedful after conduct, escaped; . . . that these statements are made to show the court that from the beginning to the end of the revolt, it was impossible for the deponent and his men to act otherwise than they did; . . . —that the third clerk, Hermenegildo Gandix, who before had been forced to live among the seamen, wearing a seaman's habit, and in all respects appearing to be one for the time; he, Gandix, was killed by a musket-ball fired through a mistake from the American boats before boarding; having in his fright ran up the mizzen-rigging, calling to the boats—"don't board," lest upon their boarding the Negroes should kill him; that this inducing the Americans to believe he some way favoured the cause of the Negroes, they fired two balls at him, so that he fell wounded from the rigging, and was drowned in the sea; . . . —that the young Don Joaquin, Marques de Arambolaza, like Hermenegildo Gandix, the third clerk, was degraded to the office and appearance of a common seaman; that upon one occasion, when Don Joaquin shrank, the Negro Babo commanded the Ashantee Lecbe to take tar and heat it, and pour it upon Don Joaquin's hands; . . . —that Don Joaquin was killed owing to another mistake of the Americans, but one impossible to be avoided, as upon the approach of the boats, Don Joaquin, with a hatchet tied edge out and upright to his hand, was made by the Negroes to appear on the bulwarks; whereupon, seen with arms in his hands and in a questionable attitude, he was shot for a renegade seaman; . . . —that on the person of Don Joaquin was found secreted a jewel, which, by papers that were discovered, proved to have been meant for the shrine of our Lady of Mercy in Lima; a votive offering, beforehand prepared and guarded, to attest his gratitude, when he should have landed in Peru, his last destination, for the safe conclusion of his entire voyage from Spain; . . . —that the jewel, with the other effects of the late Don Joaquin, is in the custody of the brethren of the Hospital de Sacerdotes, awaiting the decision of the honourable court; . . . —that, owing to the condition of the deponent, as well as the haste in which the boats departed for the attack, the Americans were not forewarned that there were, among the apparent crew, a passenger and one of the clerks disguised by the Negro Babo; . . . —that, beside the Negroes killed in the action, some were killed after the capture and re-anchoring at night, when shackled to the ring-bolts on deck; that these deaths were committed by the sailors, ere they could be prevented. That so soon as informed of it, Captain Amasa Delano used all his authority, and, in particular with his own hand, struck down Martinez Gola, who, having found a razor in the pocket of an old jacket of his, which one of the shackled Negroes had on, was aiming it at the Negro's throat; that the noble Captain Amasa Delano also wrenched from the hand of Bartholomew Barlo, a dagger secreted at the time of the massacre of the whites, with which he was in the act of stabbing a shackled

Negro, who, the same day, with another Negro, had thrown him down and jumped upon him; . . . —that, for all the events, befalling through so long a time, during which the ship was in the hands of the Negro Babo, he cannot here give account; but that, what he has said is the most substantial of what occurs to him at present, and is the truth under the oath which he has taken; which declaration he affirmed and ratified, after hearing it read to him.

He said that he is twenty-nine years of age, and broken in body and mind; that when finally dismissed by the court, he shall not return home to Chili, but betake himself to the monastery on Mount Agonia without; and signed with his honour, and crossed himself, and, for the time, departed as he came, in his litter, with the monk Infelez, to the Hospital de Sacerdotes.

BENITO CERENO.

DOCTOR ROZAS.

⚓ ⚓ ⚓ ⚓ ⚓

If the deposition of Benito Cereno has served as the key to fit into the lock of the complications which preceded it, then, as a vault whose door has been flung back, the *San Dominick's* hull lies open to-day.

Hitherto the nature of this narrative, besides rendering the intricacies in the beginning unavoidable, has more or less required that many things, instead of being set down in the order of occurrence, should be retrospectively, or irregularly given; this last is the case with the following passages, which will conclude the account:

During the long, mild voyage to Lima, there was, as before hinted, a period during which Don Benito a little recovered his health, or, at least in some degree, his tranquillity. Ere the decided relapse which came, the two captains had many cordial conversations—their fraternal unreserve in singular contrast with former withdrawments.

Again and again, it was repeated, how hard it had been to enact the part forced on the Spaniard by Babo.

"Ah, my dear Don Amasa," Don Benito once said, "at those very times when you thought me so morose and ungrateful—nay when, as you now admit, you half thought me plotting your murder—at those very times my heart was frozen; I could not look at you, thinking of what, both on board this ship and your own, hung, from other hands, over my kind benefactor. And as God lives, Don Amasa, I know not whether desire for my own safety alone could have nerved me to that leap into your boat, had it not been for the thought that, did you, unenlightened, return to your ship, you, my best friend, with all who might be with you, stolen upon, that night, in your hammocks, would never in this world have wakened again. Do but think how you walked this deck, how you sat in this cabin, every inch of ground mined into honey-combs under you. Had I dropped the least hint, made the least advance toward an understanding between us, death, explosive death—yours as mine—would have ended the scene."

"True, true," cried Captain Delano, starting, "you saved my life, Don Benito, more than I yours; saved it, too, against my knowledge and will."

"Nay, my friend," rejoined the Spaniard, courteous even to the point of religion, "God charmed your life, but you saved mine. To think of some things you did—those smilings and chattings, rash pointings and gesturings. For less than these, they slew my mate, Raneds; but you had the Prince of Heaven's safe conduct through all ambuscades."

"Yes, all is owing to Providence, I know; but the temper of my mind that morning was more than commonly pleasant, while the sight of so much suffering—more apparent than real—added to my good nature, compassion, and charity, happily interweaving the three. Had it been otherwise, doubtless, as you hint, some of my interferences with the blacks might have ended unhappily enough. Besides that, those feelings I spoke of enabled me to get the better of momentary distrust, at times when acuteness might have cost me my life, without saving another's. Only at the end did my suspicions get the better of me, and you know how wide of the mark they then proved."

"Wide, indeed," said Don Benito, sadly; "you were with me all day; stood with me, sat with me, talked with me, looked at me, ate with me, drank with me; and yet, your last act was to clutch for a villain, not only an innocent man, but the most pitiable of all men. To such degree may malign machinations and deceptions impose. So far may even the best men err, in judging the conduct of one with the recesses of whose condition he is not acquainted. But you were forced to it; and you were in time undeceived. Would that, in both respects, it was so ever, and with all men."

"I think I understand you; you generalize, Don Benito; and mournfully enough. But the past is passed; why moralize upon it? Forget it. See, yon bright sun has forgotten it all, and the blue sea, and the blue sky; these have turned over new leaves."

"Because they have no memory," he dejectedly replied; "because they are not human."

"But these mild trades that now fan your cheek, Don Benito, do they not come with a human-like healing to you? Warm friends, steadfast friends are the trades."

"With their steadfastness they but waft me to my tomb, Señor," was the foreboding response.

"You are saved, Don Benito," cried Captain Delano, more and more astonished and pained; "you are saved; what has cast such a shadow upon you?"

"The Negro."

There was silence, while the moody man sat, slowly and unconsciously gathering his mantle about him, as if it were a pall.

There was no more conversation that day.

But if the Spaniard's melancholy sometimes ended in muteness upon topics like the above, there were others upon which he never spoke at all; on which, indeed, all his old reserves were piled. Pass over the worst and, only to elucidate, let an item or two of these be cited. The dress so precise and costly, worn by him on the day whose events have been narrated, had not willingly been put on. And that silver-mounted sword, apparent symbol of despotic command, was not, indeed, a sword, but the ghost of one. The scabbard, artificially stiffened, was empty.

As for the black—whose brain, not body, had schemed and led the revolt, with the plot—his slight frame, inadequate to that which it held, had at once yielded to the superior muscular strength of his captor, in the boat. Seeing all was over, he uttered no sound, and could not be forced to. His aspect seemed to say: since I cannot do deeds, I will not speak words. Put in irons in the hold, with the rest, he was carried to Lima. During the passage Don Benito did not visit him. Nor then, nor at any time after, would he look at him. Before the tribunal he refused. When pressed by the judges he fainted. On the testimony of the sailors alone rested the legal identity of Babo. And yet the Spaniard would, upon occasion, verbally refer to the Negro, as has been shown; but look on him he would not, or could not.

Some months after, dragged to the gibbet at the tail of a mule, the black met his voiceless end. The body was burned to ashes; but for many days, the head, that hive of subtlety, fixed on a pole in the Plaza, met, unabashed, the gaze of the whites; and across the Plaza looked toward St. Bartholomew's church, in whose vaults slept then, as now, the recovered bones of Aranda; and across the Rimac bridge looked toward the monastery, on Mount Agonia without; where, three months after being dismissed by the court, Benito Cereno, borne on the bier, did, indeed, follow his leader.